MW00639312

MORE THAN A *memory*

Cover Design: Sommer Stein, Perfect Pear

Cover Photo: Stacy Powell, SP Cover Photography

Editor: My Brother's Editor

❀ Created with Vellum

MORE THAN A memory

USA TODAY BESTSELLING AUTHOR

MOLLY McLAIN

ALSO BY MOLLY MCLAIN

COLE CREEK SERIES

We're Made of Moments

Measure of a Man (Jinx's book) (Late 2022/early 2023)

The Mistakes We've Made (Amelia's book) (Coming in 2023)

RIVER BEND SERIES

Can't Shake You | Can't Hold Back

Can't Get Enough | Can't Walk Away

A River Bend Wedding | Can't Resist Him

Can't Let Go | Can't Forget Her

MASON CREEK SERIES

Perfect Secret

Perfect Chance

Perfect Scandal (Coming 9.15.22)

VELOCITY SERIES

Fly

Fight

STANDALONES

Bend

Rush

We loved like thunder
and crashed like lightning.
But you were always
my salvation in the storm.

NOTE TO READERS

Please note that this book contains discussion and references to violent death, infertility, sexual and physical assault. These activities do not happen "on the page", however, they are discussed in detail, which could be triggering for some readers.

If you are the victim of sexual assault and would like someone to talk to, please call the National Sexual Assault Hotline at 800-656-4673.

This one is for Libby, who is, hands down, the best hype girl ever. I never know how to properly thank you, so I hope this helps. Love you, lady.

PROLOGUE

TEN YEARS EARLIER...

AIDEN

"*I* don't want to sneak around anymore."

Liv's words come out of nowhere, and for a minute, I think I've imagined them. But the way she holds her breath and bites the plump bottom lip I just spent hours kissing promises I didn't. Still, I need to be sure...

"What do you mean, babe?" Because I've been in this girl's bed and in this very position with her naked body tucked against mine so many times over the past four years, I've lost count.

"I think you know," she whispers, her hand lifting to my cheek.

Every time we've been together, she's sworn me to secrecy. It's what we've done since she was seventeen and I was eighteen. Since her brother—my best friend—told me he'd kill me if I touched her. She was meant for more than our small town and a country boy like me.

1

"I need you to be clear with me, Liv. I need you to say the words."

Her slender neck, scuffed and pink from my stubble, works before she pulls in a careful breath. "I know it wasn't supposed to be this, but I think about you all the time. And I miss you when you're gone. And I..." Her eyes, suddenly full of vulnerability, flick to mine. "I'm tired of pretending I'm not in love with you."

"You love me?"

She nods, and I have her under me in a second, her rickety, secondhand mattress squeaking beneath us.

One look in her dark eyes and it's like a bullet straight to my chest without Kevlar. All the feelings I've pretended not to have for her spill from the place I've kept them hidden like warm blood seeping from a wound. A wound that could very well be my demise, but I don't care.

"Say it again."

"I love you," she repeats, and I crash my mouth to hers, claiming her confession and claiming her, too. For four long years, I've pretended she isn't everything I've ever wanted. The only girl I've ever cared about and the only one I've ever seen a future with.

"I love you, too. Fuck, Livi, I love you so much." I kiss her again and again until we're breathless.

"It's almost summer break, and I'll be home in Cole Creek for my internship," she says when she can talk again. "I want to tell Bren."

"I'll do it." I'm the one who went behind his back.

"You don't have to—"

"I need to."

Because there isn't a thing I wouldn't do for Olivia Bishop, and it's time I told my best friend exactly that.

CHAPTER 1

PRESENT DAY, TEN YEARS LATER...

AIDEN

"*A*re you shittin' me?"

Bren kicks back in his worn leather chair and folds his hands behind his head. "I wouldn't shit you about something like this, man. I know how bad you want it."

Yeah, I'm not so sure about that. As the Pine County sheriff, he may be responsible for the safety and well-being of a hell of a lot of people, but Bren Bishop has been my best friend a lot longer than either of us has had a badge. He'd give me shit all day, every day if he could.

"Remember that time you lied and told me Maddy Kaminski was waiting for me under the bleachers at the football field?" I eye him warily from the other side of his cluttered desk, full of paperwork and dirty coffee mugs. Pinned to the wall behind him is an oversized paper map of the county and a dusty framed picture of his swearing-in three years ago.

He chuckles and rocks a bit in the old, squeaky seat. "Damn, that was a long time ago. You were so gullible back then."

"Yeah, well, I was sixteen and horny as hell."

"Don't I fucking know it," he mutters, and we both know exactly what—or rather, *who*—he's thinking about.

"So, how exactly did this come about anyway?" I ask, quickly changing the subject back to the one at hand. Honestly, what he's telling me sounds too good to be true. The FBI has a ton of guys at their disposal. Why would they want me?

"I got a call from Special Agent Nolan last night. He said Bolinger—the agent we worked with on that kidnapping case last year—gave him your name. I guess they're looking for a certain kind of guy. Bolinger thought you'd be a good fit."

A certain kind of guy? I've been a detective with the county PD for as long as Bren's been sheriff and a deputy for years before that. I may be good at what I do, but there are cops like me everywhere. And a lot closer to Milwaukee, too.

"Did he say anything about the case?" I run a hand around the back of my neck, where the collar of my Pine County Sheriff's Office T-shirt is starting to feel like it shrunk a size in the wash.

"Not really. Just that they need to get more creative than usual with this one." Bren scratches at his ginger stubble. "Look, I'm not thrilled about you taking leave from your role here, but I know the bureau is your end goal. I won't be the one to hold you back from that."

Hell yeah, the FBI is my dream. But the reality is I'd have to relocate to make that happen and I'm not keen on breaking my mother's heart like that. I also wanted to be settled with a family before I took that next step, because something in the back of my mind tells me I'd end up married to the job and miss out on the rest.

4

"It's a temporary gig, though," I say, mostly for myself. "Shit, I could get down there and they could decide they don't want me."

Bren smiles. "They want you, man. They wouldn't have called if they didn't."

Maybe. Or maybe whatever they want me to do is bottom-of-the-barrel shit that they can't get anyone else to do. I'm not saying I'm not willing to sling shit if it eventually gets me where I want to go, but I'm not going to be their bitch, either.

"Just go down and talk to them. See what it's all about. No harm in that."

I ARRIVE at the FBI building just southeast of Milwaukee shortly before ten o'clock on Tuesday morning. The July sun is already hotter than hell, and I pray the air conditioning isn't broken inside, because I'm already sweating my balls off, and it has nothing to do with the weather.

I called Special Agent Nolan as soon as I left Bren's office last week, and he wasted no time telling me how badly the feds needed me. He had this meeting set up in minutes, and I suspect he would have had me come down over the weekend had it not been for the Fourth of July holiday.

As anxious as I am for this opportunity, something about the urgency and the senior agent's unwillingness to give me any information over the phone has sweat dripping down my back despite cranking the AC the entire four hours from Cole Creek.

After I get through the security gate and park, I head into the building where a preppy guy in khakis and an FBI polo greets me and immediately ushers me to a conference room with floor-to-ceiling windows overlooking Lake Michigan.

He offers me a bottle of water and a seat, but I stroll over to the windows to take in the view instead. Something about water has always called to me and given me a sense of calm, which I really friggin' need right now.

"Detective Enders," a friendly male voice sounds from the door a moment later, and I turn to face a familiar smile. The tall, dark-haired agent drops a stack of files onto the conference room table with a thud and extends his hand.

"Special Agent Bolinger." I step forward to shake, already more at ease knowing he's involved in whatever I'm about to get myself into. We worked together for a couple of weeks on a kidnapping case last year and he was an all-around decent guy. Not one of those big-dick personalities some of the federal guys like to throw around in front of us county guys, as if their work is automatically more important because they're the friggin' FBI.

"Glad you could make it." Bolinger gestures toward a chair. "Have a seat and get comfortable. Special Agent Nolan is just finishing up a team meeting, so he shouldn't be much longer."

"Thanks." I'd rather stretch my legs after the long drive and pace off some of this anxiety, but I grab a chair and crack open the bottle of water. "I hear I have you to thank for this recommendation."

A crease forms in his brow for a moment before he gives a quick nod. "I mean, I told Nolan I'd worked with you before, but you've been specifically requested—"

"Detective Enders." An older man with a receding hairline and paunchy middle pushes through the conference room door dressed in a blue suit jacket and slightly darker pants. His tie is gold and flashy, and he looks like he belongs on the PGA tour, not wearing a badge. Nonetheless, I stand and offer my hand across the table. "I'm Bernie Nolan," he says. "And I believe you already know Ian Bolinger."

"Yes, sir. Thanks so much for inviting me down."

A grin splits across Nolan's face and the lines around his eyes crinkle. "Of course, but we really should be thanking you. What we're about to propose is no easy task."

I didn't think it would be, but Bolinger's weird half statement about being requested has my curiosity amped up another notch.

"Shall we get started?" Nolan asks, and Bolinger nods as they take seats across the table from me. "As you know, the FBI is typically tasked with investigating and enforcing domestic crimes. But on occasion, our office sees cases with foreign connections. You'll be working primarily with our agents, but you should know that Interpol is assisting as well."

An international case? What the hell am I getting myself into?

"Okay." I fold my hands together on the table in front of me and wait.

"A couple months back, a UW-Milwaukee professor was found dead outside of a warehouse by the lake. It was an execution-style hit."

"So, he pissed someone off and they took him out."

Nolan nods. "He was also a Polish immigrant here on a green card, and our investigation turned up a long history of dealings with the Polish Mafia."

Ah. The good ol' Polish mob. Bren's Uncle Joe comes to mind, but that's not something I'm supposed to know about, and I'm sure it has nothing to do with this case.

"Turns out he was a bookkeeper for the SSP out of Chicago. I can't remember what SSP stands for—"

"*Samozwańczy Stróż Prawa*," I interject, and he cocks an eyebrow, either surprised that I know or that I can pronounce it. Maybe both. "Means vigilante."

"Huh. I guess that explains the Robin Hood–type crime

they're known for. Anyway, they bring in a shit ton of money, but they move it just as quickly. Rumor has it they single-handedly funded—and continue to fund—the new, nonprofit children's hospital in Chicago."

"That doesn't surprise me." Joe's a good guy, if not a little rough around the edges.

"We haven't had a lot of involvement with them until now," Nolan says. "And we're not looking to cause a fuss with them, either."

I nod, suspecting it's my Polish roots they want more than anything. But why not bring in Bren?

"The guy was pocketing money, and the organization caught on," Nolan continues. "They watched him for months and figured out he was sharing his profits with a small group of rogue members. The SSP calls them the Buntowniks, or rebels. They apparently grew tired of benevolent crime and decided to pad their own pockets instead."

"And let me guess... the SSP did him in to solve the problem."

Nolan shakes his head. "No. At some point, he quit sharing what he was skimming, and the rebel group wasn't happy about it. They took him out themselves."

"Great." I lean back in the chair. "Sounds to me like you've got it all figured out."

Bolinger clears his throat. "There's still a million dollars unaccounted for, and the SSP wants their money back. If it were for their own bank accounts, they'd probably let it go. But that money could go a long way in helping inner-city kids live a better life."

Hearing him completely ignore the fact that the money in question is still dirty, no matter where it ends up, makes me smile. I've been known to turn a blind eye a time or two, as well. Those incidents usually involve someone beating someone else's ass for doing wrong, but the principle is still the same. Not all crime is committed for nefarious reasons.

"So, how do I fit into this?" I narrow my eyes, and the agents exchange glances.

"Well," Nolan begins. "Our dead guy left a wife. She claims she had no idea he was involved with the mob, let alone playing one side off the other. We dug into her pretty deep, and we can't find a single thing to tie her to any of it. But the rogue group doesn't agree. They've been watching her like a hawk, and they're getting antsy."

Of course, they are.

"They want their money, and they think she can lead them to it." Nolan adjusts in his seat. "We have eyes on her twenty-four seven and so does the SSP. They think she's the way to the money, too, but they're not looking to hurt her in order to find it. Just the opposite actually. They want to protect her, and she wants to work with them to find the money and put this all behind her."

In other words, it's a clusterfuck.

"The problem is the rebels know she's working with both of us, and we've come to a bit of an impasse. We're not making any progress, and the longer we sit like this, the harder it's going to be to find that money."

"Maybe I'm missing something, but I'm still not sure how you think I can help."

Bolinger sucks in a careful breath and exhales just as slowly. "We think this guy's accomplices may have more information than they realize they do, but we can't get to it when they're so hyperaware of our involvement. Therefore, we need to give the illusion that we're pulling back. That this case isn't a priority anymore. And that means looking like we've pulled back on the wife without actually doing so. The only way we figure we can pull it off and make it look believ-

9

able is to have someone on the inside. Someone that's protecting her without it being obvious."

My gut tells me I'm not going to like what comes next, but I say it anyway. "And that's me."

"You'd be her bodyguard." Nolan taps his pen on the table. "But you'd need to make it look like more, if you know what I mean."

"With a woman who's just been widowed." Sounds like a horrible fucking idea.

Bolinger lifts a hand. "It's either this or we put her into witness protection, which she's already refused. She wants to help find the money, not hide."

"And you're sure she's not dirty, too? That she's not just biding her time until you get bored with the case?"

Nolan shrugs. "That's always a possibility, but her record is clean, and she seemed genuinely surprised—and pissed off, too—when she found out what her husband had been mixed up in. Between us, I get the feeling their marriage left a little something to be desired, but I'm working on my third divorce, so what the hell do I know?"

Bolinger snorts and opens the folder in front of him. "Here's the thing, Detective…" He takes out a sheet of paper and turns it upside down. "She's already agreed to personal protection and doing whatever she has to do, including pretending to be involved with you."

"Me personally?" I laugh. He makes it sound like they've already told her about me before I even agreed to do this.

Bolinger slides the sheet across the table. "She's the one who requested you. In fact, her exact words were, 'I do this with Aiden, or I don't do it at all.'"

My blood runs cold as a memory flashes through my head out of nowhere. Six weeks ago, Bren took time off for a family funeral.

His brother-in-law's funeral.

I almost laugh again at the thought of my best friend being even remotely okay with me getting anywhere near his sister, but instant rage takes over instead.

She wouldn't have the audacity to ask. Not after what she did to me.

But sure as shit, when I flip over the paper, familiar brown eyes stare back at me.

Eyes that, once upon a time, I swear could see straight into my soul.

Eyes I swore I'd never trust again.

Eyes that look terrified as hell.

Olivia Bishop wants my help?

Well, she can kiss my ass.

CHAPTER 2

OLIVIA

"*A*nd don't forget... your final projects are due by the end of the week." I smile at my laptop screen and roll my eyes when a dozen of the students looking back at me groan in unison. "Oh, come on. It's just a little paper."

"About romance novels," one of the guys grumbles.

"Hey, you could probably learn a thing or two," Jasmine, a young woman I've had in several of my classes, chimes in, and the other students laugh.

"This is where I kindly remind you that you could have taken another course this summer, Mr. Matthews." I shake a finger at him, and he gives me a sheepish smile in return. He's a good kid, though we both know he's only in my class because he thought it'd be an easy *A*. "Anyway, I'll see you all again next Tuesday. Reach out via email if you need anything sooner."

One by one, the students leave the online class, and my cell phone lights up on the desk beside me.

"Hey, Dr. Bishop…" Jasmine speaks up again. "Are you still holding virtual office hours tomorrow?"

I pick up the phone and my stomach clenches when I see Special Agent Nolan's name. He was supposed to meet with Aiden today, a little fact I've been trying not to dwell on since the feds told me he was coming down this week to talk.

"Actually, Jas, I'm not sure. Let me get back to you on that."

"Sounds good." She waves and clicks out of the class, leaving me alone with a racing heart and itchy fingers.

My husband died six weeks ago, but the prospect of seeing my first love again is all I've thought about since the FBI suggested a bodyguard boyfriend ruse to throw off the rebel group.

Yes, I suggested Aiden. No, I didn't think there was a chance in hell he'd do it. But I swallowed my pride and threw his name out there anyway. He may hate me—and rightfully so—but he's the only one I trust enough to do something crazy like this with.

Closing my eyes, I say a quick prayer and then open the message. **We met with Detective Enders today. Call me when you can.**

So he can tell me Aiden laughed in his face? Great.

I hit the agent's contact and put the call on speaker. He answers on the second ring.

"Hey, Olivia. I hope you don't mind me reaching out so late."

It's only eight o'clock, and it's not like I've been sleeping much anyway. "It's fine. I just finished a class."

"How's that going for you? The online thing, I mean?"

"Good actually. I have a few young men in my courses this summer, and I think the remote option makes showing up a little more appealing." I've been teaching freshman English and a couple of two-hundred-level literature courses at the University of Wisconsin-Milwaukee for nine years. The summer sessions have always been notorious for low attendance, especially among the students who are only enrolled for the elective credits. Curiously, attendance has been up since I started teaching online instead of in person as a safety precaution not only for myself, but for my coworkers and students, too.

"I'm glad to hear that. I know you weren't thrilled with the change of venue."

"I wasn't, but I get it." It took me a while to accept that I needed protection, but if it means keeping others safe, I'll do whatever needs to be done. Which is apparently more than Jake, my dead husband, could say.

"Anyway, you know why I'm calling." He sighs, and I hold my breath. "Special Agent Bolinger and I met with Detective Enders today, and his response wasn't what we'd hoped it would be."

Dammit. Even though I'd expected as much, the confirmation feels like a blade to the chest. "Okay." I wet my lips and shove a hand through my hair as the ache of rejection begins to burn in my throat. "So, now what?"

"We'll give him some time to reconsider, but I've gotta be honest with you, Olivia, I don't think he's going to change his mind."

And why would he? He begged me to change mine for months when I broke things off with him, but I never answered a single call or text. Why would I think he'd give me even an ounce of consideration now?

"Can we find someone else?" The mere suggestion tastes like acid on my tongue. "I know I wasn't interested before, but I won't go into hiding. I can't." I've worked too hard on my career, and I've come too far in overcoming my past. I will not run scared again. And I sure as hell won't be a victim.

"We can review our options, but we'll need to do it quickly. Word on the street is that SSP is getting antsy. They want their money."

"Should I be worried?" As if I haven't been already, despite the unmarked car that's been permanently parked in front of my house for weeks, and the surveillance cameras up and down the block.

"No, but the sooner it looks like we've backed off, the sooner the rebel group will come out from the shadows. That's the only way we're going to figure out what they're up to, let alone catch them."

Uncle Joe said the same thing when I talked to him last night, too. Of course, his interest in the men Jake was working with is a lot more dangerous than the FBI's. I may have some protection from the SSP because I'm Joe's niece and their best shot at recovering the money, but this is the mob we're talking about. They know damn well who the rebels are, but they won't divulge that information even if it would speed things up.

"Just let me know what I need to do next." I push my chair away from the desk with a defeated sigh and begin pacing.

"Keep your eyes and ears open like you've been doing, kiddo. I'll be in touch once we know more." He says a quick goodbye, and I click off the call.

A moment later, Lena, my best friend and temporary babysitter, pokes her head into my office. "Everything okay?"

"Not really."

She frowns and steps inside, her blonde hair twisted up into a messy knot that pairs well with her yoga pants and T-shirt. I have on the same pants, but I pulled on a somewhat more presentable top for my class. The two of us have been living like we're at a never-ending slumber party since Jake died and she came to stay with me.

"Sounded like you were talking to Special Agent Nolan. Not that I was eavesdropping."

I half laugh, half snort. "Isn't that your job right now? To get all up in my business?"

She tips her head from side to side, weighing the thought as if I don't know damn well that the FBI gave her strict orders to keep me in sight whenever possible, even in my own house. "Yes, but I try to give the illusion of allowing you at least a little privacy."

And if she were anyone else, I'd hate her for it. But she's been my closest friend since college, and she already knows everything about me, including what happened with Aiden at the end of my junior year. When my life changed in a single night.

"He said no."

"Aww, sweetie." She wraps me up in a sisterlike hug. "I'm so sorry."

"It's not like I actually thought he'd agree." Though I'd be lying if I said a small part of me didn't hope he'd at least hear me out before he shot me down.

"Did he say anything else?" She pulls back, her brow creased as she smooths the hair from my face.

"If he did, Bernie didn't tell me." And it's just as well. I'm not sure my heart can handle hearing all the horrible things Aiden probably had to say about me, most of which are warranted.

"Do you think Bren could help convince him?"

I shake my head adamantly. "No. I'm not dragging my brother into this any more than I already have."

"Maybe it's time you told him the truth."

The truth being my four-year, secret relationship with his best friend, which would inevitably lead to the truth about why I ended things. I'm not sure that's something I will *ever* be able to share with my brother.

"I can't," I whisper, and Lena doesn't push further. She simply pulls me in once again and lets me cry it out like she's become so good at over the past several weeks. Like she did back in college, too.

After several minutes, I pull in a deep breath and dry my tears with determination. I've come too far in the past ten years to fall apart over a man who's probably long forgotten me.

A man who is most certainly *not* the one I'm supposed to be grieving right now.

***

"So, did you talk with Wendell?" A few minutes later, I pour hot water from the teakettle into two cups in the kitchen.

"I did." Lena sighs wistfully. "I can't believe he'll be home in two weeks."

"I'm excited for you." I smile softly and choose a tea bag from the box, catching her sudden frown from the corner of my eye. "What's that look for?"

"I just realized how difficult this must be for you... my husband coming home when yours won't." She bites her lip, but there will be none of that.

"Don't you dare. Wendell has been overseas for three months, and we're going to celebrate that." If anything, I feel bad that I've monopolized so much of her time while he's been away. As an author, she was supposed to be working on her latest manuscript while Wendell finished the last stretch of his contract in Saudi Arabia. Instead, she requested an extension on her deadline and moved in with me when Jake died, partly because she's amazing like that and partly because the FBI didn't want me to be alone.

"I know you're angry about what Jake did and the position he's put you in now, but I also know you loved him. He was your partner for a long time."

He was. But he wasn't the man I thought he was either, and that's a hard pill to swallow, considering how much I'd opened up to him. How much I'd trusted him.

"It wouldn't hurt me to think about happier things, you know." I hand her a tea bag and nudge her when she takes it. "Like all the wild monkey sex you're going to have when that gorgeous husband of yours gets home."

A wide grin stretches across her face. "So much monkey sex."

"Mm-hmm." She and Wendell have been together since we were freshmen roommates at the University of Wisconsin, so I know firsthand how they like to make up for lost time. At least I won't be stuck under a pillow on the other side of the room this time, waiting for them to wear each other out.

"I've already talked with Special Agent Nolan about going home for a few days," Lena says once we're both settled at the table.

"A few days? Lena, you'll go home and stay home where you belong." And I don't care what Bernie says about it. She's given up too much of her time for me already. "We've talked about this. I don't need you to babysit me. Not that I haven't been grateful for the company."

"I know. I just hate leaving you."

"I'm a big girl. I'll be fine. And it's not like anyone has tried to get close to the house anyway." My work, now that's another story.

"I'm less concerned about something happening than I am of you being by yourself." She sticks out her bottom lip in an adorable pout, and I roll my eyes.

"We'll still talk every day, Len. When you're not having monkey sex, that is."

She snorts and dips the tea bag in and out of the water in her cup. "Not to bring him up again, but I was really hoping Aiden would have said yes."

Me too. But after the way I ended things, I can't blame him for saying no. I gave him little explanation, and what I did tell him had been a lie.

"So, what happens now?"

"They're going to review my other bodyguard options."

"To be just a bodyguard or fake boyfriend, too?"

I shrug. "I'm not sure. I guess it depends."

"On?"

"Whether or not I can bring myself to go through with it." As much as I want to help the SSP and the FBI find the money Jake took from them, it's hard to wrap my head around faking a relationship with someone I don't know to get it done, which is almost laughable considering the kind of marriage I had with Jake.

"And if you don't?"

"They'll try and push me into witness protection, which I think is completely ridiculous. I can't help them find the money if I'm in hiding." Not to mention I'd never see my family, I'd have to quit my job, move...

"You'd be safer," Lena says quietly, and I set my tea down before I spill it in frustration.

"I'm not going to spend my life looking over my shoulder because of Jake's screwups." I haven't gone through everything I have just to live in fear again.

"Have you given any more thought to what he could have done with the money?"

"Every single day. And I've quadruple-checked everything I have access to, as well, but there's nothing. Unless the feds come up with something I missed, I'm at a loss."

"The money has to be somewhere. Whether he stashed it or spent it, there has to be a clue we haven't found yet."

MOLLY MCLAIN

One would hope, but the FBI has been rehashing Jake's every move since he started working with the SSP and then the rebel group. They've come up empty-handed, as well. Whatever he did with the missing money seems to be completely off-line.

"I know I've said this before, but in the big scheme of things—at least at the mob level—a million dollars isn't all that much. Surely, the dirtbags he was in cahoots with will eventually figure out a new way to get more money and forget all about this."

As much as I'd like to think that's true, Jake's vicious assassination says they'll stop at nothing to get what they want. Even if it means taking me out, too.

"Are you sure there isn't someone else who could pull this off with you? Someone else you're comfortable with, instead of them pairing you up with some random guy?" Lena asks, and I shake my head. My circle of friends is small, and trust isn't something I hand out easily anymore.

"You know there isn't. And even if there were, it's unlikely they'd be equipped with the skills to protect me." Not like Aiden could.

"Troy would in a heartbeat, but I can't imagine him punching someone, let alone carrying a gun."

I snicker at the thought. "He'd probably shoot himself in the foot." Troy is a super sweet guy, and we've worked together at the university for as long as I've been there, but he's a teddy bear.

"Maybe witness protection wouldn't be so bad," Lena muses, and I frown. I'd rather attach myself permanently to the Polish Mafia than live the rest of my life constantly looking over my shoulder.

"I won't hide." The words come out with conviction even if they are a little shaky. Fake it 'til you make it, right?

"You're one tough bitch, you know that?" Lena sighs, and

20

I grin. I don't feel all that tough these days, but I'm determined to reclaim that title.

I reach for my mug when my phone pings with a text. "Ugh. It's probably Bernie with more bad news."

My best friend smiles sympathetically as we sip our tea, but when the second chime sounds, she gives in and grabs my phone. "Um, Olivia?"

"I'm off the clock right now. No more federal agents tonight."

She shakes her head and holds out the phone. "This cop isn't a fed."

I frown, glance at the screen, and every cell in my body goes numb.

Aiden: We need to talk.

CHAPTER 3

AIDEN

I made it to Green Bay before I cranked my truck around and did eighty all the way back to Milwaukee.

That was six hours ago.

Six hours I've spent replaying the conversation with the FBI repeatedly in my head, and six hours I've tried to forget the terrified look on Olivia's face as she stared up at me from that single sheet of paper Bolinger had slid across the table.

I should have kept driving.

I should have gone back to Cole Creek and kicked Bren's ass, because there's no way in hell he didn't know exactly what he was sending me into. Did he think it'd be funny to rub my face in what he told me I couldn't have all those years ago? Or had he figured out that I'd messed around with Olivia despite his threat and decided he wanted retribution? Either way, I hate him right now.

I don't want to do this.

I don't want to give in and play some fucking game with

Olivia. We played around enough ten years ago, and then she left me high and dry with some pathetic-ass excuse. Now she wants my help? The girl's got balls, I'll give her that. But what I won't give her is the satisfaction of finding out I said no.

She asked for me and now she's going to get me. Along with ten years' worth of pent-up anger.

Nolan gave me her number a few minutes ago when I called to tell him I was reconsidering. I warned him not to get his hopes up, because whether I actually take this job depends on Olivia understanding that *I'll* be the one in charge this time. As far as I'm concerned, she made her fair share of decisions for us years ago.

So, I send her a simple text: **We need to talk**. No name, no pleasantries, just business.

Aiden. Her one-word reply comes two minutes later and satisfaction flares in my chest. Did Nolan give her a heads-up or had she kept my number all this time?

Tamping down my twisted hope for the latter, I reply strategically. Nolan said they'd put a bug blocker on her phone, but I'm not taking any chances in saying something that might fuck up this ruse before it's even started. **I'm in town. Can we meet?**

Right now? Where are you?

The Holiday Inn on 9th. Tomorrow is fine.

No, I'll come now. Which room?

Holy shit. My chest tightens at the prospect of seeing her so soon, but I roll my shoulders and shake it off. *Business, Enders. It's business and nothing more.*

312. I hit send and then toss the phone onto the bed.

I haven't looked Olivia in the eye since she told me she loved me... and then married a mobster eleven months later.

Hope you're ready to talk, Dr. Bishop, because I've got a lot of questions.

OLIVIA

TEN YEARS.

That's how long it's been since I walked away from the only man I've ever truly loved. Yet, in a matter of minutes and a handful of miles, I'm going to come face-to-face with that decision and the decade of regret I've had since.

I should have agreed to see him tomorrow to give myself time to prepare, but no. My silly heart spoke for me, so here I am, checking my reflection in the hallway mirror as Lena hands me my keys and purse and shoves me toward the door.

"You look beautiful. Now, go before you chicken out."

"I'm not going to chicken out." I might throw up, but I'm not going to chicken out.

She grins from the door between the house and the garage as I hit the key fob and unlock my SUV. "God, I can't wait to hear how this goes."

"He probably wants to tell me to fuck off to my face."

She shrugs. "He might. But I don't think so."

My gut is screaming the opposite—that I'm about to walk into a shitstorm of rage for even mentioning his name to Special Agent Nolan. I'd deserve it, given how callous I'd been to him when we broke up. I hadn't wanted to be so cruel, but I'd had to make him hate me, so he wouldn't try to change my mind.

"Let me know when you get there and when you're on your way back, okay? And be safe."

"I'll do my best." Climbing into the driver's seat, I take several calming breaths before I put the key in the ignition.

When I finally get the nerve, I hit the garage door opener

and slowly begin to back out, immediately spotting the unmarked car in the street. The federal agent behind the wheel hops out with a scowl and I groan.

"Dammit." I forgot about him.

"Where do you think you're going at this time of night?" Agent Derek O'Reilly, my protective detail for most evenings, stops me in the driveway. He's dressed down in jeans and a Brewers T-shirt, but the gun strapped to his hip is all business.

"I have an errand to run." I smile, bat my lashes, and play dumb, like I don't know dang well I'm not allowed to leave, much less without a chaperone.

"I don't have any errands on the schedule tonight." He scowls as he scrolls through his phone and the schedule the feds have made me stick to since the rebel group started looking to me for the money Jake stole.

"Come on, Derek. It's not a big deal." I amp up the grin despite the way my hands tremble around the steering wheel.

"I can't let you do that, Dr. Bishop." He shakes his head, annoyance in his eyes. "Not without approval from Special Agent Nolan."

"Then go ahead and call him. He'll be fine with it; I know he will." Providing he can figure out where I'm really going without me having to say it. We haven't worked out all the details of this fake boyfriend bodyguard arrangement, but I know he intends to limit the number of people who know the truth, therefore I have to play dumb right now.

"I think I'll do that." The agent puts his cell to his ear, and I send up a quick prayer that Agent Nolan can think quickly on his feet. "Hey, Bernie, it's Derek. Dr. Bishop says she has an unscheduled errand to run. You know anything about this?" He glowers down at me, and I hold out my hand for the phone, immediately putting it on speaker.

"Hey. Sorry I didn't give you a heads-up, but an old friend just came to town, and I was hoping to see him."

O'Reilly's brows dart up as we both wait for Nolan to respond.

"What kind of old friend?" the senior agent asks suspiciously.

"Just someone I went to high school with. He's a good friend of my brother." Please know I mean Aiden. Please, please, please.

He responds with an annoyed huff. He may be a grumpy, old-school cop, but he's always been patient with me, so I cross my fingers and my toes that his response means he's playing along, too. "Olivia, you know I don't like these kinds of surprises."

"I know, but he just reached out tonight and…" I pause and give a dramatic sigh for Agent O'Reilly's benefit. "He's harmless, I promise. And he's staying at a hotel, so it's not like we'll be out in public."

Special Agent Nolan hums and takes a moment to consider. "You have two hours, and you'll check in with me every thirty minutes by text. O'Reilly, you'll follow her and wait outside the hotel. If she doesn't text, you'll go in after her."

O'Reilly smirks. "Noted."

"We clear, Olivia?" The senior agent grumbles and I have to hand it to him—he's a dang good actor.

"Yes. Thank you so much. And he's in Room 312, if that helps."

"You got that, Derek?" Nolan asks, and the younger agent nods.

"Ten-four, boss."

AGENT O'REILLY TAILS me into the hotel parking lot ten minutes later, not bothering with discretion as he backs his black sedan into the spot next to mine and impatiently taps his watch.

I almost roll my eyes because he's been getting paid to sit in a car and more or less play on his phone for weeks now. Instead, I refrain, because it's not that I'm ungrateful for the protection—I just want my life back.

The FBI put protective detail on me a month ago following the rebel guy's visit to the UW-Milwaukee campus with his not-so-friendly message. Two weeks later, Special Agent Nolan came up with the bodyguard boyfriend idea. He presented me with a folder full of agents he thought might fit, and I'd humored him by flipping through it. But my nausea grew with every new page. The idea of inviting a stranger into my home... knowing this *boyfriend* would probably have to touch me occasionally to make the ruse look real... it made me positively ill.

Trust is a virtue I no longer give freely, and I don't care if the men who killed Jake have their eyes set on me for what he wouldn't give them. I would rather risk my life knowing the decision was my own than trust someone who hasn't earned it.

Which is where Aiden came into play.

It took me a full week to build up the nerve to give his name to the FBI, and even then, I'd been reluctant because I knew what asking him would mean.

It would mean sliding out of my SUV in a hotel parking lot at nine o'clock on a Tuesday night while the man I've avoided for over ten years waits inside, undoubtedly wondering if I'm out of my damn mind to think he'd even consider helping me.

One week, I told Aiden I loved him, and the next, I

retracted those words because it was the only way I knew how to protect him from the truth. The truth I'm going to have to tell him, no matter how badly it hurts.

My knees tremble and my palms sweat as I enter the hotel and wave politely to the front desk clerk. The hotel is in a good part of town, and the otherwise empty lobby is a relief, knowing there's a target on my back.

I hit the button for the elevator and exhale the breath I've been holding as I step inside, only to suck it back in again when a masculine hand darts between the glossy steel as it closes.

An older man in an athletic tank top, cargo shorts, and flip-flops sways from side to side when the doors open again, his smile awkward and his body reeking of chlorine and booze.

A drunk guy coming from the pool, *not* a Polish mobster. I'd laugh if I wasn't already so close to peeing my pants.

"Going up?" he slurs, and I nod.

"Third floor. You?"

"Same." He holds on to the railing as the elevator lifts, and I cross my fingers that he doesn't puke or pass out. Fortunately, we make it upstairs without any drama, and he stumbles out ahead of me without another word.

I, however, am slower to move, because suddenly I have no idea what I'm doing.

My life these past several weeks has been so sheltered and calculated as a means to keep me out of the morgue. But coming here tonight, knowing I'm about to come face-to-face with a man whose heart I broke...

It's equally as terrifying.

I clench my eyes shut as tears begin to burn in them.

I have no business being here.

I have no business asking Aiden for a single thing.

I've put him through enough for one lifetime, haven't I?

I spin on my toes as panic rises in my chest, suddenly needing air more than I ever have when a door opens behind me and the deep, familiar voice I still hear in my dreams stops me dead in my tracks.

"Running again, Olivia?"

CHAPTER 4

AIDEN

*H*ow the hell is she more beautiful than she was ten years ago?

And why the fuck is that the first thought that runs through my head when I glance through the peephole and see her on the other side of the door, her dark eyes swimming with tears?

I should be thinking about how justified those tears are. About how she should be crying and begging and ready to do damn near anything I want as payback for giving her even a second of my time.

But one look and it's like seeing her outside my college apartment all over again. My fingers itch to touch her and my lungs crave the smell of her hair like they do my next breath. And those lips… god, what I'd give for just one more taste of her.

She spins to go almost as quickly as she arrived, and I jerk open the door, saying the first thing that comes to mind.

"Running again, Olivia?"

She goes stock-still, her long mahogany hair swinging at the middle of her back where her black top crisscrosses over creamy skin. I swallow hard, my gluttonous gaze dropping lower to her dark jeans and the curves I could map in my sleep. And her perfume... fucking hell, it's exactly like I remember. Soft, sweet, and so friggin' tempting.

She begins to turn again, and it's as if time slows. Every moment feels drawn out and heavy with the history between us. She was my first love, and I was her first everything. And yet here we are, virtual strangers.

"I didn't run," she says, with so much agony in those three words. So much pain that I didn't expect, or maybe didn't want to hear.

"But you didn't stick around either," I say tightly, because I'm not going to feel sorry for her. I'm not going to let her shitty situation now make me forget what she did to me all those years ago.

The pale, porcelain column of her neck works as she swallows and reluctantly lifts her watery gaze to mine. "I know."

My jaw tightens as we stand there for what feels like forever, the reality of being in the same space after all this time slowly sinking in. Finally, I clear my throat and step aside, waving her into my hotel room without another word.

She draws in a shaky breath and as if fighting for courage, lifts her chin before she moves past me. That gentle, familiar scent of spring flowers tickles my nose and my traitorous dick twitches, remembering all too well how quickly we used to get naked when we'd come together like this after weeks or even months apart. But this isn't high school or college, and this sure as hell isn't a happy reunion.

She goes immediately to the window, as if looking for something or someone, before she pulls out her phone. "I have to check in with Special Agent Nolan and Lena."

While she texts, I study her again. Aside from the obvious nerves, she looks damn good for someone whose husband took a bullet to the back of the head just six weeks ago. Anxious, but not devastated. Older, but still heart-stoppingly gorgeous.

"I have two hours, and I need to check in every thirty minutes or the federal agent who's parked outside gets to come inside and drag me out like a petulant child."

I almost snort. "Nolan sent you with backup?"

She nods. "The men who killed Jake hand delivered a picture of me with a target drawn on my head."

"They came to your door?"

"They came to the university, walked into the lecture hall, and handed it to me as my students were leaving class."

"No shit?" But then, this is the mob we're talking about.

"I wouldn't have asked for your help if this wasn't serious, Aiden."

My name on her tongue and the plea in her voice have my walls slipping down for a fraction of a second before I slam them back up again.

"Why me?" I demand, jaw clenched.

Her lashes flutter over those glittering eyes as she wets her glossy pink lips. "Because I don't trust anyone else."

This time I do snort. "Are you fucking kidding me? It's been ten years." She doesn't know me anymore, and I sure as hell don't know her.

"I know what you're thinking—"

"Do you?" I laugh. "Because if you had the slightest clue, you wouldn't be here right now."

I expect her to come back with some pathetic response. Some pitiful, woe-is-me excuse. But she looks up at me instead, every delicate feature on her face steeling with determination.

"I know you hate me. And asking you to do this after

what I did… it's the most selfish thing I could possibly ask of you." She pulls her shoulders back and takes a shuddery breath. "But other than Bren, you're the only one I trust with my life."

And yet she left me and married someone else.

"How?" I shake my head. "How can you say that? For all you know, I could've become a real motherfucker."

"You're here, aren't you?" She tips her head, and I want to kiss those smug words right off her lips.

"I could be here to tell you to fuck off in person."

"That's my expectation."

"And yet you still showed up."

"It's a risk I was willing to take, considering the alternative." Her eyes remain locked on mine as she swallows, and as much as I want to despise her assurance, I can't help but respect her for it. Any other person would have gone into hiding, but for some reason, she'd rather fight.

"I'm not sure how I feel about you deciding I'm worth your time again because you need something from me," I admit, and then immediately regret showing her that vulnerability. I'm done being weak for her, dammit.

"I never thought you weren't worth my time." She takes a step toward me, and I ball my hands into fists to keep from reaching out and touching her.

"But I wasn't enough, was I? If I had been, you wouldn't have left."

OLIVIA

THE GOOD NEWS is I knew the question was coming.

The bad news is I've had a week to think about it, and I'm still not sure how to explain to him that he's always been

33

enough. That in some ways he was too much, and I was the one who felt unworthy. But telling him that would mean having to tell him why I felt that way in the first place, and I'm not ready for that. At least not entirely.

"I lied to you," I admit quietly. "When I broke things off, I told you I didn't love you… that I'd misunderstood my feelings when I'd said those words, but that wasn't true."

He crosses his arms over his chest, drawing my attention to the dark tattoos and thick muscles in his forearms, both of which are more abundant than I remember. "I'm listening."

"I did love you. So freaking much." A wave of emotion rises in my throat, and I glance to the carpeted floor. Foolishly, I want him to come to me and put his comforting hands on my shoulders and ease away the pain like he used to. But he doesn't move. "Things were complicated, and it was easier to pretend I didn't care than to tell the truth."

"You were that afraid of what Bren would say?" He scowls and I shake my head. That isn't the truth I'm referring to.

"I didn't want to put either of you in a position…" I pause, trying to find the words without saying more than I'm prepared to explain, at least right now. "In a position to have to choose."

"Choose? Jesus, we talked about that."

He's right—we *did* talk about wanting our relationship despite the damage it might cause to each of ours with Bren, but we hadn't talked about the choice I had to make for both of them, so they wouldn't have to.

"I know. We did, but—" I'm saved from having to skirt around the truth when my phone chirps in my purse. "That's probably Agent Nolan."

Aiden's eyes, which are a darker blue than I remember, narrow, and I shiver. Every bit of him is darker and more intense now. Edgier. More dangerous. From the tattoos to the beard to the stern set of his broad shoulders, there's no doubt he could—and would—do some serious damage to anything or anyone who got in his way.

Is he going to do it? the agent's text reads.

I don't know yet.

When he doesn't reply, I tuck the phone away and glance back to Aiden, who's still watching me intently, like he can't figure out if I'm really here or if he hallucinated this whole screwed-up mess.

"Are the feds about to break down my door?"

"No, but Agent Nolan does want to know if you're going to help."

That broody gaze sweeps down the length of my body and back up again, and butterflies flutter in my stomach. My nerves are on the verge of bursting into flames, and my body decides to add butterflies to the mix? Seriously?

"What happens if I don't?" He cocks an eyebrow.

"They'll assign someone else to or force me into a witness protection program."

"And you don't like those options because…?"

"Because I've worked too hard on my career to give it up, and as far as someone else…" The butterflies turn to nausea in an instant. "I don't know if I could do that."

"But you'd do it with me?"

I do anything with him. Anything.

I shove a hand through my hair and bite my lips together to keep them from trembling. "I need to be comfortable with whoever they pair me with."

"And you'd be comfortable with me? After all this time?" A disbelieving smirk flickers across his face and I close my eyes, fighting for courage. How do I tell him he's the only one I've ever been comfortable with?

"It's a risk I'm willing to take."

He gives a humorless laugh. "What about Bren? You

weren't willing to risk him finding out about us then, and I guarantee he won't be any happier about it now."

"He already knows."

His brows dart up. "What?"

"Not about before," I clarify quickly. I haven't been that brave. "But he knows the FBI wants to give me a bodyguard who looks like more."

"And he's okay with that guy being me?" He gives me a skeptical look, and I nod.

"I guess he's not a big fan of funerals."

The thick tendons in his neck flex as his stubbled jaw pulses. "I left, you know. I told Nolan and Bolinger there was no way in hell I would do it."

"I know."

He studies me for a moment. "But for some reason, I couldn't keep going. I couldn't walk away, knowing that if something happened to you, it would kill your family."

Tears well in my eyes, but I nod. Of course, I wish he was here for me and not because he's a cop and my brother's best friend, but I'll take what I can get right now and hope I can show him I'm not the horrible person he thinks I am along the way.

"I'm here for them."

"I understand."

"This isn't going to be easy," he says with gritty concession, and I almost weep. Instead, I lift my chin with false confidence.

"Nothing about my life for the past month and a half has been easy."

"And if we're going to do this, you're going to need to be honest with me."

I nod once again, even as the ache in my stomach twists into an impossible knot.

"Starting now."

CHAPTER 5

AIDEN

"*I* met him on the train in Prague." From the chair by the desk, Liv wrings her hands together in her lap. "I'd thought my Czech was decent until I got to the Czech Republic and couldn't understand anyone. They talked too fast, and I ended up missing my stop because I'd mistranslated what I thought I'd heard. Jakub saved me from a meltdown and helped me get to the hostel I was staying at until I could move into my dorm."

When we'd been together, she'd talked about visiting Europe with her mom someday, so they could explore their Bohemian and Polish ancestry. Privately, I'd been jealous. I would have loved to plan a trip with Liv, but we'd never talked about the future like that. We only thought as far ahead as our next stolen weekend together.

"I thought he was Polish," I say from the edge of the bed, elbows dug so deeply into my knees that the denim from my jeans abrades my skin.

"He was, but he was in Prague for college, too. We both went to Charles University. He was a history major."

I'd Googled the guy as soon as I got to the hotel earlier. There wasn't a ton of information, just a short bio still posted on the University of Milwaukee's website. *Jakub Jelanovich, PhD. Professor of World and European History.* There were a few random news articles about his work with the college's student groups and his involvement with the Polish Exhibition House in Chicago, which was the only thing of interest that had come up.

"So, he helped you and then what? You start dating?"

"No." She shakes her head, and her hair reflects the light from the bedside lamp. "We were just friends."

"Until you weren't." I don't want to sound bitter, but I am and there's no point in denying it.

She blows out a breath, her gaze transfixed on her knotted hands. "I wasn't in a good place when I got to Europe. I was still hung up on you, and I wasn't interested in dating. Jake wasn't either. His girlfriend had been killed the year before and he was still grieving."

She'd been hung up on me? Then why hadn't she taken my calls? Why the hell had she left me at all?

I tamp down the urge to demand those answers just yet. "How'd she die?" I ask instead.

"She was snatched from outside a club, they think by a sex trafficking group. Her body was found a couple days later in a hotel in Kraków."

"Fuck. That's tough."

She nods. "Jake was with her the night she was taken, so he felt guilty for not protecting her."

I would, too, not that I feel an ounce of sympathy for the guy. He was a mobster, for Christ's sake. "What are the chances he was involved with the Mafia back then, and her murder had something to do with his involvement?"

Liv shakes her head. "I don't think so. He was a quiet person. Kept to himself most of the time and didn't have a lot of friends."

"You don't have to be loud and outgoing to be in the Mafia." Hell, most of those bastards are the strong, silent type. They keep to themselves because they're busy watching everybody. Waiting to make their move.

"I know, I'm just saying I don't think he was mixed up with anything back then. I suppose it's possible, but my gut says he wasn't. I don't think that happened until he came to the States."

Maybe, but I'm not ruling anything out. "If you were just friends, how'd you end up married?"

"Is that relevant to the case or are you asking for yourself?" she counters, and I pin her with an unyielding glare instead of answering. She huffs out an annoyed breath. "We became close while I was abroad. I'd made other friends, too, but Jake and I... we just connected. He told me about wanting to come to the US for his master's degree and doctorate, but he'd had issues with his student visa."

"And what, you offered to marry him to make it easier?" I give a short laugh, never expecting her to stare back at me, unfazed. "Are you fucking kidding me?" She married this asshole just so he could come to the US.

"He was one of my best friends. I wanted to help."

We'd been friends, too, and we'd shared a fuck lot more than a connection.

"I know that's probably hard to hear," she says quietly. "But you wanted the truth. Neither Jake nor I were interested in a romantic relationship, with each other or with other people, so it didn't seem like such a crazy idea. And it worked."

"For nine years?" She's telling me she was in a loveless, sexless marriage for close to a decade? As much as my scorned pride likes hearing that she didn't ditch me and fall madly in love with someone else, I can't wrap my head around living that kind of life she's describing for so long either.

She tucks a strand of hair behind her ear and mutters, "It wasn't like I didn't love him."

Fucking hell.

"He and Lena were my best friends, but he was my partner, too."

"Partner?" I grit out, the word feeling like sand on my tongue.

"He was my husband, Aiden. I may not have been in love with him in the traditional sense, but I *did* love him." Her voice cracks, and she pulls in a shaky breath. "I thought I knew him, but now…" She breaks off and bites her lip. "I feel so betrayed."

Yeah, well, welcome to the club. "You really had no idea he was involved with the mob?"

"Not a clue. I've gone back through everything, and I can't figure out when it started. The SSP, as much as they want my help in finding their money, won't tell me or the FBI anything. They've only confirmed that Jake was an 'associate,' and that they'd only realized he was siphoning money from the organization a couple of months before he was killed."

He'd obviously had access, which meant he must've had a role in the organization they're not willing to own up to. Annoying, but not surprising. "Have you talked to your uncle?"

"Yes, but he claims he doesn't know anything more about Jake than I do. Part of me believes him, because he's not as involved in the SSP as he used to be, but the other part thinks he's just trying to protect me."

Knowing Joe, she's probably right. "What about your parents? Do they know the truth about why he was killed?"

"I had to tell them when the FBI put security on me, and Uncle Joe, in turn, put surveillance on them."

Good. I'd thought about that, as well. If these assholes get desperate enough for their money, they'll go to any length to get it.

"What about your marriage? Do your parents know the truth about that?"

She shakes her head adamantly. "No, and I don't want them to know. It's bad enough I was married to a mobster. I don't want them to know it wasn't a traditional relationship on top of that. Like, how much worse could it get? I'd married a man to help him out, and he turned out to be a criminal who put my life in danger."

For a woman like Olivia, who's always wanted her family's approval, I can see how coming clean about being so reckless would be difficult. But the selfish part of me wants them to know the truth. And then I want them to find out about us, because I *did* love her and I'm the one who's stepping up to keep her safe now.

Not good enough for her, my ass.

"We may have to tell them the truth about this, too, if it comes to that point."

She nods. "I can live with that. Lena knows, too. And obviously Bren, because the FBI had to talk to him before they talked to you."

At least that'll keep him from hunting me down and castrating me like he'd promised he'd do when we were kids. He'd caught me with my arm around Liv one night at a bonfire, and he'd vowed it'd be the last time I'd touch her.

"You know these guys are going to look into me when I start coming around. They're going to figure out I'm a cop."

"Yes, but if they dig deep enough, they'll also figure out that we have a history, too, and maybe they'll believe that I'm a grieving widow who's reached out to an old friend for comfort."

We share a silent stare before I fold my hands together between my knees. "If they can figure it out, so can Bren."

"Then he figures it out." She lifts a shoulder like it's not a big deal and I bite my tongue.

She was the one who hadn't wanted anyone to know about us all those years ago, and I played along because I loved having her to myself when we were together. But her nonchalance now pisses me off. If she hadn't cared so much then, maybe we wouldn't be having this conversation now.

"I hope you know this isn't easy for me," she offers quietly, glancing up with watery eyes. "I hurt you, and I realize that asking you to do anything for me, let alone something so significant, is incredibly selfish after everything I've done. But I know you care about my brother, and you'd do anything for him, no matter how much you might hate me."

"I don't hate you, Livi." Her old nickname spills out with far too much ease, and if I hate anything, it's that no matter how hard I try to fight it, she always finds a way to bring me to my knees.

The tears she's fought to keep in finally break free and it takes everything in me not to go to her, wrap her up in my arms, and promise that I'll do whatever it takes to keep her safe.

But if I'm going to survive this, I can only touch her and offer her comfort for show. The minute I cross the line and do it for real is the minute I write my own obituary. And if I'm not careful, hers, too.

CHAPTER 6

AIDEN

"You son of a bitch."

Bren glances up from a stack of reports with the ease of a man who's not only been expecting this visit, but who's been looking forward to it, too.

"Aiden." He casually closes a manila file folder and leans back in his chair. "How was Milwaukee?"

"Why the hell didn't you tell me?" I slam his office door hard enough to rattle the pictures on the walls.

"Wasn't my place." He lifts a shoulder and then folds his hands behind his head.

"Fuck that." I stalk to his desk. I've spent the last four hours on the road, rehashing our conversation from last week and counting the number of opportunities he'd had to tell me what I was headed into. "We've always said we were friends before we were cops, and this was one of those times when you should have given me a goddamn heads-up."

"It's just a job."

"It's your sister!" I roar, slamming both hands down onto

his files. "Whose husband was just murdered by the fucking mob!"

"Hey…" He sits forward abruptly, jutting his ginger-bristled chin toward the door while he grits his teeth. "Keep that shit down."

"You should have told me," I seethe.

"I couldn't. Nolan and Bolinger gave me explicit instructions not to say anything more than I did. You think that was easy, all things considered?"

"All things being what exactly? That it's Olivia who needs protection, or the fact that the feds want me to do the very thing you made me promise I'd never do?"

His jaw tightens and his eyes narrow. "Don't tell me you're still hung up on that."

Fuck yes, I'm still hung up on it, but I'm damn sure not going to tell him that now and kill this thing before it starts.

He shakes his head as he gets to his feet. "Look, I don't want to think too much about why that still bothers you, because I don't want to regret telling the feds you're the best man for the job. But Olivia needs someone she can trust, and I need to know she's in good hands when I close my eyes at night."

I stand tall and level with him, eye to eye. "Then you're fucking lucky I said yes."

A smug smile slashes across his face. "Good."

"Good," I mock him and then take a step back, running a hand around the back of my neck to calm down before I stroke out. "How the hell did she get messed up with a fucking mobster anyway?"

He lifts his hands. "I don't know, man, but something tells me you're gonna find out."

"Damn right, I am. And you never suspected anything?" I find it hard to believe that he didn't get at least a bad vibe from the guy. Bren's a cop, and a damn good one at that.

"Nope. Didn't know him well enough. Olivia never brought him home, and I only ever talked to him once a year at Christmas."

"That alone didn't strike you as funny?" The Liv I knew lived for spending time with her family, and she'd find every excuse possible to go home on the weekends we weren't together in college.

"It did, but she was married, working on her doctorate, and teaching. I figured she was too busy."

I'm not buying it. "Was he controlling? Maybe he didn't want her coming back for some reason."

He shrugs. "Again, I can't say. I didn't get that impression, but I spent less than twenty days with the guy in nine years. What do I know?"

That's exactly what I'm saying. Bren and Liv were as close as two siblings could be. The fact that he doesn't know anything about the man she was married to rubs me the wrong way, but he won't like the reason why, so I let it go.

"I'm going to need some time off for this. I assume that won't be a problem."

"I wouldn't have sent you down there if it was."

I glare at him from across the desk, wanting so goddamn badly to tell him that Liv wouldn't be in this situation if he'd let her choose a man who actually gave a shit about her all those years ago.

But I'd make an ass out of myself if I did, because if anyone is to blame for this mess, it's me.

IN A DESPERATE ATTEMPT TO lower my blood pressure, I walk into my childhood home a half hour later to see some of my favorite people.

"Honey!" Ma jumps up from the couch where she's

45

working on a puzzle with my nephew, her mess of gray-and-blonde curls almost as wild as her neon floral T-shirt. "What are you doing here in the middle of the day?"

"Just taking a late lunch. Figured I'd see what's good here." I tuck my hands into my jeans and sidle casually into the living room despite the chaos in my head.

"Oh, I'm glad." She rushes over and wraps her arms around my neck while I press a kiss to the top of her head. "I have leftover Polish sausage and sauerkraut from supper. How's that sound?"

"That's perfect, Ma. Thank you." I never did eat dinner last night, and I was too fired up this morning on the drive back from Milwaukee to ingest more than coffee.

She pats my cheek. "I'll go warm it up if you wouldn't mind helping Jett finish his puzzle."

"You got it." A kid's puzzle is all I have the capacity for right now anyway. "Whatcha working on, Jettster?"

"Dump truck puzzle," he says without looking up as I take a seat next to him, his concentration on point. "Wanna help?"

"Sure. Slide some of those pieces over."

He does, and I snap a piece into place to appease him while I watch him work and greedily soak up some of his sunshine. I haven't thought too much about having kids of my own, other than Ma being on my case about settling down, but I'd be lying if I said I wasn't at least a little envious of the relationship Jesse has with his boy.

"So, I heard you and your mom are moving into your dad's house. You excited?"

He nods so fiercely, I swear his teeth clack together. "Yup! I getta bring all my toys and put 'em in my room."

"That's awesome. I bet it's nice to spend more time with your dad, huh?"

"Uh-huh. Mama likes Daddy."

I chuckle. "Oh yeah? How do you know that?"

46

"She gives him kisses."

I bet she does. Among other things. "Grown-ups do that sometimes. It's best to close your eyes and pretend you don't see."

Jett giggles. "You're silly, Uncle Aiden."

"Hey, I'm just trying to help you out, little dude." Because if I know my younger brother, he's going to do his damnedest to make up for all the time he and Hayden missed out on when she'd been in Green Bay.

"How are my boys doing?" Ma returns to the living room with a steaming plate of food and a glass of iced tea. She sets both on the coffee table next to the puzzle, and my stomach growls.

"This looks great, Ma. Thanks again."

"You know, you're more than welcome to come over and have dinner with us. Now that Jett and Hayden are here, your brother doesn't come over as often, so there's always plenty."

I nod, though we both know I won't. My work schedule is too erratic, and Jesse and our youngest brother, Justin, a.k.a Jinx, have always been the ones to stick close to home. My baby sister, Amelia, and I are the independent ones who prefer to do our own thing.

"So, how is work going?" Ma asks as I swallow down a too-hot mouthful of sausage and kraut and quickly reach for the tea.

"Same as always," I lie when I can finally talk. I don't like bending the truth, but in my line of work, it's best I don't tell her more than she needs to know. She's a worrywart by nature, but add in my law enforcement career, and she's on the verge of stroking out every time I talk to her. "But I do have to make a few trips downstate over the next couple of weeks. I shouldn't be gone more than a day or two at a time, but if I go off-grid here and there, that's probably where I am."

"Okay. It's nothing I need to worry about, right?"

"Ma, you never need to worry about me."

She tips her head to the side and glares at me with the same blue eyes she passed down to three out of four of us kids. "Don't lie to me, Aiden Alexander."

"Hey, that's my name!" Jett shouts, and I give the kid a mental fist bump for changing the subject and saving my ass.

"You're right. Our middle names are both Alexander. After Grampy."

"You talking about me in there?" my old man calls from the rear of the house.

"Yup!" Jett giggles again.

"Better be about how good-lookin' I am." Dad appears in the doorway, blotting sweat from his brow with a handkerchief. I thought I'd heard the mower going when I'd walked in, and it looks like I was right.

"When are you gonna let Jinx take over the yard work like he's offered a hundred times?" I ask, and Dad glares at me like he always does when I bring up the subject.

"I'm retired, not crippled."

"I know, but you also have a son who oversees the lawn care portion of the family business." Jesse technically owns Enders Excavating, but Jinx handles the landscaping side of the company while Jesse deals with the bigger, earth-moving jobs.

"Your brother isn't touching my grass until I'm six feet under."

"Stubborn old man."

"And don't you forget it." He points a finger at me, and Jett's eyes go wide.

"Uh-oh, Uncle Aiden. Better behave."

"You tell him, Jettster." Dad kicks off his shoes in the hall and then claims his recliner.

48

"Aiden was just telling me that he'll be traveling a bit for work over the next few weeks."

"Yeah?" My old man cocks an eyebrow.

"Nothing serious. I just have a few meetings lined up." Meetings, fake dates, whatever.

"For the sheriff's department or your PI work?" Dad asks.

"The county." I'd love to tell them about the FBI gig, but it'll have to wait until Liv's case is over.

"You been doing much private work lately?"

I nod. "Busier than ever. Who knew northern Wisconsin had so many shady people?"

My old man laughs. "You'll find 'em everywhere if you look close enough."

No kidding. I started my own private investigation business a year ago, and I already have enough work that I could resign from the sheriff's office and not lose a cent. Unfortunately, I'm going to have to pull back on it for a while, but it should all shake out in the end.

Polishing off the rest of my lunch, I get to my feet with my empty plate and glass in hand. "Any chance I can get a refill on the iced tea?"

"Of course. Here, I'll get it for you." Ma reaches for the glass, but I hold it away from her.

"Ma, I'm thirty-two. I can pour my own tea."

She sticks her tongue out at me, and I grin as I head to the kitchen and my phone buzzes in my pocket. A text from Olivia. **It was nice seeing you last night.**

So, what, we're friends now? I set the plate in the sink and almost reply with something sarcastic when I remember that I was the one who said we'd need to be *on* at all times, and this is the kind of text she'd probably send if we'd genuinely met up as old acquaintances.

Was thinking the same. I'll be back down that way later in the week. We should grab a drink, I text back.

I doubt the feds will let me out for another visit. Maybe you could come over instead?

Come over? To her place? Why the hell did I think this was a good idea again? Oh, that's right—*I didn't.*

I'm down for that. Friday night work?

Perfect. 3434 Riverview Court. 6 pm?

6 pm it is. See you then.

She sends a heart emoji, and I shove the phone back in my pocket like the damn thing zapped my hand.

Hearts? Is that the kind of shit I'm going to be expected to do?

"I suppose you have to get back to work now, huh?" Mom strolls into the kitchen behind me.

"Yeah, I've got some reports to finish up." And a plan to make.

"I made Grandma Kowalcyzk's *chlodnik* recipe to have with chicken salad sandwiches if you'd like to come back for dinner tonight." She offers with a bright smile, as if she's forgotten how much I despise that friggin' soup.

"No offense, Ma, but I'd rather drink motor oil than cold beet soup."

She scoffs and smacks my arm. "Rude!"

I chuckle and bend to kiss her cheek. "Sorry. I love you, if that helps."

"*Hmmph.*" She narrows her eyes, but it doesn't hide the sparkle in them. The four of us kids are her pride and joy, even if we do annoy the hell out of her sometimes. "You're lucky you're so handsome."

"Oh, so you only forgive me because I'm your best-looking child?"

She rolls her eyes and shoves me toward the front door. "Get out of my house before you get your bullcrap all over!"

Laughing, I do as she says, pausing only to say goodbye to Jett and Dad.

It isn't until I climb into my police SUV and turn over the engine that it occurs to me...

If this gig with Liv ends up taking longer than a few weeks, there's a chance I'm going to have to tell my family that I'm seeing her, and that's going to be the best news I've ever given my mother.

I'm not sure what bothers me more... knowing I'm going to have to break her heart when this fake relationship is over...

Or knowing that once upon a time it had been real, and I couldn't tell her about it.

CHAPTER 7

OLIVIA

"I still can't believe he's going to do it." Lena looks up from her coffee cup with bright eyes.

"You and me both." I flip the last of our crepes and then slide it from the pan and onto the plate with the other five. It's been two days since I met with Aiden, and I'm still walking around like I'm in a dream, waiting for someone to pinch me.

"I was thinking I'd go home for a while on Friday night. I don't want to be the awkward third wheel while the two of you catch up."

I frown. "Len, you don't have to leave. It's not like it's a real date."

"Maybe not, but you need time to get reacquainted. And to talk. About private things."

"You know everything there is to know."

She smiles gently. "I do, but he doesn't."

It takes me a second to realize what she's insinuating, and

52

my stomach turns. "I'm not dumping all that on him right out of the gate."

"He should know, sweetie, and the sooner, the better."

"I know. And I will tell him. Eventually." But the thought of upsetting him right after he's agreed to help makes me sick to my stomach. "I'd like the chance to show him I'm not an awful person first."

"You aren't an awful person." Her brow pinches as she shakes her head. "You didn't ask for what happened—"

"I'm not talking about that part."

"Olivia…" She's on her feet and at my side in seconds. "You couldn't control that part, either." Her voice as insistent as her hands on my shoulders.

"I know that, too." But that's the part I regret not telling him about the most, and it's the part I'm afraid he'll hate me for even more.

Lena pulls me in for a hug and I close my eyes as the reality of what Aiden and I are about to do sinks in. He said this wouldn't be easy and he was right. Pretending to care about him while actually caring about him—still—may very well be the hardest thing I've ever done.

"Let's fill these crepes, eat, and talk about happier things." My best friend stands back and gives me her best reassuring smile. "Like the fact that you have two weeks of classes left and then the rest of the summer to yourself."

"And let's not forget about your handsome hubby coming home," I add, and her grin turns all lovesick and dopey.

"He called this morning, by the way. He'll be home a few days early."

"Len, that's great!"

"I know. I can't wait." Her cheeks flush and her eyes grow misty, and I'm so damn happy for her. She and Wendell are the real deal, and he's promised this stint overseas will be his last. That means they're probably going to get started on that family they've been putting off, and nothing makes me happier than imagining Lena as a mom.

"I'm so excited for you. And I give you three months."

She frowns. "Three months?"

"Before you're pregnant."

"Oh my god, stop." She swats my arm as she laughs, the gleam in her eyes promising she's had the same thought.

My phone rings on the counter, interrupting our giggles, and I sigh when I read the screen. "It's Bernie."

"Go and talk, and I'll stuff these bad boys. Do you want strawberries or chocolate on top?"

"Surprise me." Then I stick the phone to my ear. "Good morning, Special Agent."

"Good morning, kiddo. I'm about to ring your doorbell."

At eight o'clock on a Thursday morning? "Is everything okay?"

"Yep, just thought it'd be nice to chat in person."

"Oh. Um, any chance you're hungry?"

"Always. Whatcha got?"

"Homemade crepes."

"Sounds like I picked the perfect time to visit. See ya in two."

"DAMN, THOSE WERE GOOD." The FBI agent pushes his plate to the side and reaches for his coffee less than fifteen minutes later.

"Olivia made them, but they're my mom's recipe." Lena beams as she gets to her feet and collects our plates.

"Is your mom single?" he teases, and Lena laughs. I, however, gesture to the wedding ring on his finger with a curious smile.

"What would your wife say about that?"

54

He glances at his hand and winces. "Don't know. She filed for divorce a month ago. Said I work too damn much."

Oh. Well, that doesn't make me feel guilty or anything, jeez. "I, um, am sorry to hear that."

"Eh. She put up with me longer than I expected she would." He lifts a shoulder and rests an ankle on his knee. "Anyway, I figured we should talk about Detective Enders now that he's on board."

"All right." Never did I think I'd be so relieved to talk about my ex-unofficial-boyfriend turned fake-boyfriend-slash-bodyguard.

"He and I spoke for quite a while yesterday."

I can just imagine how that conversation went. "And?"

"You picked well, kiddo. He has some good ideas, and he certainly seems to know a lot about you."

Heat creeps up my neck and into my cheeks. "It's been a while, but yes, he knew me very well, once upon a time." I'd told him as much when I suggested Aiden as an option for our ruse, minus the details about how our relationship ended.

Special Agent Nolan's eyes narrow with concern like my Grandpa Zieliński's used to, reminding me why I've taken such a liking to the man. "Are you going to be able to do this, Olivia?"

"Of course, I am." I don't have a choice.

"You've been through a lot these past couple of months, and while I have a job to do, I don't want to cause you more pain to get it done."

Lena clears her throat and gets to her feet. "And that's my cue to go and put some laundry in."

Ugh, thanks, Len. "I'll be fine, Bernie."

He eyes me for another beat before he sighs. "He seems like a good guy."

"He is." Without a doubt, the kindest, most loving man

I've ever known. At least, until I broke his heart. "I promise I can handle this, Bernie. Even if it hurts a little."

He studies me for a long beat. "Anyone ever tell you you're stubborn as hell?"

I laugh. "A bunch of people, a bunch of times."

He grins and gives his head a conceding shake. "Well, I hope it works out in our favor this time."

I lift my coffee cup in a mock toast. "You and me both."

"Anyway, like I said, Enders has put some thought into this, and I like where he's going with it."

I didn't realize Aiden would be calling any of the shots, but if I'm honest, there's another layer of comfort in knowing I'll be under his watch in more ways than one.

"And what is he thinking exactly?"

"Nothing too crazy, but we're on the same page about getting this rolling. You two have a past, so it would make sense that you'd jump into things."

Jump into things? "Are you sure that's a good idea? I thought you wanted to go slow." And I thought I had time to get used to the idea of spending time with Aiden again.

He lifts a hand. "Something tells me this isn't a *no news is good news* situation. I suspect the rebels are up to something, and we need to get a jump on them."

I rub my suddenly sweaty palms on my leggings. "So, we're going from zero to a hundred, is that what you're saying?"

He inclines his chin.

"Does that mean going out in public sooner, too?"

"It does."

Thank god. As nervous as I am about being a target, I'm dying for social interaction. I love Lena to death, but I need people and sunlight. And coffee. God, what I wouldn't do for a fancy cup of coffee.

"You two made plans for him to come over tomorrow night, correct?"

"We did. I hope that's okay. I didn't think you'd be willing to let me go out yet."

"No, I think it's a good plan. I'm sure you and Detective Enders will want to spend some time getting reacquainted before you go under the microscope."

Right, because alone time with my ex is going to be *so much easier* than having people who want me dead watching me from a distance.

"How is Aiden going to get past whoever is on duty?"

"I was thinking about that." Agent Nolan rubs at the gray stubble on his jaw. "How good of an actress are you?"

Oh boy.

AIDEN

"Hey man, haven't seen you in a few days. How'd your meeting go in Milwaukee?" Craig Perry, my temporary roommate and old high school friend, cracks open a beer as soon as I walk through my front door on Thursday night. Given he's already swapped out his dingy work clothes for basketball shorts and nothing more, he's clearly been here a while. Again.

"The meeting went fine." I go to the fridge for a beer of my own, not bothering to kick off my boots or drop my holster on the table. It's been a long week, and the hardest part is yet to come. "The feds need someone unknown for an undercover gig." It isn't a complete lie, not that Craig would give a shit either way. He's got too much going on in his own life to pay attention to mine.

"Yeah? You gonna do it?" He flashes a grin while I twist the top off my bottle.

"Here and there. It's nothing serious." As in, I won't be gone long enough for him to get any more comfortable in my house than he already has. I love the guy like a brother, but I'm at the end of my rope with this roommate arrangement. "How's the hunt for a rental going?"

"Eh. There's a one-bedroom apartment above the hardware store, but it's barely big enough for me, let alone the kids when they come over. That house next to Cady's is still open, too, but I don't think that's a good idea."

"Why not?" I'd think a place next door to his girlfriend would be perfect. Easier to run back and forth between booty calls.

"Rachel would have my ass if I had the kids staying that close to Cady."

I lift my beer with a snort. "She's gonna hate any interaction they have with Cady regardless of where it's at." Craig and Rachel split up five months ago, and within two, he was seeing his high school sweetheart again. How the hell he could go from his wife of twelve years to his first love in the blink of an eye is beyond me.

"I know, but right next door would be like rubbing salt in a wound, you know? I'm not trying to hurt Rach like that."

Yeah, well, maybe he should have thought about that before he hooked up with Cady again.

"Look, man, I don't want to make shit harder on you, but I think that one-bedroom apartment might be worth looking into. At least for the time being. You've already been seeing the kids at your folks', and I'm sure they enjoy the time with them, too."

He rubs a hand over his bald head and nods. "Yeah, probably. I know you're anxious to get your couch back."

"It's more like I need my privacy back, if ya know what I

mean." If this ruse with Olivia takes longer than I'm hoping, I'm going to have to bring her around. I sure as hell don't want to continue the charade in my own damn home just because he's here.

He arches an eyebrow. "You seeing someone?"

"Maybe."

"Well, I'll be damned." A bark of laughter rattles his burly chest. "Who is it?"

"Nope." I shake my head before he even finishes the question. I might know all of his dirt, but I'm not sharing mine. Especially when it's not real. "I'm not saying shit."

Craig chuckles again. "That's all right. It'll come out eventually. Nothing ever stays quiet for too long in this town."

I don't know about that. Some things can remain secrets for years if you hide them well enough.

"I'll stop by and talk to Karl about the apartment tomorrow. I won't be accused of cockblocking you in your own house."

"Appreciate that, man." Though, the only action my cock is gonna get is with my hand in the shower. And given how good Liv looked the other night, probably lots of it.

BY THE TIME I polish off a frozen pizza and grab a shower, Craig is stretched out on the couch in front of a Brewers game. Normally, I'd kick back in the recliner and join him, but there's no room in my head for baseball tonight.

I drop into the leather chair behind the old desk in my home office, plug in my laptop, and send a handful of follow-up emails and invoices for my private investigation work. I hate to put the PI gig on hold when I've finally hit my stride, but a few weeks off shouldn't set me back too much. After all, the point of venturing out on my own was to build my résumé and list of references, so if the time came that I wanted to leave Pine County for bigger and better opportunities, I'd have the experience I needed. Helping the FBI and Interpol with Jakub Jelanovich's case is going to do a hell of a lot more for my career than catching a bunch of cheating husbands with their pants down.

Speaking of Jelanovich, I dig into my laptop bag and retrieve the flash drive Special Agent Nolan had overnighted to me after we talked on Wednesday.

"Here's everything you need to know about Jelanovich," he'd said. *"You lose it or leak it, and your sister will be helping your mother pick out your headstone while your father and brothers carry your casket."*

Not gonna lie… I'd been on the fence about the guy until that moment. He'd come off almost tired during our first meeting. Like he had one foot out the door to retirement and wanted this case over with so he could swap his badge for a fishing pole. Part of me wanted to jump on board for that fact alone, because if he wasn't going to take this seriously, someone had to.

But after talking with Olivia on Monday night and him this morning, it's obvious the guy has been working this case twenty-four seven from the start. He may be tired, but it's only because he's so damn invested.

The flash drive confirms it. It's full of files organized by date, stemming all the way back to Jelanovich's birth in Katowice, Poland. There's detailed information about his parents, grandparents, aunts, uncles, everyone. He was an only child, and both of his parents died in a factory fire when he was eleven. He moved in with a maternal aunt and remained there until he was sixteen and ran away. Social services located him a month later with his girlfriend and her family almost sixty miles away in Kraków. A year and a half later, that same girlfriend was kidnapped and found dead, just like Olivia had said.

Naturally, my gut says he ran away because he was up to no good. Mixed up in something he shouldn't have been. But the only police report with his name on it is the runaway complaint from his aunt and the follow-up when he was located. The guy had even enrolled himself in high school in Kraków, and he'd had a job at a bookstore. Not exactly criminally suspicious behavior, unless it was a well-designed cover.

He went on to become an honor student at Charles University, and eventually received his doctorate from Loyola only three years after coming to the United States as Mr. Olivia Bishop. Olivia had said she'd started working at UW-Milwaukee as a part-time adjunct instructor as soon as they'd returned to the States, but Jelanovich didn't start teaching there until he received his PhD. In fact, for those three years, he spent more time in Chicago than he did with her in Milwaukee, working at the Polish Exhibition House while he was in grad school.

That museum stint and the fact that he remained so connected after he'd finished his doctorate doesn't sit well. I can't shake the feeling that it's where his involvement with the SSP began. Or maybe continued, if he'd been involved before he left Europe. It could also be nothing. He was a Polish immigrant with a traumatic past, losing both his parents and the girl he loved in horrific ways. Maybe the museum was just a way to stay connected to his roots.

His work record at UW-Milwaukee is also clean. An exemplary professor with a great reputation among his coworkers and students. Not a single traffic ticket. Not a single credit card or loan paid late. He was a member of the St. James Catholic Church, the gym down the street from the university, and the neighborhood watch group in the subdivision where he and Olivia lived. For chrissakes, the only red mark on the guy's background was a friggin' overdue library book from his Loyola days.

I lean back in the chair, fold my arms behind my head, and stare at the picture filling up my laptop screen. The fucking guy was even good-looking. A young David Beckham with half the tattoos. Jake, Olivia had called him. A man she'd trusted and had grown to love, at least platonically, during the course of their relationship.

There's no way in hell they weren't fucking.

Marriage of convenience or not, a guy like this would have a sidepiece if he wasn't getting it at home, and his list of friends is even shorter than mine. Unless he hid a mistress as well as he hid his mob involvement, all signs point to the wife at home.

Fuuck. I dig the heels of my hands into my eyes and try to erase the thought—and the subsequent images—from my head. I haven't lived like a monk for the past ten years, but I can guaran-damn-tee that every woman who's invited me into her bed wanted me there.

It's bad enough Olivia married this asshole to get him across the Atlantic, but if she'd been fucking him for any reason other than she dug his Beckham vibe, I'll exhume his body and cut his dick off myself.

Then again, her doing him because she wanted to doesn't bode well either.

She might've been his in the legal sense, but part of Olivia Bishop will always be mine. She gave it to me when she gave me her virginity fourteen years ago.

And I'll be damned if I'm giving it back.

CHAPTER 8

THIRTEEN YEARS EARLIER...

AIDEN

"What the hell, man, you're leaving already?" Craig scowls from the other side of the campfire, one hand wrapped around a beer and the other around Rachel.

"Yeah, I'm not feeling great tonight." It's total bullshit. I feel better than I have in months, since summer break is finally here, and Bren and I are home from college.

But my head is somewhere else. Hell, it's been somewhere else for a long time.

"Is your old man kicking your ass at work or what?" Bren snickers, and just because I can, I kick the chunk of wood he's sitting on out from under him. "The fuck!" he scoffs, hurrying to his feet as I start toward my truck. "You're lucky you're leaving, you prick!"

My only response is a single-finger salute into the night

air. If he knew where I was really headed, he wouldn't let me walk away. Hell, he'd never let me walk again.

"Feel better!" Rachel calls after me and I blow her a kiss over my shoulder, making Craig snarl.

I hop into my truck, parked at the back edge of the field on Craig's family's land, where we've gathered like this since we were old enough to steal beer from our dads or bribe someone older to buy. When I peel out, my destination is as clear in my mind as the stars in the sky.

I find her about a half mile from her house, walking down the side of the road in a pair of cutoff jean shorts, a tank top, and a pair of Converse shoes. She doesn't bother turning around as I approach, just sticks out her thumb like she's done at least a dozen times in the past year.

"Need a ride, pretty girl?" I call from the truck with all the windows rolled down.

She turns a flirty smile my way, her long ponytail swinging as her dark eyes shine beneath the streetlight. "You're late."

"And you're fucking gorgeous."

She purses her lips. "I bet you say that to all the girls you pick up on the side of the road, don't you, Enders?"

"Just you, Livi. Now, get your ass in here before someone sees us."

She rolls her eyes, but pops the passenger door open and hops in. "You know the prospect of getting caught is half the fun, right?"

"And you know that the second we get caught, it's over."

She scoffs as she fastens her seat belt. "Well, I'm eighteen now, so my brother can kiss my butt."

"I'd rather do that myself." I reach across the cab and palm her bare thigh. I swear she wears these shorts to drive me out of my damn mind.

"You've been home for three days and you're already thinking about getting me naked?"

"I was thinking about getting you naked long before we started this, babe, and now I do it no less than a hundred times a day."

She bites her lip, and in my peripheral, I catch her watching me carefully. We started sneaking out like this last summer shortly after I graduated. Bren had caught me looking at her once and with my arm around her another, and he'd promised he'd end me if he caught me doing either again. But something about turning eighteen and knowing I'd be gone to college while she'd be here with every other swinging dick in Cole Creek made it damn near impossible not to at least try and stake my claim.

Now, she's the one who's just finished high school. She'll be off to college in the fall, too, and we'll be farther apart than we are now. But at least she'll have the privacy of her dorm room. Since I share an apartment with Bren, I have a feeling I'll be knocking on her door in Madison plenty.

"Where are we going tonight?" she asks as my truck bounces down a back road.

We have a half dozen different hiding places in Cole Creek with varying degrees of privacy, but tonight, I'm feeling brave and a little reminiscent.

"You'll see." I squeeze her thigh gently, the feel of her soft skin beneath my fingers already making me hard.

"Oh-kay." She draws out the word suspiciously. "What do you plan on doing when we get there?"

"Kissing every inch of your body."

"Oh really?" She shoots me a naughty glance, the shadows and the streetlights playing across her face as we get closer to our destination.

We've done a lot together. Explored each other's bodies. Learned things together. But we've yet to take it all the way.

I've wanted to. Fucking hell, I've wanted to. But we take that part of our relationship at Liv's pace, and it's been the best kind of torture I can imagine.

"The lake, huh?" She grins when I crank the truck onto the dirt road that goes around to the backside of Amber Lake. Cabins and a few year-round houses surround the lake, but there's a sliver of undeveloped property with a trail just wide enough for a single vehicle. Well, a single vehicle if you don't mind getting a few scratches. The property belongs to the Cole family, Cole Creek's founders, and there are no less than five *No Trespassing* signs posted on the property. They've never stopped me before and they won't tonight, either.

"We haven't been out here since last summer, and I don't know about you, but I could go for a dip."

"I didn't bring a suit." She bites her lip with feigned innocence, and I give a low, knowing laugh.

"Babe, that's never stopped you before."

Her timid expression turns devious, and I'm rock hard in seconds, just thinking about her stripping out of those clothes. We haven't had time alone in months because of her softball schedule and me being a couple of hours away for school, and I fully intend to make up for lost time tonight.

I stop the truck at a small clearing in the trees that's just wide enough to park. Olivia pops her door open and is out of the truck, ditching her flip-flops in the grass so she can dip her toes in the water before my boots even hit the ground.

"You boys and those boots. You know it's June, right?"

I grin as I bend to untie them. "And you know I'm working with my old man, right?"

She scoffs. "During the week, yes. But it's Friday night. Put some sandals on. Or sneakers. You know, relax."

I roll my eyes while I kick off the boots and unzip my

jeans, dropping them right there in the grass. "Not going to give me shit about wearing pants?"

She eyes the straining bulge in my boxer briefs and sighs. "Nope."

"Dirty girl." I yank my T-shirt over my head and charge her, throwing her over my shoulder and spinning us around in the water. I fucking love touching this girl. It's literally my favorite thing to do, and I can't wait to do it as often as we can get away with for the next three months.

"I'm still dressed!" she squeals. "If I go home wet, I'll give us away!"

Good point.

I trudge through the water and deposit her back in the grass, doing my damnedest to unbutton her shorts while she strips off her tank top.

"Fuck." I groan at the sight of her pale bra, pushing those pretty tits up like an offering. My greedy hands and fingers waste no time cupping them and stroking her nipples through the fabric. "Missed this."

"Groping my boobs?" She tips her head to the side, her dark eyes sparkling playfully in the moonlight.

I shake my head. "Just being with you."

"Aww." Her fingers feather back into my hair before her lips find mine in a slow, welcoming kiss. She tastes like mangoes from the gum she's always chewing, and I deepen the kiss to get even more of her until we're both gasping for air. "Wow." She pulls back to catch her breath. "You really did miss me."

"Hell yeah, I did." Sure, we've texted and shared a few late-night conversations that ended up with us both losing our underwear, but getting off alone only curbs the craving for so long. It's not the same as holding her. And touching her. And feeling her body against mine. "How about you? Did you miss me or are those boyfriends of yours keeping you preoccupied?"

"Hmm…" She twists her lips thoughtfully as her fingers work against my scalp, giving me goose bumps. "They've kept me busy, but I still had time to miss you."

"Oh really." Palming her ass, I lift her and her legs naturally wrap around my waist. "Tell me about 'em."

"Which one should I start with?" She starts naming random guys in town, and I half laugh, half growl.

I don't think she's seeing anyone else, other than the guy she went to Prom with a couple months back, but we've never said we're exclusive, and as much as I want us to be, I'm not sure it'd be fair to ask her for that. *Hey, Livi, I don't want us to date other people, but we still can't tell anyone we're sneaking around. You cool with that?* It's shitty, and I'm not gonna be that guy. I won't ask her to be mine and only mine until I can tell everyone else she belongs to me, too.

"Sounds like you've been busy." I carry her into the water until we're waist deep.

"Probably not as busy as you." She smiles, but there's something about the way she says it that doesn't align.

"I haven't been busy, Liv. Not the way you're thinking." I may be nineteen, in college, and perpetually fucking horny, but the second I realized there was something more between us than the juvenile need to do what we were told we couldn't, the other girls lost their appeal.

"You haven't been with anyone else?" Her brows lift above skeptical eyes.

"Not in a long time." I wish I could say there's been no one at all, but I went off to college last fall hell-bent on living like a guy who'd just been given his freedom. Liv and I had only shared a few stolen hours together last summer. A few kisses and tentative touches. It wasn't until Thanksgiving break when we were both home that things changed. When those exploratory moments became purposeful. Desperate. Greedy.

"How long?" she dares to ask, and I answer without hesitation.

"Last fall."

Her dark eyes widen at the same time she shoves at my shoulder. "You're lying."

I chuckle and turn us in the water so I can see her face better in the moonlight. "Babe, if I was going to lie, I would have told you I was a virgin."

She laughs softly, her tits shaking against my chest. "Yeah, right. I've experienced enough to know that's not true."

"Uh-huh." My fingers dig deep into the soft flesh of her ass, hungrily tugging her body closer to mine. The mere thought of all the shit we've done since Thanksgiving has my balls aching for more.

"More proof that you've missed me, I see." She flexes her hips and grinds intentionally against my cock, making us both groan into the night. "God, that feels good."

"You want me to make it feel even better?" I husk against her lips. "You want me to make you come with my mouth?"

"*Aidennn.*" Her head falls back as her hips pulse in time with mine, her breath already coming in short, desperate pants. "I want to make you feel good, too."

"I can get on board with that."

"Then get me out of this water," she commands, and I obey like the whipped guy I am.

Spreading my T-shirt out in the grass, I guide her down and immediately wedge myself between her thighs, so we can continue what we started in the water with nothing but our wet underwear between us. She's so fucking soft and warm, accepting every one of my thrusts with a breathy little grunt.

"You drive me crazy." I slide my mouth from her lips to her neck, nipping and teasing her skin. She always smells like flowers. Sweet and delicate, which is a reminder that no matter how much shit she likes to give me—one of my favorite things about her—she also has a soft and tender side, too. She's fucking everything, this girl.

"Touch me," she begs, her heaving chest rising and falling beneath my own. "I need it. I need you."

I groan and clench my eyes shut. Words like that make it hard not to ask for more. I want to give her everything. I want to show her just how good it could be between us, but I've taken so much from her already, by playing this game.

"Show me." I slide to the side, so I can watch, my own hand finding my throbbing cock and rubbing through my boxers.

She bites her lip, but her eyes never stray from mine as her hand lifts to her breast. Her touch is tentative at first. Featherlike fingertips on the swell of flesh rising from her bra before they stroke over her nipple still covered in pale lace.

Her breath hitches as she becomes bolder, tweaking that hardened peak until her body trembles with arousal. Then she tugs at the fabric, exposing that pretty pink bud to me and the moon and those knowing fingers.

My mouth goes dry as I watch her play until I can't take it any longer. I give in and dip my head, laving my tongue across the nub and then sucking it into my mouth.

"Oh god…" She pants, her hands diving back into my hair as her back arches off my T-shirt. "More," she pleads, and I give it to her. Tugging down the other cup, I go back and forth between her breasts, toying and sucking until she's gasping for breath. Only then do I give her what she really wants, sliding a hand into her panties and finding her already so slick and swollen for me.

"Who missed who, huh, Livi?" I tease, nipping at her lips

with a kiss as I stroke her clit in that slow, torturous way I know she likes.

"I've been waiting for you to come home," she rasps as she closes her eyes and lets her legs fall open for me.

"So I could do this?" I slip a finger inside, and she hisses.

"*Yesss.* Aiden, I need more."

I chuckle and slide down the length of her body to position my shoulders between her thighs. "Like this?" Pulling her panties to the side, I flick my tongue across her clit. She cries out into the night, and I grin against the inside of her leg. "Shh, baby. No getting caught, remember?"

A low guttural laugh rolls in her chest as she grips my T-shirt at her sides and gives herself over to me, trying her damnedest not to be too loud as I dive back in, eating her pussy under the stars like it's my last goddamn meal.

"Aiden," she cries softly, and I know what she needs. I feel it in the tension in her body, but fuck if I don't love hearing her call my name, begging me to give it to her.

"You're so wet," I tell her, slipping that finger back in again. "But still so fucking tight."

"More," she pants, flexing her hips just slightly, like she wants to fuck my hand, but isn't quite brave enough to do it.

"More?" I chuckle. "You sure?"

"Yes, dammit!" Her eyes fly open and lock on mine as I give her another finger and fuck them in and out of her as her nostrils flare and she grits her teeth. "I want you," she rasps. "I want to feel you."

"You are feeling me, baby."

She gives her head the slightest shake. "I want *you*," she says again and my dick throbs in realization. "I'm ready."

"Livi—"

"I want it to be you."

I want that, too. In fact, the idea of anyone else touching

her makes me want to do something that'll put me in the back of a cop car, not behind the wheel.

"The more we keep doing this, the riskier it's going to get. I want it to be you before—"

I press a finger to her lips before she can say it. I'm not ready for this to be over. Fuck, it feels like we've barely started.

"You have a condom, right?"

"I do, but—"

She sits up, tits spilling from her bra, and cups my face. "We've come too far not to finish what we've started."

Jesus fucking Christ.

"I want to feel you inside me," she whispers. "I want to know all of you, Aiden. And I want you to know me."

She's going to kill me. Right here on the shore of Amber Lake.

"You're sure." It's not a question. I see the certainty in her dark eyes. I know she means it, and that excites me and scares the hell out of me at the same time. "I don't want to hurt you."

"It'll only hurt for a little while. And then you'll make me feel better, I know you will." She presses a kiss to my lips. "I can't imagine it being anyone else."

Fuck that shit. She'll *never* know another man if I have anything to say about it.

She reaches down and palms my dick through my wet boxer briefs. "I've thought about this so many times," she whispers. "When I lie alone in bed at night, wishing you were here."

"Me, too," I admit. "I want you so fucking badly, Liv."

"Then have me."

That's all I need to hear. I'm so far gone with her tonight that I couldn't turn back even if I'd wanted to. Not with her practically begging me to fuck her for the first time.

I kiss her hard, our mouths as frantic as our hands, tugging off each other's underwear right there in the grass beside the lake. I'd imagined our first time together to be a hell of a lot more romantic than this, but somehow this is fitting, too. This is our spot. The first place we snuck off to, the first place we kissed, and now the first place we'll make love.

She strokes me as I reach for my jeans and grab the condom from my wallet. She's so confident in herself now. Knows how to touch me and drive me insane, which I fucking love and not just because I taught her how to do it, but because I've learned as much from her as she has from me.

And now we're going to share this. I may not be a virgin like she is, but I might as well be, because this is the first time I actually give a shit. The other girls were a means to an end, but Liv... fuck. It feels like the beginning.

"You're shaking," she whispers as she watches me tear open the packet and try to roll the rubber over my dick with fumbling hands. "Let me."

I laugh. "If I let you keep touching me, I'm gonna be done before we even get started."

She smiles and leans back on one hand while the other strokes lazily over one of her breasts, making her already hard nipple tighten into a puckered bud. I groan and her grin hitches a little higher to one side.

"Quit playing with me," I grumble, finally getting the damn condom on and lunging for her. She falls back on my T-shirt with a soft squeak as I hover above her, hands planted on either side of her head. Her dark hair is splayed out in the grass just like her legs are for me.

"I feel like I've waited forever for this," she rasps as I widen my knees so I can control the stroke of my shaft against her wet heat. If she were anyone else, I'd be buried inside already, chasing release.

"We can't undo this, Livi," I warn her, teeth gritted as she pulses her hips in time with mine, her breath hitching every time my cock rubs her clit. "You let me inside and we can't take that back."

"I want you." Her nails score down my arms as she pulls in a shaky breath and her lashes flutter in that way I've come to know all too well. She's close to coming from friction alone, and she wants me inside when she does it. But I know better. It'll hurt too much and she won't come at all.

"You're not ready yet." I reach between us and stroke my thumb over her clit instead of fucking her.

"Aiden," she whimpers in frustration that quickly dissipates when I find the perfect spot just to the left of her clit. "Oh god!" She flies in minutes, her hips bucking up to mine and damn near making me come just from watching her.

"Good girl. Now you're ready." With her body still humming from her orgasm, I line up and press in until she takes just the tip of my dick. She's so fucking tight and hot, and all I can think about is how good she's going to feel gripping me when I'm seated all the way inside. But I can't be greedy. Not with her.

"O-oh," she stammered, her brow furrowed slightly. "That's... wow."

"Too much?"

She shakes her head and licks her lips. "No. Just... you're big."

I laugh, because I'm pretty sure she has no reference material to base that on.

"Give me more," she rasps, so I inch in a little farther but feel her body go rigid beneath me.

"Relax for me, Livi." Lowering down to my elbows, I can claim her mouth to distract her, and she gasps against my lips as I retreat and push in again. But the hazy look in her eyes assures me that she's begun to feel the pleasure with the pain. The promise of something better to come.

"Better," she pants, her hips slowly beginning to work with mine, and amping up that pressure at the base of my spine.

"You feel fucking amazing." Better than amazing. Fucking perfect. And having her like this… knowing she's giving me something that will be mine and mine alone forever… it's everything. "Fuck, Livi," I grunt, my body humming as we fall into a rhythm. "I'm not going to last."

"I don't care," she whispers as her hands thread into my hair and hold my face close to hers. "Come inside me. Show me what that feels like."

Jesus Christ. I close my eyes and lose myself in the sensation of her body welcoming mine. Of knowing that what she's given me tonight, she can never give to anyone else. This is ours and ours alone, and it means more to me than I ever thought possible.

I come with one last thrust, spilling myself inside of her and feeling her body tremble beneath mine as she realizes the magnitude of what we've done as well.

She might've given me her body, but she took my heart in return.

CHAPTER 9

PRESENT...

AIDEN

The sun is still shining in a blue and orange sky when I pull into Liv's driveway on Friday night. I've been on edge since we planned this so-called date, but the weather and my '90s country playlist have at least dulled my nerves to a tolerable buzz instead of the live wires they've been.

Something tells me the agent hurrying from his unmarked car in the street to my truck is going to charge them back up again. I roll my window down before he can knock on the glass, or worse, smash it in.

"Wrong house, asshole." His eyes narrow to slits as he rests his hand on his holster. He's probably my age, maybe a little younger. Built like a brick house, too.

I give him my best shit-eating grin. "Nah, I'm pretty sure it's the right house. I'm here to see Olivia."

He scowls and removes the Glock. "The fuck you are. No one steps foot on this property without clearance."

"Ah." I chuckle. He takes his job seriously, and I like that. But if he lifts that gun any higher, we're going to have a problem. "Guess I should've thought of that, huh?"

"Yeah, I guess you should have," the guy mutters as the front door of the white, two-story colonial opens and Olivia appears, dressed in a pair of snug jeans and an off-the-shoulder pink sweater.

"It's okay, Derek," she calls out, and her use of his first name makes my lip curl. Is she this familiar with all of her security? "He's my friend from the hotel."

"Don't care. No one goes inside without clearance."

Her shoulders drop as she steps onto the porch in bare feet. "Does it matter that he's a cop?"

The agent's eyebrows lift. "Then needing clearance shouldn't be a surprise."

I sigh, pull out my badge, and hand it over. "Do what you gotta do, man."

"It doesn't work like that."

Obviously, but I have a role to play. "Then how does it work, Agent? You want to frisk me?"

His scowl hardens, but he reholsters the gun. "Don't fucking move."

"Wouldn't think of it."

He pulls out his phone and hits a contact. A few seconds later, he barks into the line, "Dr. Bishop has unexpected company. She says it's the guy from the hotel."

I can't hear the other end of the call, but I know he's called Nolan to tattle just like we'd hoped.

A smug grin spreads across his face as he listens. "Ah, well, that's perfect then. See you soon." He disconnects and shoves the phone back in his pocket. "Special Agent Nolan happens to be nearby. You can plead your case to him yourself."

I snort. "Fine by me. Oh, and I don't believe I got your full name, *Derek*. I have a feeling we're going to be seeing a lot of each other, so we might as well get acquainted."

He glowers for a long beat before answering. "O'Reilly."

"Aiden Enders." I offer my hand through the open window, but he doesn't so much as glance at the gesture.

"What's your interest here?" he grumbles instead.

I glance to Olivia, still standing on the front stoop with her arms crossed over her chest anxiously. "Her."

His jaw tightens in a way I'm not sure I like.

"She should really be inside, don't you think? Standing out here like this where she's an easy target isn't the best idea, all things considered."

Color rises in his neck and he quickly glances at Olivia. "Go inside. I'll take care of this."

She looks to me for confirmation, and I dip my chin. Whether seeking my approval is part of her act or because she genuinely trusts me more, I'm not sure. But I'll take it regardless.

A minute later, a dark sedan pulls up behind my truck, and O'Reilly steps back as Nolan gets out.

"He says he's a cop," the younger agent says. "Badge looks legit, but I wasn't taking chances."

Nolan marches up to the driver's door and props his hands on his hips. "Detective Enders, right?"

"Yes, sir."

"You ought to know you can't just show up like this." His eyes remain as stoic as his set jaw. "I don't give a shit if you're a cop, an old friend, or the President of the fucking United States. She's protected, and I'm pretty sure she told you that."

"She did, but I didn't realize I needed to schedule a visit."

His gaze narrows. "You're damn lucky I already checked

78

you out the other day or your ass would be in cuffs right now."

Uh-huh. "Well, I appreciate your consideration." I stick my tongue in my cheek to keep from grinning. He could play one of those shitty cops on TV if he ever decides to give up the bureau.

"Is this gonna be a regular thing?"

I lift a shoulder. "Not sure."

He takes a step closer and lowers his voice, but not so much that O'Reilly can't hear. "I know you two have history, and I swear to god if you're trying to play on her vulnerability..."

"You've got nothing to worry about, Special Agent," I grind out. Acting or not, he's hit a nerve. If anyone's going to get hurt in this mess, it's me, not Olivia.

Still glowering, he shifts back and nods to O'Reilly. "He's clear, but I want to be notified every time he comes and goes."

I snort. "Wow."

He points a finger at me. "Don't push your luck, Enders."

O'Reilly continues to watch me as I hop out of the truck with a bottle of wine in hand. Something about the guy pisses me off, but I can't put my finger on it.

Olivia opens the front door as I climb the porch, taking in the potted flowers and the chairs that look brand new. The house is definitely on the upscale side, with its well-maintained yard and exterior. Jinx would be impressed.

"Sorry about that." She glances quickly to the agents still conversing in the driveway. "Special Agent Nolan thought it would be more believable."

"He's probably right. Having me go down to the station for clearance probably would have garnered attention we don't need."

She clears her throat and steps aside, gesturing toward the foyer. "Come in."

"Thanks. Is Lena here?"

"Ah, no. She went home for the night."

"The night?"

"Her husband Wendell—you might remember him from college—is coming home from overseas in a few days and she wanted to get things in order. Since you're going to be here for a while, it seemed like a good opportunity."

"Right." And hopefully I'll be able to completely relieve Lena of her babysitting duties sooner than later, because let's be honest—she's in as much danger as Liv is when she's here, and that doesn't bode well.

Clearing my throat, I glance around the foyer and the living room off to the left. "Nice place."

She follows my perusal around the modern but comfortable-looking space. It's immaculately clean and white. Very, very white. The walls, the chair rail, the carpeting in the living room... hell, even the furniture. The only color comes from the honey-colored floors and the sporadic splash of color in the pictures on the walls.

"Thanks." She gives a small smile. "I love the style, but I've always thought it could use some color."

I give in to a laugh, despite the awkwardness of being in the home she shared with another man. "You said it, not me."

She tips her head to the side and gives me a wry grin. "Ha ha. If you must know, Jake had a thing for white. Said it looked cleaner. More organized."

Yeah, well, Jake was also embezzling money from one of the most powerful underground organizations in the world, but hey, what do I know?

"Here..." I pass her the wine. "Couldn't come empty-handed."

"Thank you." Our fingers brush when she takes the bottle,

and I pretend not to notice her quick intake of breath. "I'll pour us a glass while we wait for dinner to finish."

"You didn't have to cook, Liv."

"Of course, I did. You came all the way down here for me. The least I can do is feed you."

"I'm getting paid to be here, remember?"

"Are you?" She glances over her shoulder as I follow her to the kitchen. "I mean, obviously you are, but from the FBI?"

"I was sworn in as a federal agent this morning via Zoom."

"No kidding."

"Had to keep it on the down low, but it's official." Not quite how I imagined it would happen, but it happened and that's all that matters. The only part that bugs me is that I couldn't share the news with my folks or siblings, and risk them asking questions I can't answer.

Liv bites her lip, her thoughts as clear in her eyes as if she'd said them out loud. She knew the FBI was my dream. We'd talked about it as often as we'd talked about her wanting to become a professor. Neither of us imagined this was how I'd get in.

"Anyway, it smells good in here." I change the subject before I get pissed all over again about the circumstances. If I don't make the best of this situation, it's going to be one hell of a long assignment.

"Nothing special. Just garlic and herb chicken and roasted vegetables. I wanted to grill it, but even the back patio is off-limits these days." She sighs and I feel her frustration. The Liv I knew was a free spirit. The girl who loved the sun on her face and the wind in her hair.

"You've gotta be going crazy in here like this." I nod toward the windows overlooking the backyard, where the blinds are pulled just like the rest of the house.

She makes a throaty sound as she takes two wineglasses

down from the cupboard. "I steal peeks every now and then, but for the most part, they have me living like a vampire. I'm afraid that when I do finally get the chance to go outside for any amount of time, I'm going to catch fire and burn up on the spot."

I chuckle and lean a hip against the counter. "You always did sunburn easily."

Our eyes meet and her cheeks turn the slightest shade of pink. "Still do."

Fuck, the places on her I've seen turn pink like that.

I clear my throat. "Anyway, you said the picture they took of you was from your bedroom window?"

She nods and uncorks the wine. "Hence living in the dark."

"Is your room upstairs or downstairs?"

"Upstairs."

"At the front or the back of the house?"

"The back. Why?" She frowns curiously as I recall the picture I'd seen in the file. It was a close-up shot of her in a bra that looked straight on, like whoever had taken it had been at the same level as her.

"Just gathering information." And making a mental note to check whether or not the feds tried to replicate the shot from any of the neighbors' houses.

"Okay." She hands me a glass of wine but then hesitates, eyes narrowed. "Are you actually going to drink that?"

"I brought it, didn't I?" I prefer the kind of alcohol that comes in brown, twelve-ounce bottles, but I can be classy every now and then when I have to be.

She presses her lips into a knowing smile. "I have Bud Light in the fridge if you'd rather."

No shit. Did she buy it for me or is it left over from her dead husband?

"I had Lena run out for it earlier before she went home."

Well, damn. "In that case, I'll take a beer."

Satisfaction dances across her face as she goes to the fridge. "Some things never change, do they?"

Apparently not, and the way my gaze drops to her ass when she bends to retrieve the beer is no exception. She's always been a beautiful woman, and time has been good to her physically. Too bad it's been so cruel otherwise.

"Damn bottle." She struggles to open it for a solid thirty seconds before she hands it over with a huff and then rolls her eyes when I twist it off with ease. "Men."

"Don't be hatin'." I wink and lift the beer for a toast. "Here's to keeping you alive."

Her drink clinks against mine before my words hit her and her jaw drops. "Really? That's your toast?"

"It's what we're doing, isn't it?" I take a pull from the beer and recline back against the counter once again.

"Yes, but it sounds awful when you say it like that."

"Hate to break it to you, Liv, but you're gonna be hearing a lot of awful shit in the coming weeks."

"What do you mean?" She frowns before she sips.

"If we can't wrap this up quickly, people back home are bound to find out about us seeing each other." I air quote the last three words, and she wets her lips nervously.

"I guess I didn't think of that."

"You gonna be all right with it?" Her husband has been gone for less than two months, and in no time, everyone's going to think she's banging her brother's best friend. Not the kind of reputation a lady probably wants to make for herself.

"It can't possibly get any worse than the truth." She distractedly swirls the red liquid around in her glass and forces a smile. "You know?"

Yep, but I'm not going to agree and rub salt in the wound. "Let's hope that's a bridge we don't have to cross."

AFTER DINNER, we move into the living room with full bellies and a basic recap of everything she'd told me at the hotel earlier in the week.

"Now that you've had time to think about things, I suppose you have more questions." She settles onto one corner of the couch while I claim the other.

"Tell me more about Jake." Leaning back, I stretch an arm along the top of the cushions as casually as I can. No part of hearing her recall her life with another man is going to relax me, but I'll try. For her.

"What do you want to know?" She pulls her legs up to sit cross-legged and then picks at a string on the bottom of her jeans.

"Whatever you want to tell me. Maybe his hobbies, habits… that kind of thing."

She blows out a breath and rattles off a bunch of basic stuff I'd already gathered. His love of history and his involvement with the museum in Chicago, his introverted personality, his preference for reading over watching football or baseball on TV…

"He didn't have a ton of friends, but those he did have, he was close with."

"Okay, tell me about them."

"His friend Eli in Chicago, for one. He's a law professor at Columbia, but he's involved with the museum, too. And Victor, who lives on the next street over. He's Czech, so they bonded over that. And I suppose Troy from the university. He was actually a friend of mine first, but he and Jake grew close over the years, too."

"This Eli guy… is he Polish, as well?"

"I assume so, but I'm not sure. I don't even know what he

does at the museum. We talked mostly about teaching whenever we saw each other."

"How often did Jake go to Chicago?"

"At least once a month for museum board meetings. Sometimes more often if he and Eli had a golf date."

Prime opportunity to discuss matters like swindling money from the SSP. "And the neighbor? Victor?"

"He's quiet and super sweet. He blushes about everything. I can't imagine he'd be involved with anything crazier than the neighborhood poker ring."

"You didn't think Jake would be either."

Her eyes flick to mine before she glances down with a sigh. "True."

"What about your friend at work?"

"Troy. He and Jake are more work friends than anything. They grabbed lunch together every now and then when their schedules allowed it, and we'd sometimes meet up with him for drinks after work."

I study her for a moment, watching the worry line form in the center of her forehead. "What's wrong?"

"Nothing really. It's just... Lena thinks Troy has a thing for me."

"What do you mean?"

She pulls in a breath and then exhales heavily. "I don't know. I guess he's a little flirty, and I've caught him staring a few times, though he's never been inappropriate."

Inappropriate or not, he made her feel uncomfortable and that automatically makes me dislike the guy. "You said you knew him before Jake did?"

"I started teaching at the university as an adjunct instructor while I worked on my doctorate. Troy was new, too. We went through orientation together. And then when Jake started working for the university a few years later, they became friends, as well."

But something about the guy doesn't sit right with her. Maybe there's a reason for that.

"I should have known," she says abruptly as she pushes a hand through her hair. "That Jake was involved with the SSP, at the very least, even if I didn't know exactly what he was doing."

"Guys like that go out of their way to make sure they don't get caught. You can't beat yourself up about it, Liv."

"Maybe he'd still be here if I'd realized..." She clenches her eyes shut, and the regret in her voice... the pain... it's hard to hear even after all this time. But letting it get to me won't do either of us any good.

"Can you show me around? I assume you still have his things here."

She nods and quickly gets to her feet, like she's grateful for the distraction. "The FBI went through everything, but Special Agent Nolan told me not to get rid of anything just in case."

"I'd like to take a look myself, if you don't mind. Just to put things into perspective."

"Of course." She gestures toward a short hall running to the left between the kitchen and living room. "He used the master bedroom, and his office is right across the hall."

Separate bedrooms? Interesting.

"Here." She leads the way to the rooms and opens one of the dark oak doors, revealing a neat and tidy bedroom that's just as white and unassuming as the rest of the house. But the second the scent of masculine cologne that isn't mine hits my nose, the hair on the back of my neck rises. This guy might've put on a good show, but he was a dirty crook who obviously didn't give a shit about his wife. He's damn lucky he'll never meet me face to face.

"This is how he left it?" I ask, my voice gruff.

"Mostly. Like I said, Special Agent Nolan and his team

went through everything, but they left it pretty much how it was."

I nod, and take it all in. The stack of books on the dresser, the framed pictures on the wall—European scenes if my geography recollection is correct—and the four-poster bed that I imagine Liv shared at least occasionally.

"Mind if I take a closer look?" I crane my head to the side until my neck snaps while my hands flex at my sides.

"Not at all." She steps aside, and I make my way around the room, taking measured breaths to keep the mental pictures of Liv with another man from playing out in my head.

I hate everything about this asshole. His obsession with white. How fucking organized he was. For fuck's sake, even his clothes are hung in order of color and garment type in his closet. What kind of guy does that? Either a control freak or someone who's trying a little too hard to look *clean*.

"How about the office?"

"Sure."

Like the bedroom, the office is tidy but far more lived in. The built-in bookcases on the side walls are full of history books and literature, and the desk has a couple stacks of files and paperwork and a single computer monitor.

"The FBI took his laptop and external hard drives." Liv leans into the doorway. "They also took a few files, but I don't think they ever found anything in them."

"They're in the electronic records Nolan shared with me the other day."

"Ah, okay."

"And these were deemed irrelevant?" I gesture to the remaining folders, and she nods.

"Those are just the household finances and his paperwork from the university. Grades, advising info… that kind of thing."

"I'm going to want to check all of this over myself. I hope that's okay with you."

"Of course." She nods again. "Right now?"

"No, but eventually."

Our eyes lock and she blinks, as if realizing just how much time we're going to have to spend together over the next few weeks.

"How are we going to do this?" she asks suddenly. "With us, I mean? Are you going to keep coming back every week? Or a couple times a week? We live on opposite ends of the state, and you can't stay down here without it being obvious that you're working with the FBI."

I shrug from behind the desk. "I guess that depends."

"On?"

"How quickly we fall into old habits."

Her lips part and her cheeks flush at the same time her breathing kicks up just a notch. Between that perfect little pout and the slight flare of her nostrils, it's almost like the thought turned her on. Hell, maybe it does. The prospect of touching her and kissing her sure as fuck has my blood pumping a little faster.

But this isn't real, and I'd do well not to forget that.

CHAPTER 10

OLIVIA

*N*ever in a million years did I think Aiden Enders would be walking around my house in his socks, drinking my beer, and breathing my air. At least not since I was a fool-hearted twenty-one-year-old girl who'd thought we'd actually end up sharing a life together.

"How about the rest of the house?" he asks, pulling Jake's office door closed behind us.

"My bedroom and office are upstairs. Lena has the small guest room on the other side of this level, near the laundry room."

"Anything else upstairs?" he asks.

"Another guest room and a bathroom."

"Can I take a look?"

"Of course." Though, the thought of Aiden in my bedroom… well, let's just say he's been there lots of times already in my dreams and in my imagination.

We head upstairs, and it's possible I put a little extra sway in my hips, knowing he's behind me. I'm not the youthful college girl I was ten years ago, but I've done well to keep in shape, and it wouldn't hurt my feelings if he took notice. You know, to help this fake relationship of ours seem more authentic.

The first stop is the guest bedroom, which has nothing more than basic furniture, and the second is my bathroom.

"For the record, I would have cleaned if I had known you'd want to see it." I flip on the light to reveal the evidence of my obsessive primping session before he arrived. My curling iron, hair products, and makeup are spread across the counter, and there's a lacy black bra and panties set sitting on top of the hamper, because I'd almost convinced myself that I should wear them *just in case*.

"I assume the feds went through everything in here, too?" He glances around, and yep, his gaze drops to my underwear. Great.

"Uh, why would they?" I skirt around him and quickly shove the black lace into the hamper.

He cocks an eyebrow. "They didn't look in here?"

"I suppose they could have, but I assumed they didn't. Jake never used my bathroom."

He lifts his chin and something dark flashes in his eyes. "Never?"

"Never. He—" *Shit*. He might've used it a time or two to clean up after sex the few times we'd had it up here, but that had been forever ago. "Not anytime recently."

Those stormy blue eyes narrow knowingly, and I want to shrink away in shame. But I shouldn't feel ashamed, dammit. We were married and being intimate with my husband was far more appropriate than sleeping with other men for the sake of getting off. Not that I'd had much interest in sex at all, especially early on.

"Your office?" Aiden steps back, as if the awkwardness of

the moment is more than he wants to deal with right now, too.

"Yep, over here. It's a little messy, because I've been spending most of my time up here between teaching and trying to figure out what Jake did with the money." I hug my arms around myself as Aiden's perceptive eyes take everything in.

"Have you come up with anything?"

"About Jake?" I shake my head. "Only that he covered his tracks really well."

"Or he had an accomplice."

I frown. "There's been no evidence of that."

"A million dollars doesn't just up and walk away, Liv."

"Well, no, but—"

"If there's no evidence of Jake spending it or stashing it, maybe that's because someone else did."

Obviously, I'd wondered the same thing when we couldn't find the money, but there's been literally no sign that Jake ever had the funds, let alone gave them to someone else.

Unless that other person had the money all along. But who?

"Is that what you think happened?"

He shrugs. "We can't rule anything out at this point."

"I guess not." I bite my lip and sigh.

"Do you still talk to his friends?" He opens a folder on my desk and casually flips through a syllabus for one of my courses this semester.

"Victor and his wife came over a couple of times for coffee, and like I said, I work with Troy, so we correspond via email like we've always done. I haven't seen or talked to Eli since the funeral, but his wife has texted a couple of times to check in."

"Eli is the guy in Chicago, right? The one at the museum?"

I nod.

"What else do you know about him?"

"He's a professor at Columbia like I told you. He teaches a few law classes. His wife's name is Melanie, and he golfs. He's really nice. A family kind of guy."

"Sounds like a trip to Chicago might be warranted."

"Why?" I pull back in surprise. "The FBI has already talked to him. If there was any concern, they would have told me."

He lifts an easy shoulder. "Something about that museum doesn't feel right. I'd rather look into him myself to make sure nothing was missed."

"Won't you give yourself away if you talk to him?"

"There's this cool thing cops do called undercover work…" One corner of his mouth lifts into a cocky smile, and I roll my eyes.

"Ha ha." I understand feeling like he needs to double-check some things, because I'd probably be the same way if I jumped into teaching a class in the middle of a semester. But if Eli is up to something—and I don't believe he is—then Aiden would be putting himself in front of the firing squad. This job is risky enough without doing his own investigation.

"Look, I can see the hesitation in your eyes, but there has to be something they're missing."

I don't disagree, but… "Driving down to Chicago isn't part of your job."

His jaw sets tight, and I shiver, because there's something about that determined *try and stop me* look in his eyes that always gets to me. "Saving your ass is my job, Liv, and I'll do whatever it takes to make that happen."

"Aiden…"

"You're not going to win this argument." His fierce expression leaves no room for debate. I suppose I should have known better than to try and say otherwise, because he's always been the hardheaded kind. The kind who doesn't like to be told he can't do something, case in point, when my brother told him to stay away from me all those years ago.

"You're still bullheaded, I see."

"Born and raised with no plans to change." He grins, and I give in to a soft laugh. He's right—I'm not going to win this debate and I'm not even going to try.

"So, what are you going to do? What's your big undercover plan, Detective?"

"Not sure yet, but I *am* Polish, so I'm sure I can come up with a reason to pay the museum a visit."

"You know, your mom would probably love it. It's quite beautiful. Lots of history to explore."

"I'm sure she would, but I'm not dragging my mother along on an investigation."

"Maybe some other time." I offer a small smile, and we share an extended stare, the momentary step into personal conversation feeling foreign and yet familiar at the same time.

"Anyway, I'm going to want to look through everything in here, too.

"Uh, sure. Whatever you need." I nibble on the corner of my lip and pray I have enough time to move the one file I don't want him to see just yet.

"I know it feels like an invasion of privacy, but if I'm going to be useful in this case, I need to do some of my own work."

"I understand. It's just..." I glance down, unable to look him in the eye when I lie.

"It's just what?" He sits on the edge of my desk, and even though he's still halfway across the room, another shiver of awareness slides down my spine. He's so big and imposing, and he should look and feel out of place in my personal space, but he doesn't. In fact, nothing about him being here in my home feels wrong. Sure, it's different, but there's still a familiarity between us. A level of comfort that relieves me as much as it makes me nervous. But the comfort isn't quite enough just yet to tell him my big, bad, ugly secret.

"I'd just like to organize things a bit first. I'm in the middle of grading assignments and I don't want to lose my place. Anyway, let me show you my room and then we can head back downstairs to make a plan for what's to come."

I spin away and start down the hall ahead of him, reaching into my dark room for the light, when Aiden's hand suddenly shoots out from behind me and grabs my wrist.

I gasp, and not just because he scared the shit out of me, but because I can feel his big body behind me, radiating heat and something that feels a heck of a lot more dangerous.

"Don't," he rasps as he pushes around me and hurries to the window beside my bed. The blinds are closed, but something must have caught his attention because he carefully opens them just a sliver to peek outside. "The outside light came on as soon as we stepped into the doorway. It wasn't on when we were in your office."

"Oh." How could he tell that with the blinds closed?

"I'm going to go downstairs and check it out."

"It's probably a stray cat. There are lots in this neighborhood."

"Maybe, but I'm gonna look anyway."

"The FBI has surveillance out there. If you poke around, Derek will see you. He might get suspicious."

He cocks an eyebrow. "You mean Agent O'Reilly?"

I nod. "Yes. In fact, he probably already knows what's out back. He can see the feed on his laptop."

"Are you on a first-name basis with all of the agents who park out front?"

"What?"

"Are you friendly with the agents, or do you know this guy personally?"

"I don't understand…"

He shakes his head. "We'll talk about that later. Right now, I'm taking out your trash."

He pushes past me and bounds down the stairs. I hear him in the kitchen, gathering up the garbage, before I reach the bottom of the stairs myself.

"Stay here," he commands.

"Do you want me to tell Derek—"

"No." And then he's gone out the back door.

Sighing, I refill my wine and toss his empty beer into the recycling bin, waiting for the brawl to begin outside when Agent O'Reilly goes to investigate. But there's nothing. At least, not until Aiden slams back into the house a few minutes later, the red fury on his face making my stomach turn.

"What is it?" I'm almost afraid to know given his scowl.

He doesn't answer, just whips out his phone, hits a couple buttons and sticks it to his ear, nostrils flaring. "Nolan, this is Enders. We have a situation."

Oh god. I drop onto a stool, watching him pace as the anger rolls off his broad shoulders in palpable waves. What in the heck did he find? And where is Derek?

"No, I haven't talked to O'Reilly, because he's sitting in his fucking car playing games on his goddamn phone!" He pinches the bridge of his nose and grinds his teeth. "Yeah, you do that." Then he hangs up and continues to pace as if I'm not even here.

"Aiden, what's going on?"

He pauses and rubs at his forehead, his jaw pulsing with tension. "I just walked the entire perimeter of your property, and not once did the asshole parked out front so much as look up from his phone. And it was a cat. A fucking decapitated one in your trash can. Still warm."

"Oh my god." I slam my hand to my mouth as bile rises.

He grimaces at my reaction and softens his expression. "Whoever left it probably expected you or Lena to find it."

Uh-huh. "Do you think...?" I can't say the rest.

He scrubs a hand over his face. "That someone is trying to send a message? Yeah, I do." He pulls a piece of paper out of his pocket and holds it up for me to read.

The ink—rather the blood—gives an ominous message: *See what happens to pussy when it doesn't play nice?*

"I'm going to be sick." I press my fingers to my lips to hold back the bile and sprint to the bathroom in just enough time to lose my dinner every ounce of false safety I'd convinced myself I'd had.

Someone left a mutilated cat in my backyard.

Someone used its blood to pen a disgusting note.

Someone had been close enough to get to the backside of my garage, just feet away from my car and from my back door.

Jesus.

"Hey." Aiden quietly enters the small room a minute later and hands me a glass of water. While I sip and try to wash away the taste of vomit, he wets a washcloth and then squats beside me, pressing it to my forehead. "I'm not gonna let these bastards get to you, Liv. I promise."

"I-I know." My voice trembles and I hate that he has to see me like this, curled up in the corner of the bathroom like a scared little girl instead of the strong, fearless woman I've worked so damn hard to become. "They were right outside."

He nods and brushes the hair back from my face. While his touch is gentle enough, he still vibrates with suppressed anger, and that somehow soothes my fear and heightens it at the same time.

"Thank you," I whisper, and his gaze lifts to mine. "I'm glad you're here."

"And I'm glad to hear you say that, because I'm staying the night."

"What? No. You don't have to do that." He's already doing so much.

Readjusting his stance so his elbows are on his knees, his piercing eyes never leave mine. "Yes, I do, Liv. Whoever did this isn't going to come back tonight because they've already accomplished their goal. But making a bold move like this... it means we need to up our game, too."

"More than the fast-track Special Agent Nolan mentioned earlier?"

"Probably."

Crap. "Is going out in public even a good idea anymore? The whole point was to draw them out, so they'd make a move, which they've done."

"We still don't know who they are."

And that's becoming more and more unsettling. What if these guys *are* people I know? Could it really be Eli, Victor, or even Troy? The possibility seems as unlikely as Jake having acquaintances I knew nothing about, but one of those options has to be true.

"I assume Nolan is on his way over?"

Aiden gets to his feet and offers me a hand. "It's better he talks to O'Reilly, because I might kill him if I have to."

"Derek is usually on top of things. I don't understand how he didn't notice the light."

"I don't know, but he's done a bang-up job pissing me off tonight." He hesitates at the door while I rewet the washcloth and wipe the rest of my face. "You call him by his first name. Is that your choice or his?"

I shrug. "Mine, I guess. He was the first agent to take watch out front and he's the one who's usually here at night."

"How well do you know him?"

"He comes in every now and then to say hi when he's on shift. I let him use the bathroom, and sometimes he watches TV with me and Lena. He's always friendly. And for the record, I call Special Agent Nolan 'Bernie' sometimes, too."

A scowl creases Aiden's brow as our eyes meet in the mirror. "He watches TV with you?"

"Yeah, I feel bad that he has to sit outside for so long."

"He's supposed to make sure no one's outside lurking around your house, Liv, not enjoying free entertainment."

"I didn't realize it was a big deal."

He folds his thick, inked arms over his chest and glowers.

"You don't trust him, do you?"

"Not one damn bit." He gives his head a single shake. "I can count the number of people I trust on one hand, and he sure as hell isn't one of them."

I'm sure I'm not either, but fortunately the trust in this arrangement only needs to go one way.

My trust in him is all that matters.

AIDEN

"He claims he never saw the motion light on. The sun was almost down, and from the front yard, the light might not have been noticeable."

"That's bullshit. I saw it from upstairs with the goddamn blinds closed."

Special Agent Nolan raises his hands, palms up. "I know. And I'm glad you did. I've got our surveillance team looking at all of the footage from around the block right now."

"I want access to the surveillance, since I obviously can't trust that asshole to keep an eye on it for me." In order to

98

keep a lid on this ruse, Nolan talked to O'Reilly privately before he came inside and sent a forensics crew to the back to take care of the cat, dust for prints, and look for anything else that might give us some idea of who the hell had the audacity to walk onto Olivia's property before the sun had fully set.

"All right. I can arrange for that."

"He should have been watching, Nolan. Who the fuck knows what else he's missed."

The senior agent holds up a hand. "We review the footage daily."

"Reviewing it after the fact isn't going to keep her alive." I stab my finger toward the stairs, where Liv escaped to take a bath and calm her nerves. "And I'll be damned if something is going to happen on my watch less than three fucking hours into this job."

"Detective, I understand your frustration. In fact, I'm just as upset that this happened. But it's exactly why you're here."

I can't imagine if I hadn't been. The thought of Liv or Lena finding that mess and the nasty note that went along with it… no one should have to see that shit, let alone a woman who hasn't done a damn thing to deserve it.

"I'm staying over tonight, and probably the weekend. Hell, I might even move in."

Nolan has the nerve to crack a smile. "Let's not get ahead of ourselves."

I'll do whatever the fuck I want if it means keeping Liv safe, and I don't give a shit what he has to say about it.

"I'll let you know as soon as the surveillance team has something on the footage. Until then, I'm going to need you to simmer down and let us do our job. If anyone else sees you like this—"

"They'll think I'm the concerned fucking boyfriend you hired me to be."

He eyes me for a moment before he nods and inclines his head toward the back door. "Lock up behind me, and like I said, I'll be in touch."

Yeah, well, not soon enough.

I see him out and triple-check the locks and the security system before I grab a beer from the fridge and down half of it in two gulps.

I promised myself I wouldn't let this case get the best of me. I'd do my job, and when it was over, I'd walk away like Liv did ten years ago.

But seeing that bloody message flipped a switch inside of me.

This isn't just a job—it's personal. And it has been from day one, when Olivia's terrified eyes stared up at me from the single sheet of paper Bolinger had slid across the desk. The same terrified eyes that stared up at me tonight from her bathroom floor.

If something happened to her... if someone got close enough to put hands on her, or god forbid, hurt her...

The mental images of what I'd do to that pathetic bastard make that cat look like child's play. I'd lose my badge in a heartbeat, and I wouldn't think twice about it.

It'd be worth it.

Because she is worth it.

Always has been, always will be.

CHAPTER 11

OLIVIA

I wake before dawn like I always do, beating the sunrise and the timer on the coffeepot. One of these days, I'll remember to reset the dang thing, so I don't have to drag around the kitchen like a zombie, waiting for that first cup to brew.

The only difference this morning is that, today, I'm not dying for that coffee. I didn't toss and turn once last night, and the last time I'd looked at the clock, it had only been eleven.

Someone murdered my husband seven weeks ago, and last night they left a mutilated cat in my trash can. Yet, I slept better than I have in years.

All because Aiden had been downstairs, keeping watch.

I can't let myself think too much about his effect on me, because letting him into my home and back into my life is difficult enough. To acknowledge that he still has so much power over me... well, that's dangerous territory, and I'm already in plenty of trouble.

Quickly brushing my teeth and pulling my hair into a fresh ponytail, I make my way downstairs, expecting to find my fake boyfriend crashed on the couch since he refused to take the guest room I'd offered him. Instead, he's sitting in an armchair facing the dining room and the back door with his eyes closed.

His chest rises and falls with slow and steady breaths, but his posture is rigid and tense. Even asleep, he can't relax, and I feel guilty about that, knowing his presence has had the opposite effect on me, at least where sleep is concerned.

I retrieve a blanket from the ottoman and begin to drape it over him when his eyes snap open, scaring the crap out of me. "Dang it, I thought you were sleeping!"

"You're lucky I heard you come down the stairs," he says without an ounce of sleepiness in his voice.

"Have you been awake this entire time?"

"Yep."

"Aiden, you need sleep," I snap, refolding the blanket with frustration that's aimed more at myself than him, because a small, twisted part of me secretly loves that he stayed up for me. "Why don't you go upstairs and rest? Nothing is going to happen in the daylight."

"I'm good."

"You're full of shit." I pin him with a glare, and my stupid nipples tighten when one corner of his mouth lifts in a smirk that looks downright sinful amid that dark, trimmed beard.

"Bossy." The single word slides down my spine like a caress… with the tip of his tongue.

"You're damn right I'm bossy. How are you going to help me if you're dead-ass tired?" And how am I going to keep my panties on if he keeps looking at me like that?

He continues to smirk as he gets to his feet and stretches his arms above his head. The movement reveals a sliver of abs that are even more defined than they were at twenty-two. Sexy jerk.

"You're right." He stifles a yawn. "It's gonna be a long day if I don't get at least a couple hours of shut-eye."

"See, I told you."

"Don't get smart, Livi—I'm only agreeing because O'Reilly clocked out a half hour ago and the new guy started his shift with a walk around. I like him better already."

Probably Agent Morales. He usually works day shift on the weekends.

"Did Agent Nolan let you know if they saw anything on the footage from last night?" I ask, setting the blanket back on the ottoman.

"Yup. Someone in a dark hoodie walked into the back-yard from the alley and dumped the cat. Didn't so much as flinch when the motion light came on. Just walked right back out and disappeared from the street surveillance."

"Jesus." The lack of fear is unnerving. And so is the knowledge of the camera placement.

"The feds dusted the garbage can lid for prints and came up with a partial that doesn't belong to me, you, or Lena, but they couldn't find another match in the system either. For all we know, it could be from a trash collector."

"They were here yesterday."

He nods. "That's what Nolan thought."

I sigh and tip my head toward the stairs. "All right. Go and sleep. We'll talk more after you get some rest."

"All right, boss lady." He offers a sleepy smile before he turns away, only to glance right back over his shoulder. "Oh, and Liv?"

"Yeah?"

"You might want to call Lena and tell her she's off the hook until Monday."

"Why?"

"I'm staying the weekend."

God help me.

AIDEN

As soon as I'd seen his office, I knew I wasn't going back to Cole Creek until I had a chance to go through every last piece of the dead mobster's shit. Finding the surprise in the trash can only solidified my plan, and as soon as Liv went to bed, I grabbed my overnight bag from the truck and got to work.

I spent five hours cross-referencing everything I found in Jake's desk to the information Special Agent Nolan had shared with me. Just like the feds, I couldn't find anything that didn't immediately lead to a dead end. In fact, the guy kept his shit so clean that I'd started to wonder if maybe he hadn't done anything wrong after all.

But then I remembered that Joe Zieliński had insisted the feds protect Olivia, and he'd gone as far as to put surveillance on her parents, too. Joe might not be able to give us the details we need without violating the trust of the SSP, but he wouldn't have taken those precautions if he didn't know exactly what Jake had done and what Liv was up against now.

After grabbing a three-hour nap and a quick shower in her bathroom, I head back downstairs to find Liv sitting cross-legged on an oversized chair in the living room with her laptop. Her hair is twisted up in a messy bun and her glasses are perched at the end of her nose, in full-on Dr. Bishop mode.

"Good morning for real this time," she offers in a soft voice with a pretty smile to match.

"Morning." I thumb toward the kitchen to distract myself from how goddamn gorgeous she looks. "Coffee?"

"Just made a new pot, along with a ham and cheese quiche. Help yourself."

"Thanks." I open a few cupboards until I find the mugs and plates, and then cut into the egg dish. "Can I bring you some, too?"

"Oh, that would be sweet of you. Thanks."

Sweet is not how I'd describe myself right now, with my thoughts skipping back to all the times she'd donned that sexy, studious look when she'd study on the weekends we were together in college. Or more specifically, all the times I'd rewarded her for getting her work done by making her come on her desk.

"So, how come you never changed your name?" I ask, strolling into the living room with our food and my coffee.

"Excuse me?" She glances, lashes fluttering behind those prim glasses, as I hand her a plate.

"Didn't Immigration give you shit for not taking his last name?"

"Oh, um, yeah, I guess." She sets her laptop aside to eat. "They were curious, but I told them the truth. Dr. Bishop had been my dream since I was a little girl."

She'd told me that, too, however, she'd also teased that Dr. Olivia Enders had a ring to it, as well. "And they believed you?"

She lifts a shoulder and gathers a bite of quiche on her fork. "Eventually."

Interesting. Taking a bite of my own, I watch her while she eats. She tries hard to seem relaxed, but the furrow in her brow gives her away. Does talking about her marriage make her anxious, or is talking about it with *me* the real culprit?

"Most couples who are actually in love struggle to convince Immigration. How did you two pull it off?"

She pushes another bite around on the plate and sighs. "Jake and I were close, so it wasn't that difficult. We cared about each other even if it wasn't love in the traditional sense."

I snort because that's *not* what I wanted to hear.

"What?" She looks up at me with a soft scowl. "Do you want me to say it was a struggle? That it had been hard to show affection for my husband?" She flinches as soon as the words are out of her mouth. "I'm sorry. It's just—"

"Not something you want to talk about with your ex?" I've done my best to leave our past out of this, but the need to know more—about why she chose another man over me—is always there, simmering beneath the surface.

"Not really, but I know you have questions and I owe you answers, so why don't you just ask what it is you really want to know?"

"Were you sleeping with him?" The question rolls off my tongue without hesitation. She opened the door, and I'm damn well going to take the invitation.

Her face turns as pink as her coral T-shirt while her knuckles pale with the death grip on her plate. "Sometimes."

"Sometimes." I laugh bitterly. I'd already guessed but hearing her say it still pisses me off.

"We were married," she rasps, and it feels like a stab to the gut.

"Believe me, I know." I set my plate aside to scrub my hands over my face. "I just don't understand how you were fucking the guy and so oblivious to the shit he was doing."

"Yeah, well I was fucking you for a long time and no one knew about us, either" she counters, and I grimace.

"Two completely different things, Liv."

"Not really." Her gaze locks on mine. "Look, there are things you don't know, okay? Things I want to tell you... things I will tell you. But not yet."

Things like what? I search her face, but she glances away, hiding her secrets.

"Things about him?"

"Things about us," she whispers, and that knife buried in my stomach twists. "You'd think that after ten years, it'd be easier, but no."

She glances away and blinks back tears. The agony in her voice and the emotion in her eyes grip at my heart, and I want to shake the truth from her as much as I want to pull her close and take it all away.

"You put your feelings aside to help me, and the least I can do is tell you the truth about what happened. I'm just so scared that you'll hate me all over again, and I—"

Fuck it. I get to my feet and pull her up from the chair, my hands curling around her jaw to tip her face to mine.

"I do not hate you," I say sternly, as her watery eyes dart back and forth between mine. "Yes, I was hurt. And pissed. Really fucking pissed. But that was only because you hid from me instead of talking to me about it. That wasn't hate, Livi, that was a broken heart."

Her body trembles against mine as a soft hiccup rises in her chest. "I'm sorry."

"I am, too." Taking her glasses off, I toss them onto her chair and swipe her tears away with my thumbs. "I wish we could go back and change things, if for nothing else than for you to have known that you could have come to me with anything. Anything at all, and I would have never hated you for it."

She closes her eyes, slides her hands around to my back, and gives in to her emotions with her face buried in my T-shirt.

We stand there for what feels like forever until her tears become sniffles, her breathing steadies, and the air around us feels a little lighter. She hasn't given me the answers I want—

the answers I think she needs to share for her own peace of mind, too—but we're at least one step closer.

"Thank you," she whispers with her cheek pressed against my chest and her fingers gently caressing my back.

"You don't need to thank me, Livi." I close my eyes and press a kiss on top of her head. "In fact, I'm glad you asked me."

"You are?" She glances up at me, her nose red and her eyes just as bloodshot.

"I'm really fucking good at what I do." I wink, and she laughs before resting her cheek against my chest once again.

"Then I'm glad you're here."

"So am I."

OLIVIA

Aiden spent most of the day going through Jake's office and bedroom while I graded midterm projects for one class and discussion board posts for another. Normally, I enjoy reading through my students' work, but it's been harder and harder to concentrate, the more the days and weeks tick by without any progress on Jake's case.

Lena was right—I desperately need a vacation. Unfortunately, relaxation won't be a luxury I can truly enjoy until we find the missing money and the men who killed Jake behind bars.

"What do you think about going out tonight?" Aiden's voice precedes him before he appears in the doorway of my office. His hair is messed on top like he's been running his hands through it, and the stubble on his jaw seems darker and thicker than it had just this morning.

"Did you find something?"

"No, but after last night's visit, it might throw these guys off if you go out in public. Make them anxious so they do something sloppy."

"You want to bait them? With me?" I've always known I was a pawn in this case, but now that it's time to actually play the game, I think I'd rather sit out.

"That's one way of looking at it, but another is that it'd give us the upper hand for a bit."

"At my expense." I take off my glasses and rub my eyes. "Remind me again why I thought this was a good idea?"

"Because you want these guys off your back so you can live your life again?" He takes a step into my office. "I promise I will never put you in a situation where I don't think I can keep you safe."

It's not him that I doubt. In fact, after this morning, I trust him more than ever. It's me I'm worried about. The more time we spend together, the more I question whether or not I can keep my head—and my heart—where they belong.

"Where would we go?" I ask. "Dinner? Drinks?"

"Wherever you're comfortable."

"Not to sound like a wuss, but I'm not sure I'm comfortable anywhere anymore."

He gives me a reassuring smile. "I'll be by your side the entire time, Liv."

Uh-huh. Exactly. "Bernie probably wouldn't allow it anyway."

"I already talked to him. He was reluctant but saw my point and agreed."

"So, it's already been decided." Well, at least now I'm annoyed enough to argue properly. "Is it too much to ask that I have some say in these things? This is my life, after all."

"Think of it as a date." He grins like he's being cute and that irritates me even more.

"A date with a target painted on my back."

"A date between two lovers who've rekindled an old flame."

My cheeks heat like a twelve-year-old at his use of "lovers," and my brief annoyance evaporates.

"I wasn't stroking my ego when I said I was good at what I do." He leans down, placing his big hands on the papers on my desk, and my heart begins to race. "But you already know that, or I wouldn't be here right now."

Lovers. Stroking. Hands.

"This is risky." So, so risky.

His blue eyes darken in a way that's all too familiar and far too dangerous. "You used to love taking risks with me, Liv. Tonight won't be any different."

That's exactly what I'm afraid of.

CHAPTER 12

AIDEN

*T*he Speakeasy.

I have to hand it to Olivia–choosing a place that's an obvious tribute to the mobster lifestyle is ballsy. And it's also exactly the kind of place I would have chosen myself had I known it existed.

The bar is rustic, but modern. Full of sleek, dark wood and rich leather, accented with brushed chrome. The music is old-school jazz, and the waitstaff is dressed in 1920s flapper dresses and pin-striped pants with matching vests. It's classy and fun at the same time.

"How the hell did you go from not wanting to go out to picking a place like this?" With my hand on the small of her back, I guide her from the front of the establishment toward a booth at the back, nearest the rear exit and the restrooms.

"Troy's sister and brother-in-law own it. I'm comfortable here," she says under her breath before she stops short to let a waitress with a feather in her hair pass by with a tray full of drinks.

The abrupt halt has my hand instinctively sliding around her waist to steady her and pull her back against me. I grit my teeth when her ass, barely covered in a one-piece outfit she called a romper, connects with my crotch. She's quite a bit shorter than I am, but the heels she's wearing put her at the perfect height for accidents like this to drive me insane. And the night's barely started.

I clear my throat. "Any chance the brother-in-law is Polish?"

"Actually, I think he is."

Great. "Remind me to never let you pick the place again."

"Cami and Frank aren't mobsters. They have four kids, for Pete's sake."

"What? Mobsters don't fuck?"

She shoots me a narrow-eyed glare as we reach the tall semicircle booth situated in the corner. "Would you cut me some slack, please? I'm not stupid. Besides, I thought you'd like it here."

"I do." And now I feel like a prick for giving her a hard time. In fact, if she's wrong and her friends *are* shady, this is probably the best place she could have chosen, if we really want to get this show started. "It's a cool vibe. A helluva lot classier than the pub back home."

Her lips purse into a satisfied smile as she slides into one side of the sleek black leather booth while I take the other. We meet in the middle just as a waitress with a blonde bob, a sequin headband, and cherry red lipstick sashays up to the table.

"Evening, folks. Can I interest you in one of our local brews?"

"Do you still have the peach IPA?" Liv asks.

"Sure do."

"I'll take that, please."

"Absolutely. And how about you, handsome?" The waitress shifts her gaze to me, and in my peripheral, Liv's smile tightens just like the hand she places on my leg.

"Something dark and uncomplicated, if you've got it."

The blonde flashes a flirty grin. "I've got everything you could ever want, sugar."

Liv laughs even as her fingertips dig into my thigh through my jeans.

"Surprise me then," I say with a wink, because who the hell knew I'd like possessive Olivia so much?

"You got it." The waitress nods to the menus tucked between a flickering candle and a caddy of napkins in the middle of the table. "Feel free to take a peek at the menus while I get your drinks."

I dip my chin, and she turns to spin away, the tassels on her short dress swinging around her thighs. She's a pretty girl, but her legs have nothing on Olivia's, especially tonight in those shorts and heels.

"You're a really shitty fake date." Liv gives my leg one last purposeful squeeze before letting go.

"Aww, are you jealous?" I tease, missing her touch the second it's gone.

"No, but you're supposed to be into me, remember?"

I chuckle and adjust in my seat, because I'm definitely into her in that skimpy fucking outfit.

"Anyway, I assume you've already scoped out the back-up?" she says quietly as she reaches for a menu.

"Yep. O'Reilly's up front in the corner, and Getty's talking to the bald guy at the bar." I haven't met Agent Getty yet, but Nolan shared her picture earlier. There's another agent parked outside, too, keeping an eye on my truck and the front door.

"What are you hoping will happen tonight, exactly?"

"I don't think anything will happen yet. They're not

prepared." I lean in and scan the menu with her, but she pulls back, frowning.

"Then what are we doing here?"

"We need them to think you're getting sick of living in fear. That you're ready to get out and put this all behind you."

"I'm all of those things, but I thought having a new guy in my life was supposed to show them that."

"Can't show 'em if we don't flaunt it a little, Liv." I lift my gaze to hers and she blinks, her eyelashes fluttering anxiously. She did her hair and makeup tonight, and there's a sparkle to her skin that makes me itch to lean in and kiss it.

So I do.

She gasps the moment my lips graze her cheek on my way to the soft spot behind her ear. She smells amazing, and my dick twitches. Fucking thing obviously didn't get the memo that this isn't real.

"There's a guy watching us from the bar," I say softly, my hand lifting to her cheek as I nuzzle her neck. "Black button-down. Dark hair."

"Um… what? I don't see…" She shivers and goose bumps rise on her bare skin as I nip lightly.

"Two o'clock, but don't look now. Pretend you're into this."

Her quick intake of breath is lost the moment I turn her face to mine and brush my lips across hers. I expect her to freak out, so I tighten my grip to keep her with me, but she doesn't go rigid at all. She fucking melts. Melts right into the kiss like it's the most natural thing in the world.

"Mmm." She moans softly as she opens for me, the tip of her tongue teasing mine just as she digs those damn fingers into my leg again like she's trying to excavate my friggin' femur.

She chuckles against my lips when I flinch. "Give me a little warning next time, huh?"

Fucking hell. "There was no time."

"Uh-huh." She pulls back with mischief in her eyes. "There's no one at two o'clock."

"That's because he walked past to go to the bathroom when you stuck your tongue down my throat."

"Sure he did." She purses those wicked lips as the waitress returns with our drinks, setting a bottle of pale beer in front of Liv and a tall glass of dark ale in front of me.

"Here's your dark and uncomplicated," the blonde says. "Otherwise known as our Boss Black Ale."

"Tall, dark, and handsome just like you." Liv flashes a sexy grin before she wipes the remnants of her lipstick from the corner of my mouth.

The waitress laughs. "Just the drinks tonight or can I get you something to eat, too?"

Shit, we never finished looking at the menu.

"We haven't had dinner," Olivia reminds me, and my stomach growls as confirmation. "They have the best Chicago-style pizza. Do you trust me to order for us?"

Like old times? Sure, I'll bite. "Go ahead. Let's see how well you remember what I like."

The glimmer of a challenge sparkles in her eyes before she pulls her shoulders back and orders without hesitation. "We'll take a medium, light on the sauce, with sausage, pepperoni, black olives, and red onion. And can we get the bruschetta as an appetizer? With fresh mozzarella?"

Well, hell.

"Absolutely." The waitress smiles and shifts her gaze to me. "How'd she do?"

"Not bad."

"Good." She winks at Olivia. "I'll have that bruschetta out for you shortly."

"Not bad," Olivia mocks when we're alone again. "I nailed that."

"Awfully confident for someone who hasn't had pizza with me in ten years."

"But did I get it wrong?" One eyebrow lifts over a sexy smoky eye, and I want to kiss her all over again. Hell, I want to do a lot more than kiss her.

Before I can do something stupid, like give in to that urge, the guy in the black button-down exits the bathroom with his focus immediately on me. His lip curls as our eyes lock, and I have a guess who he is without an introduction, though it appears I'm going to get one.

"Well, well…" he says as he approaches the booth, his scathing expression turning sweet as he looks from me to Olivia. "You're the last person I expected to see out tonight, Dr. Bishop."

"Troy." Her shoulders sag in relief before she slides out of the booth to greet him with a hug that lasts a couple seconds too long. "It's so good to see you. How have you been?"

"I can't complain." He holds her at a distance and takes her in with more than platonic interest. Lena was right—he's got a hard-on for her, and I don't like it one fucking bit. "You look amazing."

"Aw, thank you." She laughs softly, tucking her hair behind her ear before she gestures to me. "Troy, this is my friend, Aiden. Aiden, Troy McAllister. We work together at UWM."

"Oh, right. You've mentioned him." I get to my feet to offer a hand, because this asshole needs to see exactly what he's going to get if he decides to try something stupid. He's a decent-sized guy, but I've got at least three inches and thirty pounds on him. "Nice to finally meet you."

"She's mentioned me, huh? Unfortunately, I can't say the same about you." That friggin' lip curls again, and I almost growl.

"I don't imagine she would have, out of respect for her

husband, of course. But Liv and I, we go way back, don't we?" I give her my best adoring smile and her cheeks turn pink. "High school sweethearts," I add with a wink.

Olivia blinks fast for a moment, like it's the first time she's thought of us that way. But whether we were official or not, it's true. She was my high school infatuation, and I'm pretty sure I was hers.

"Ah, I see." Her friend gives a dismissive laugh that has me biting back a smile. He doesn't view me as a threat, and that's just as well. I love proving people wrong. "Now that the feds have loosened your leash, we should meet for coffee soon. Catch up on everything."

"I'd like that," she agrees, though we both know that's not going to happen.

"I'll call you next week then." He grins down at her before pulling her in for another hug while he glares at me over her shoulder. "Nice to meet you, Ethan."

"Aiden," Olivia corrects naively. The fucker knows my name, but he'd rather play games instead.

"Anyway, I'll let you get back to your evening," he says before he forces himself to let go of her.

"Have a good night." Olivia gives a little finger wave as he backs away and then finally turns to go. Sighing, she slips back into the booth and then pats the seat next to her for me to follow. "So, he was the guy, huh?"

"Yeah, and Lena's right. In fact, I'm surprised he didn't whip out his dick and piss on your shoes to mark his territory."

"Oh, stop it." She swats my arm when I sit again. "He's harmless."

"He may not be a mobster, but he's after you, Liv. Not sure how you've missed that."

She reaches for her beer but hesitates before taking a

drink. "It's not that I didn't notice. I just figured it was better if I didn't acknowledge it."

"You've worked with him for nine years now?"

She nods.

"If he hasn't gotten over his little schoolboy crush by now, he's not going to. You need to tell him you're not interested. Unless you are…" Fuck. She isn't, is she?

She rolls her eyes. "I'm not."

Thank god.

"He's not even my type." She finally takes a drink, and my gaze homes in on the way her delicate neck works as she swallows, instigating an old memory.

Heavy breathing. Damp skin. My face buried in the curve of her neck and shoulder as I drive into her over and over again…

"He's too uptight. Kinda like someone else I know."

"Huh?" I blink away the flashback.

Olivia gives a small snort and rolls her eyes. "Nothing."

"I'm pretty sure you just called me uptight."

"I thought you didn't hear me."

"My mind was somewhere else, so it took a second to sink in. Rest assured, I don't miss anything, Liv." I grin and her brows lift above mischievous eyes.

"Oh really."

"Nope." Like the way her pulse had picked up beneath my thumb when we kissed. And the way her pupils had dilated, too.

"Hmm." A playful smile plays at her mouth as the waitress returns with our bruschetta. Olivia thanks her and then adds a couple pieces of the bread covered in cheese, tomato, and basil on a small plate before setting it in front of me.

"I could have done that myself."

"I know, but we're on a date, and I'm playing the part of a

woman who's trying to woo you, remember? Let me do my thing."

A low chuckle rolls in my chest. Enjoying this time with her feels wrong, considering it's a job, but I'm finding it hard not to.

We're ten years older. We've lived completely different lives for a decade. But somehow, we're still the same people we've always been. I still like her. I'm still drawn to her. And despite trying to tell myself otherwise, I've fucking missed her.

Clearing my throat, I grab a napkin and eye the appetizers. "So, how many weeks of classes do you have left again?"

"Two." She crosses her legs beneath the table, and when her shoe bumps my shin, she doesn't bother to move it. Just keeps it there even though no one is going to pay attention to what's going on beneath our table other than us. And I like it. "I can't believe how fast the summer term has gone. In some ways, this past month has dragged, but as far as teaching goes, it's flown by."

"How many classes do you have?"

"Right now, three, but I usually teach four during a normal semester."

"Is that a lot?"

"Pretty average for a state university, but it's more work when the classes are online, which all of mine are right now. You know, for safety reasons."

I'd seen that in the file. "Are you teaching online in the fall, too, or going back to campus?"

She lifts a shoulder and reaches for a piece of bruschetta. "I guess that depends. Right now, they're in person, but I have the option to move them online if I need to. Honestly, I don't want to do that to my students. Some of them don't do well in an online setting, and I don't want to disappoint them."

"Better to disappoint them than to end up dead."

She winces before she takes a bite and mulls over her response. "Sometimes I wonder if things will ever go back to normal."

"As far as teaching?"

"As far as everything." Her brow creases as her dark eyes meet mine. "I'm worried I'll never be able to stop looking over my shoulder. Or that I'll have to triple-check the locks and alarm every night before bed. Or don't get me started on taking out the trash."

And I want nothing more than to ease her mind on all accounts. Fear radiates off of her at all times, but she tries so damn hard to pretend it's not there, lingering beneath the surface of everything she does. And I hate that for her. I'd hate it for anyone I was working with, but it's personal with her. There's no way for it not to be.

I place my hand on her knee beneath the table and stroke my thumb over her silky skin. "I'm going to do my best to make you feel safe again, Liv."

She blinks fast as if to keep from tearing up, and it takes everything in me not to reach out and pull her in for another kiss. A kiss that would be for comfort and not show.

"I don't know if I'll ever be able to thank you enough for this." Her hand covers mine and squeezes gently.

"You don't have to thank me, Liv."

Her lips curl into a soft smile. "Because it's your job, right?"

I give my head a single shake. "Because asking me instead of someone else is all the thanks I need."

CHAPTER 13

OLIVIA

*A*iden isn't the same man tonight as he was in his hotel room.

I'd been prepared—as I could have been, anyway—to deal with that version of him during this fake relationship of ours. And there'd been some comfort in believing his hardened exterior would keep me from seeing too many glimpses of the man I once loved.

I didn't expect this softer side of him. Certainly not yet, if at all.

But this man... this guarded but gentle man is something I could have only hoped to see again. It's the Aiden I remember best. The Aiden I fell in love with all those years ago.

As much as seeing this side of him gives me hope that maybe we'll come out of this without all the hurt from the past, it stirs my guilty conscience, too.

I owe him answers.

And I can't expect him to step out of his comfort zone and open up to me when I haven't done the same for him.

He turns his truck into my driveway at nearly ten o'clock with Agent O'Reilly behind us in his unmarked car. The agent parks and gets out before strolling up the driveway as Aiden and I climb out.

"The surveillance team said everything was quiet, but I'll do a quick sweep of the perimeter to be sure." His tone is stiff and begrudged, probably because of the scolding he received from Special Agent Nolan last night.

"Appreciate that, man." Aiden takes my hand and leads me up the porch steps while Agent O'Reilly treks toward the garage.

The sky is clear, dotted with glittering silver stars and a bright summer moon. The cool air is soothing to my lungs, and dread whirls in my belly at the thought of going inside only to be locked away again for god only knows how long.

"It's a nice night. Too bad we can't sit out here and relax."

"Funny, I was just thinking the same thing." With a sigh, I hand him my keys and he opens the door for me to step inside. "I love sitting out back during the summer. It's the closest thing I've found to life back home in Cole Creek."

"Yeah?" He toes off his shoes and offers a steadying hand while I unstrap my heels.

"The fence hides all the houses, and the traffic is far enough away that it's almost quiet sometimes. If I close my eyes, I can almost pretend I'm sitting on my parents' porch in the country."

He surveys me with kind eyes. "You haven't been home much, have you?"

I kick off my second shoe and shake my head. "No. My parents usually come down here for the holidays."

"That's a surprise," he says as he leads the way to the kitchen, silently checking to make sure there aren't any bogeymen hiding around the corners. "Your folks hated driving in Green Bay. I can't imagine them in Milwaukee."

"Once Dad discovered the casino and the easiest way to get there, that changed."

Aiden gives a short laugh while I go to the fridge for wine. We only had one drink each at the bar in order to stay alert, and mine had gone down far too well with everything on my mind. "You want a beer?"

"Sure." He checks Jake's office, the bedrooms, and the bathroom, and by the time he returns, I have his beer opened and my glass of red poured.

"I'm going to change, and then enjoy this wine while I watch something completely pointless on TV. You're welcome to join me if you'd like." He probably wants to pick up where he left off with Jake's things, but I don't want to be rude and not offer him a break, either.

"Yeah." He takes the beer and nods agreeably. "I think I could use some pointless TV tonight."

"Great." I grab my glass and head for the stairs. "I'll be back in two shakes."

"Actually, I should clear the second floor, too, just in case." He flashes an apologetic smile, and I roll my eyes but let him do his thing.

While he checks every room on the second floor, I linger by the top of the stairs, trying not to notice how sexy he is floating from room to room like a bearded and tattooed ninja, ready to fight off intruders on my behalf.

"Thank you," I tell him when he's finished, hoping he doesn't notice the blush that's crept into my cheeks or the way my nipples tightened just thinking about him roughing someone up for me.

"Just doing my job." He winks before he jogs down the steps, and I swear to god, if I weren't leaning against the wall, I'd have melted into a puddle on the hardwood floor.

I'm not supposed to be attracted to my fake boyfriend, but I kind of set myself up for failure on that one, didn't I? Aiden always was the cutest boy in high school, the hottest guy in college, and he's still the most handsome man I've ever met, a decade later.

It doesn't hurt that he's also softening up to our arrangement, and maybe even to me, which I know better than to assume means anything. Like he said, he's just doing his job, and I'd be foolish to think his kindness is anything more.

Especially after I tell him what it is I'm hoping to tell him tonight. Because that? That could change everything.

By the time I slip into my sleep shorts and a tank top, wash my face, and pull up my hair, my glass of wine is empty and the warm tingle of a buzz hums along my nerves. Another glass, maybe two, and I should have just enough liquid courage to accomplish my goal.

Aiden is relaxed on the couch, with his knees spread wide and an arm draped lazily along the top of the cushions, remote control in one hand and his beer in the other, when I join him again.

"What's your pointless poison tonight?" he asks while I go to the kitchen for a refill. "A movie or a sitcom?"

"Surprise me."

"*Rambo* it is then."

"Ugh. You still like those same old war movies?"

He chuckles. "Yes, but I'm kidding. *Rambo* isn't even on." He clicks to the Food Network—my favorite—and sets the remote aside. Bonus points for the detective. "O'Reilly cleared the backyard, by the way. No surprises in the trash tonight."

"Thank god." I drop down onto the opposite end of the couch, my glass in one hand and the rest of the bottle in the other. Aiden lifts an eyebrow as I set it on the side table.

"Double fisting?"

"Liquid courage," I admit. I'd rather he know I'm building up my nerve rather than assume I've become an alcoholic.

"Ah." He eyes me curiously for a moment before glancing to the TV where Bobby Flay goes head to head with another chef over a Beef Wellington recipe. "This guy's still alive?"

"He's not even old."

"Christ, he was seventy ten years ago."

"No, he wasn't." I laugh. "He's only, like, fifty-something."

"Oh, and how do you know that? Don't tell me you still think he's hot?"

My cheeks warm. "Can we please forget I ever told you that?"

"Nope." He shakes his head, pure delight in his eyes. "And from the look on your face right now, you'd still let him baste your turkey."

"Baste my turkey?"

"Glaze your ham."

"Aiden Enders!" I swing a throw pillow at him, but he snatches it away before it makes contact.

"Cream your corn. Toss your salad. Frost your cake," he rattles off like a kid trying to get out as many swear words as he can before his mom breaks out the dish soap.

"Will you stop?" I laugh so hard that I almost spill my wine. "Merlot will not come out of this fabric, you know."

"Eh, you're the one who said the place could use more color."

Silent giggles continue to shake my body for a solid minute before I finally get it together enough to take a deep breath and focus again.

"Honestly, we can watch something else. I don't mind."

"I'm good." He lifts a shoulder and takes a pull from his beer. "Besides, I'm pretty sure you're not armoring yourself with an entire bottle of wine just to watch TV."

I raise my glass to him. "You're right—you really don't miss anything, do you?"

His lopsided grin is only halfhearted, the ease of our shared laughter already slipping away. "Is what you have to say really so bad that you have to get shit-faced to spit it out?"

"Yep."

"Liv…" He turns to me. "We don't have to do this now. It's not going to change anything."

Maybe not, but if we're going to have any chance of putting the past behind us when this charade is over, I have to tell him. For my own peace of mind and because he deserves to know.

"I was assaulted." The words tumble from my mouth on their own accord, and for a moment, I'm not sure if I said them out loud or just in my head. His frown confirms.

"You what?"

"I was assaulted. The weekend after I told you I loved you and didn't want to sneak around anymore." Holy shit, I said it. I actually said it.

"What do you mean *assaulted*?" He sits forward, his shoulders and arms tightening with aggravation as he pins me with an intense glare.

I close my eyes and suck in a shuddered breath. "I can't look at you and say this."

"Liv…" His fingers graze my knee, and I flinch.

"Please don't. Just let me say it."

"Jesus Christ." He shifts, and I imagine him leaning forward, elbows on his knees while he scrubs his hands over his face.

"Lena and I went to a party. She wanted to stay longer with Wendell, and I wanted to go home so I could call you. A guy from one of my classes was leaving too, and he offered to walk me home." My throat begins to constrict at the memory, but I swallow against it. "When we got to my apartment, he asked to use the bathroom, and when he realized no one else was home..." My voice rises as the pressure in my chest builds, leaving no room for air. But I have to get it out. I have to say the words. "He raped me. Twice."

As traumatizing as that part had been, forcing himself on me hadn't been the worst of it. My fingers lift to the invisible scar on my bottom lip. The one I can feel but no one can see. Like the one above my temple, hidden in my hairline. The slightly raised line required fifteen stitches and a month to heal.

"He beat me up between rounds. Said he'd been watching me, and he knew you and I were sneaking around. He told me that he'd tell Bren and my parents about what a slut I'd been if I went to the police."

When Aiden doesn't move or make a sound, I peek through watery eyes and find him glaring ahead at the TV, his jaw and his fists tight, his face red, and his body vibrating with precisely the kind of rage I'd worried about, especially back then.

"I didn't believe him. And if he was telling the truth, I didn't care." I swallow hard, but the vise around my throat... it feels like Kyle Weston's hand did that night. "I knew how you would react. I knew it would kill you and that you'd want to kill him in return. And I couldn't do that to you. I couldn't let you risk your career because of him. *Because of me.*"

Aiden pushes off the couch in an angry rush, his empty beer bottle clanking against the side table as he tosses it and paces toward the kitchen, rage rolling off his wide shoulders in deadly waves.

"I'm sorry." My voice is a strangled, garbled cry. "That's why I cut you off and wouldn't see you when you came to Madison. I was a mess. My body, my face..." *My heart.*

He stops just inside the dining room, his back to me as he pulls in one ominous breath after the other. When he laces his hands behind his head so tightly that his knuckles bleach white, I brace myself for the wrath I've avoided for ten years. His anger, his frustration, his promise of vengeance...

But instead of angry words, his only response is an anguished, gut-wrenching roar that vibrates the windows and chills me to the bone, not in fear, but in heartache.

Before I can get to my feet to offer him comfort, he storms to the back door, disarms the alarm, and disappears into the night.

Like I did ten years ago.

CHAPTER 14

AIDEN

*T*he images in my head... the absolute fucking nightmare that bastard had put her through... it replays over and over again in my mind like a twisted horror movie I can't look away from.

I should've known.

I should've been there.

I should've protected her.

But instead, I brought that shit to her doorstep.

Instead of telling my best friend the truth, I took the coward's way out. I snuck around behind his back when all it would have taken was a single fucking conversation. But I'd been too selfish to do even that.

And she paid the price.

"Motherfucker!" My fist connects with the wooden gate between the backyard and the alley, the crack of my knuckles echoing through the night. But I don't stop. I push through the gate on a tirade, blood and rage whooshing in my ears like a turbulent sea.

To think I'd accused her of being the selfish one. Of carelessly ripping out my heart and digging her heel into it like my love meant nothing at all. All the while *she'd* been the one in pain. The one who'd suffered through the worst kind of hell by herself because of me.

"Aiden, stop!" Her voice carries down the dark alley, and my boots grind to a halt on the asphalt.

I spin to find her standing barefoot by the gate, her chest heaving in her tank top as the streetlight shines down on her tearstained face.

"Get back in the house!" Jesus Christ, she couldn't make herself an easier target if she tried. With a single shot from any of these houses, she could be dead.

But instead of listening, she gives her head a defiant shake, and a red veil of fury falls over my gaze.

"What in the hell is wrong with you?" I march back down the alley and reach for her arm, but she jerks away, nostrils flaring and hands tightening into angry fists.

"Dammit, Aiden, don't talk to me like I'm a child!"

"You shouldn't be out here," I growl, glancing around for the red dot I half expect to find floating in the air.

"I didn't ask you to come here for this!" Her voice is shaky but determined. "And I sure as hell didn't tell you what happened so you'd feel sorry for me!"

"What?" I recoil, because I may be feeling a lot of things right now, but pity sure as hell isn't one of them.

"What's going on out here?" a gruff voice sounds from the backyard before Agent O'Reilly steps through the gate, his weapon drawn. He homes in on Olivia immediately—specifically, her barely clothed body—and a slimy grin curls one corner of his mouth.

"Just a misunderstanding." Teeth clenched, I step between them and stare him down. This guy grows creepier and creepier by the day, and I'm in no mood to play his games tonight.

"Is that so?" he asks Olivia over my shoulder, and I feel her shift behind me before tentative fingertips brush my forearm and slide down to my hand.

"Yes." She leans into my side as she tangles our fingers, and it takes me a second to realize she's using me as a shield from his prying eyes. "I, uh, got mad because the waitress was flirty earlier. I just... I had a moment."

O'Reilly's gaze slides from her to me and back again. "Well, take it back inside before I decide to call it into Nolan."

She nods and squeezes my hand. "Okay. Thank you. I promise I'm done throwing tantrums tonight."

He dips his chin and I tug her quickly back to the house, locking the doors and resetting the alarms behind us.

For several drawn-out moments, we stand in the darkened kitchen, tension crackling between us like electricity.

"Do you realize how dangerous that was?" I rasp, my throat raw with simmering anger and guilt. So much fucking guilt.

"Do you realize I'm not as helpless as everyone thinks I am?" she counters, lifting her chin defiantly though her words are still unsteady.

"I never said you were helpless."

She wets her lips and wraps her arms around herself as if cold. "You're right. Out of everyone, you were the only one who didn't treat me like some fragile flower."

I scowl. "What the hell are you talking about?"

"You never treated me like a kid. You were protective, yes, but it was a different kind of protective than my brother."

I stare at her, failing to comprehend what this has to do with anything.

"Bren sheltered me to keep me from getting hurt, but

you… you walked beside me. You held my hand and helped me find my own way."

"Liv, I don't understand—"

"That's why I asked you to do this. Because you saw my strength where others saw weakness."

"I thought…" I thought she asked for me because we had history. Because she was comfortable with me.

She nods, seemingly reading my thoughts. "That, too. But mostly…" She closes her eyes and swallows. "Mostly because I'd hoped you'd be the one person who wouldn't treat me like a victim in all of this."

Jesus, I had no idea she'd felt that way.

Her eyes spring open again, and the defeat in those dark depths wraps around my heart like a fist. She's hanging on by a thread, and she's reaching out to me, of all people, to be her lifeline.

"Why didn't you tell me what happened?" I see her pain. I feel it, too. But what she's saying doesn't add up. If I was that person for her then and she thinks I can still be now, then why hadn't she come to me when she'd been so brutally attacked? Why hadn't she let me help her?

She rubs her arms and takes a seat at the end of the table, her body curving protectively into itself. "Because I became someone else that night. I wasn't the girl you knew anymore. I didn't even know myself." She breaks off and glances away but not before I see the shame in her eyes. "That night broke me. And humiliated me in the worst way possible. I couldn't let you see me like that."

"Livi, I loved you." I pull out the chair beside her, pleading as I sit. "I would have helped you through it."

"How could you help me when I couldn't even help myself?"

"That's what I was there for. To be your strength until you found your own again."

132

She shakes her head. "I didn't want to lean on you like that."

"But that's what people who love each other do, Liv. They support each other no matter what, especially in moments of weakness."

"That's not how it was with us. Not really."

I recoil. "What?"

"We were barely together, we—"

"We were as together as two people can be. We may not have gone public with our relationship, and it might've taken four years to admit how we felt about each other, but I was yours and you were mine."

Tears spill down her cheeks as her eyes search mine. "I didn't know. I—"

"I loved you for every one of those years, Liv. Every. Single. One. So don't tell me it wasn't like that with us, because it was. It fucking was."

"PENNY FOR YOUR THOUGHTS." An hour later, sitting shoulder to shoulder on the floor in front of the couch, Liv adjusts the ice pack she insisted I put on my hand before she picks up her third—or is it her fourth?—glass of wine.

"You're so fucking brave." I bring my beer to my mouth and take a pull. I hadn't planned on getting drunk tonight— the only time I drink at all when I'm undercover is when I have to—but Liv's confession has my head all sorts of screwed up. Without something to take the edge off and calm me down, I'd probably be halfway to whichever prison the fucker that violated her ended up in.

She snorts. "I am not brave."

"Are you kidding me?" I bump my bent knee against hers. "You went through literal fucking hell and look at you now."

She blinks at me and heat creeps up the back of my neck.

"Okay, maybe not now, as in the past two months, but in general. You still got your PhD, and you're doing the job you always wanted to do."

She lifts a shoulder. "Yeah, but don't forget that I also married Jake so neither of us would have to deal with a real relationship again. And then, you know, he turned out to be in the mob."

Silent laughter shakes my chest. "You always did have questionable taste in men."

"Oh really?" She whirls around to face me, long tendrils of dark hair flitting against her cheeks.

"Yep. Heard the guy you snuck around with in college turned out to be a real prick."

She rolls her still-puffy eyes, a ghost of smile on her lips. "Ugh. Him."

I become serious again. "Tell me you put that bastard away for a long fucking time, Livi."

She stills at my plea and glances down to her red-polished toes.

"Liv…" I sit up rigidly and turn to her, but she keeps her gaze trained on her feet.

"I couldn't," she says quietly.

"What do you mean you couldn't? You went to court, right? Did they not believe you?"

She shakes her head. "No, that's not it."

"Then what is it?" Because if that son of a bitch is still walking the streets, he won't be for much longer, I'll make damn sure of that.

"He died."

Her words hit me like a punch to the gut. "What?"

"He was in an accident a couple weeks after… you know." She sets her wineglass to the coffee table we'd pushed off to the side and tugs the hair tie from her bun. "The car caught fire and he wasn't able to get out. He was pronounced dead at the scene."

She says it so easily—quietly but easily—like it's not a big deal. Like that fucker got exactly what he had coming to him, and she's not wrong. I hope he felt every flick of fire against his rapist fucking skin.

"Anyway, I didn't go to the police before that. I—"

"*Livi.*"

"I know. I should have. I just…" She huffs out a breath as she retwists her hair. "I was in a bad place for those couple of weeks, and by the time I decided to say something, it was too late."

Fucking hell. I set my beer aside and dig the heels of my hands into my eyes. The only solace I'd had in this was knowing—or rather assuming—she'd gone to the police. That justice had been served.

"I hate it." The distant look settles over her eyes once again, the distraction of fussing with her hair gone. "I was glad he was dead, and in a way, it felt like he got what he deserved. But that faded. And then I was angry that he never had to look me in the eye, knowing what he did to me. It was like, by dying before I could confront him, he got away with it."

Jesus Christ. As if shit wasn't bad enough, she'd had that to deal with, too. I'd only had my heart broken, but I know all too well how the lack of closure can eat away at you.

"That's when I decided to go to Europe and spend my last year of college abroad."

Every muscle in my body tightens all over again. "I fucking hate this story."

"I do, too, but it felt like the only choice I had at the time."

"You could have told me," I tell her once again, and she lifts a hand only to let it drop back to her lap.

"Yes, but you have to understand why I didn't. Even if I

could have gotten past you seeing me like that and feeling sorry for me, I never would have forgiven myself for what you would have done."

My lip curls as I imagine how good it would have felt to knock that bastard's teeth in. I would have cut his dick off, too, and made him choke to death on the fucking thing.

"You would have gone after him and you would have retaliated, and you would have put your career at risk."

I give a resolute nod. "You're damn right I would have."

"Aiden, no." She grips my thigh. "You've wanted to be a detective since you were a little boy. You and Bren both. I wasn't going to take that away from you."

"And you thought taking yourself away was better?"

She closes her eyes for a moment before she pulls back her shoulders and steels herself against any further emotion. "I had to make a choice, and I did what I thought was best."

"For who?"

"For both of us!"

I laugh, but there's no humor in it. She didn't tell me because she didn't trust how I felt about her. She didn't think I could handle it, so she left me before I could leave her. "That's not how it works, Liv. Not when we had what we had."

"Aiden—"

"Did you tell Jake?" The question is out of my mouth before I can decide whether or not I even want the answer. But when she blinks, the guilt as clear as the pink in her bloodshot eyes, I get one anyway. "Fuck!" I push to my feet as blind rage clouds my vision.

"Aiden, we were married," she pleads. "He and Lena were my best friends."

"What the hell was I?" My temper flares but she holds her own.

"You were more than my best friend."

"You're damn right I was." I ball my hands into fists. "I knew you felt it, Livi. I fucking knew you did."

She glances down. "I did. I'm not denying that. I wanted to be everything for you, but I didn't know how to do that when I couldn't even look at myself in the mirror."

"Livi— "

"But I can now." She nods adamantly. "And asking you to do this is me proving to myself that I won't be that girl again. I won't let someone else's decisions knock me down. I've come too far."

I stare down at her, my chest aching. I loved this girl with every part of myself, and she'd questioned that.

"I wanted to reach out to you for so long. To show you that I'd found myself again, but I couldn't because..." She shakes her head, unable to say the words. She'd been married. Fucking married. "And then he was gone, and I was in trouble, and it all made sense." She tries to smile but the tears spill down her cheeks instead. "This is my chance to show both of us that I can be strong again, no matter what. Just like I was before that night."

"Baby..." I pull her to her feet, and she curls into my chest, giving in to the emotion she's tried all night to contain.

All this time, she'd been worried about being enough for me, but the truth is if I had been enough for her, she would have known that it didn't matter if she was broken or whole, battered, bruised, or fucking perfect, I would have loved her anyway.

As far as I'm concerned, she has nothing to prove. But me...

I wasn't the man she needed then, but I'm damn sure going to be now.

CHAPTER 15

OLIVIA

I wake before the alarm again on Sunday morning, not because I slept well but because I didn't sleep at all.

Last night after Aiden held me and let me cry what felt like years' worth of tears, he demanded the name of my attacker, so he could verify for himself that he was no longer a threat. While he opened his laptop, I said good night and climbed into bed with the false hope that I'd actually get some rest.

I thought that finally telling him would relieve some of the guilt I've carried, but instead, telling him what happened only added to it. The hurt in his eyes and in his words… it had been more than I'd expected, because until that point, I wasn't sure he still cared.

Last night made it very clear that we've both tried but neither of us has truly found closure with the past, and this venture together is our chance to lay those demons to rest once and for all.

Shortly after my head hit the pillow, he came upstairs. He showered, and I thought maybe he'd try to sleep, too, but then my office door creaked open down the hall, and I gave up hope on getting a single wink of sleep.

Kyle Weston's obituary and the newspaper articles about his death have been in a folder at the front of my file cabinet since Jake died. I put them there as a reminder of everything I've overcome. The situation I'm in now isn't an easy one, but I'd still like to think I've put my darkest days behind me.

With the exception of the day I tell Aiden the final piece of the story.

I suppose that's the real reason I tossed and turned all night, and the reason why, at eight o'clock in the morning, I've already finished an entire pot of coffee by myself.

Some secrets are easier to share than others, and who would have thought that telling him I'd been raped would be the less painful of the two I kept?

I drop a cinnamon raisin bagel into the toaster with a sigh and grab my phone to call Lena when there's a soft knock on the front door. I smile, knowing immediately who it is, and hurry to the foyer to let Agent Morales in before his second knock wakes Aiden.

Quickly checking the peephole, I disengage the alarm and open the door to the salt-and-pepper-haired agent holding my *Wall Street Journal* like he does every Sunday morning.

"My company is still sleeping," I whisper. "But if we're quiet, we can share a cup of coffee."

"Ah, that's okay, doc. The fresh cup I have in the car will do." He hands over the newspaper. "How have you been?"

"Honestly, I think I'm a little better than I was last week, though it feels strange to finally say that."

The lines around his dark eyes crinkle as he smiles. "You've been through a lot, doc. It's gonna take some time, so give yourself a little grace."

"I'm trying." And I think I might finally be on the right track.

"Oh, I meant to tell you that your friend Victor stopped by earlier when he was walking his dog. He asked about the truck in the driveway."

"He did?" I've never seen Victor walk his dog down this street, though his wife Elena does every now and then.

"I didn't tell him anything, of course. Your company is none of my business."

"Thank you." My company technically *is* his business, but I appreciate the sentiment, nonetheless. I also make a mental note to check in with Elena so she can assure Victor that he has nothing to worry about.

"Anyway, I just wanted to make sure you got your paper."

"Thank you for that. You definitely make my Sunday mornings a little brighter." I smile and offer him the sports section like I always do. It's our deal. He brings the paper to the door since I can't go outside, and I give him the sports pages.

"You're welcome, doc. Looks like I should let you get back inside." He winks and then turns back to his car while I shut the door and reset the alarm. When I turn, I run smack into a bare-chested, rumple-haired Aiden.

"Jesus!" I hold the newspaper to my throat as all the air I inhaled rushes from my body at once. "Are you trying to give me a heart attack?"

"You're too damn friendly with your security detail." He glowers, his husky, sleep-thickened voice sounding far sexier than it should considering the scowl. Then again, my face had been smashed into the center of his rock-hard pecs a few seconds ago, so maybe I'm slightly concussed.

"He brought me the paper."

"You offered him coffee."

"So?" I shove past him before I do something stupid like

reach out to see if the dark dusting of hair on that hard-as-nails chest is as soft as I remember. "I already told you—I feel bad that these guys spend so much time sitting outside, babysitting me. The least I can do is be hospitable every now and then."

"They get paid to babysit you," he calls out in frustration before following me to the kitchen.

"Yeah, well, so do you, but you're sleeping in my guest room, aren't you?"

He snorts. "I'm getting paid to do a helluva lot more than babysit you, babe."

My bark of laughter is short but a whole lot of snarky. "You did not just say that."

He smirks, crosses his arms over his chest, and leans his hip against the counter, drawing my attention to the fact that his jeans aren't buttoned, and he is one hundred percent not wearing underwear.

"I am not having this discussion with you like that. Go put some clothes on, for god's sake." I wave him off and head for the coffeepot, only to find it empty, because—hello—I already drank it all.

"I think you should come home with me."

I spin like I'm on roller skates. "What?"

He lifts the shoulder covered in tattoos. "If we want to draw these guys out, we need to remove the obstacles."

"I don't follow." Spending time with him here is hard enough. Doing so at home, where it all began, would be ten times harder.

"There are fifteen hundred people in Cole Creek, and even during the summer, everyone in town knows when someone new shows up."

True enough, but... "That also means there would be fewer obstacles between me and whoever wants their money or my head. Not to sound vain, but I wouldn't look very good without a face." I shudder, thinking about that poor cat.

"I happen to like your face where it is, too, but if we want to get this done and over with, going home is our best bet. Bren is there, and you know he'll help. Nolan will probably put a couple undercover feds in the area, as well. I doubt he'll let me do this without backup."

"I don't think he'll let you do it *at all*."

"He will." He dips his chin confidently and tucks his thumbs into his jeans, inching them even lower on his hips.

I gulp hard and glance away from all that toned muscle. "This isn't your case, remember?"

"The feds brought me in for a reason and that's because I know you better than they do. I have a different perspective, and right now, that's what this case needs."

I can't argue with that. We need to do something different, but bringing danger to my family's doorstep?

"I don't want to put my parents in harm's way. If something happened to them…"

"Liv, listen…" He steps forward and reaches for me, his warm, calloused hand wrapping gently around my wrist. "Besides you, they'll be my number one priority. And your uncle already has them under surveillance, right?"

He does. The day the FBI put surveillance on me, Uncle Joe had a high-tech security system installed at my parents' house with cameras all around their property. My dad was salty at first, because who needs security when you have a shotgun? But in no time, he was watching the wildlife on the monitors like it was the big screen.

"You'll need to stay with me," Aiden adds. "And people in town are going to have to believe we're together just like they do here."

Gulp. I knew there was a possibility it would come to this, but I didn't think it'd be so soon. I've only been widowed for seven weeks, and Aiden is the only one who knows that my marriage wasn't the kind built on love.

"Even our parents?" I can tolerate the judgment of people I haven't talked to in years, but I'm not sure I can handle my parents thinking I'm using another man to grieve. Especially not when that other man is Aiden.

"For their safety, I think we should tell them the truth." His hand slides down to mine, giving it a light squeeze before he lets go. "But we can give my parents a varied version of the truth."

I tip my head. "What's the varied version of a fake relationship?"

His eyes dart back and forth between mine before he swallows. "We'll tell them that we were together before."

"Oh." Well, that's certainly going to make things interesting.

"They don't need the details but turning to an old friend for comfort is perfectly normal. They won't give us shit about it."

I hope not. "And what about Bren?"

His eyes darken at the same time his jaw tightens. "I'll take care of that."

"And that means...?"

"I'm going to tell him the truth."

Oh god. I know it's the right thing to do but telling him at the same time we ask him for help feels manipulative. *Hey, Bren, I need you to help save my ass. But also, Aiden and I were boning in college. Sorry!*

"He's going to figure it out the second he sees us together anyway, Liv."

Guilt slides down my spine, and I shiver. "I hate that we lied to him."

"I hate a lot of what we did, but there's nothing we can do about it now." He lifts a hand, and I frown.

143

"Do you really?"

"I just mean that I'd do a lot of things differently if I could." He takes a step forward and lifts his calloused palm to my cheek. "It's gonna be okay, Livi. I promise."

I nod as my throat begins to ache. "Be careful, Detective, or I might think you're starting to enjoy this."

A slow grin curls at one side of his mouth. "You might, huh?"

"Uh-huh."

His gaze drops to my lips before he opens his mouth only to snap it shut again.

"What?" I step into him, my fingertips pressing against his chest. "Say it."

But he doesn't. He shakes his head instead and takes a step back. "Some things are better left unsaid."

"Not always," I remind him. I think my confession last night proved that.

He still resists, and I know better than to push.

"I'm going to call Special Agent Nolan. I'd like to tell him you're on board with going back home." He rubs at his stubbled jaw and pulls his phone from his pocket, drawing a line in the sand and reverting our conversation back to safer territory.

Except I'm not sure it's safer at all. Going home with him. *Staying* with him. Nothing about that seems safe.

In fact, I'd say it's downright dangerous.

CHAPTER 16

AIDEN

"I don't like this." Special Agent Nolan scowls through my laptop screen on Sunday afternoon. "We can't protect her up there like we can down here."

Elbows on my knees, I lace my fingers together and nod. I may be overstepping, but I don't give a shit. "I understand your concern, but you brought me on board to make it look like you were backing off. At some point, you need to do that."

He surveys me through narrowed eyes. "This feels a lot more like actually backing off, not pretending to do it."

"Yeah, well, sometimes you gotta take chances to get the job done."

"And you're willing to take chances with her life?"

Hell no. The only thing I'm taking a chance on is my sanity, because bringing Liv into my home—the one place in Cole Creek that *doesn't* remind me of her—is like walking onto a psych ward and asking for a straitjacket.

Or at the very least a damn good reason to move when this is over.

"I would never suggest this if I wasn't one hundred and ten percent confident that I can handle it. Remember, I won't be alone. Her brother is there. And her uncle, though you probably don't want to think too much about how he might help."

The older agent scoffs. "You're right—I don't."

"He's on our side, Nolan. He just plays by the mob's rules instead of ours."

"Like I said, I'd rather not think about it." Relaxing back so that most of the screen is full of his rotund belly, he sighs. "What exactly do you think taking her to Cole Creek will accomplish?"

For one, it'd let her live again. After everything she shared last night, being cooped up like a prisoner in her own home is the last thing she needs. As if worrying about whether the next flash of headlights on the street or knock at the door is going to be someone to hurt her again isn't bad enough, she'd had no one but Lena and the feds to talk to.

Liv needs her family. Hell, she's needed them for ten years, but she's avoided Cole Creek because of me and the secret she's kept. I can't let her do that anymore. She wants me to remind her of how fearless she used to be? This is step one.

"Pine County is small, and Cole Creek is smaller. Even in the summer with tourists everywhere, it's a helluva lot easier to see who's doing what than it is here. My hope is that these assholes come looking for her, and up there, we'll be able to narrow down who doesn't belong a lot faster than you can here."

"We have more manpower down here, Enders."

"Yes, but the SSP said only a few guys were involved in the embezzlement, and one of them is already dead. I could handle a few on my own, but I'll bring the sheriff in to ease your mind."

He snorts. "Watch it, Detective. Arrogance isn't going to win me over here."

"It's confidence, not arrogance." Because whether either of us wants it to be or not, I have a personal interest in how this turns out. I'll take a bullet to the head myself before I let someone else touch Liv.

"And she'd stay with you?" One bushy eyebrow lifts.

"Yeah. I already have a security system, and the sheriff's office is just a couple blocks away."

"She'd have to be with you or her brother at all times."

I shake my head. "I disagree."

"That's too damn bad."

"You're gonna kill her yourself if you don't lighten up," I snap, and his lip curls.

"What the hell do you mean by that?"

"She's going stir crazy. I already see it in her. And when it gets to be too much, she could do something careless. You need to give her some breathing room now before that happens."

"Going with you is enough breathing room," he grumbles.

"She needs time with her family right now. There's a lot of shit you don't know."

"What kind of shit?" He leans forward again.

"Nothing that has to do with this case." Fuck, I never should've said anything. "Look, I need you to trust me on this."

"I barely know you, Detective." Those dark eyes narrow again, and his continued skepticism spurs my determination.

"Maybe not, but I know her, and let's not forget that's why you brought me into this." I'm a good cop, and there isn't a person in this world I'd go down fighting for as hard as I would for Liv.

He glances away, and while he exhales a long breath, I hold mine. "You know I can't let you do this without backup."

"I figured as much, but with all due respect, you can't put someone on her twenty-four seven up there. No one will believe we're really together."

"You're pushing your luck, Enders."

Yep, and again, I don't give a shit.

"I'll station someone at the sheriff's office," he concedes, and I dip my chin instead of fist-pumping the air.

"Bren will be fine with that. In fact, they can use my office since I'll be on 'vacation' as of tomorrow." The other guys aren't going to be happy about it, but they're going to have to suck it up since we can't tell them the truth.

"How long do you anticipate this *vacation* of yours to last?"

"Depends. I plan on going to Chicago in the morning to pay Eli Nowak a visit."

"Nowak..." Nolan frowns as he thinks back, trying to recall the name. "The professor at Columbia?"

"I read his interview report in the file. It was shorter than I expected." And completed by Agent O'Reilly instead of Special Agents Nolan or Bolinger. "Did you even talk to him yourself?"

The agent's ruddy cheeks pale. "There was nothing to talk to him about. He has a clean record, and there was nothing to indicate Mafia involvement."

"Looking at him on paper, you would have said the same thing about Jakub Jelanovich." And I can't believe we're having this conversation. "No offense, but I'd rather talk to him myself than take O'Reilly's word."

"What makes you think there's more to him?"

I don't have more than a hunch, but I'm not telling him

that. "He had the most in common with Jelanovich. They both went to Loyola, they're professors, and they were both involved with the Polish Exhibition House."

"Was he an immigrant, too?"

I shake my head. "Born and raised in the Chicago suburbs."

Nolan nods and scrubs a hand over his jaw. "I assume you're going undercover?"

"Yep. Turns out I was adopted as a kid. Just found out I'm Polish and want to know more about my roots."

The older man chuckles. "How do you know you'll find him at the museum?"

"He's on summer break and spending a lot of his time there, volunteering as a genealogy expert." Funny how much you can find out about a person when you actually dig into them rather than glossing shit over on a drive-by visit. "So, my vacation depends on how long it takes him to figure out that Olivia and my Polish friend, who's coming back to Cole Creek after her husband died, are one and the same."

The corners of his mouth tip up into a smile. "Sounds like you've got it all figured out."

"Just doing my job."

OLIVIA

"I told him about Kyle."

Lena's head snaps up from where she's kneeling on my closet floor, helping me pack. I called and asked her to come over when Aiden said we'd leave after he visits Eli tomorrow, providing Special Agent Nolan gives his approval.

"And?" She sits back on her heels with wide blue eyes, her blonde bun a little crooked from bending over.

"I thought he was going to take my back gate off the hinges." I tell her about chasing after him and how it probably helped defuse his anger, even if it had been a stupid move on my part.

"Oh, honey." She worries her bottom lip as she searches my face. "How are you holding up?"

"I'm fine. Mostly." I shift to sit cross-legged beside her, my suitcase and a mess of clothing options in front of us. "I mean, it brought up a lot of old memories for me, which I expected, but I didn't think he'd be so angry. He took it personally. Like he'd failed me somehow."

Lena's jaw drops as she presses her hand to her chest and falls sideways to her butt. "Oh god, I knew it."

I frown. "Knew what?"

"He still cares about you."

I roll my eyes. "Don't make this into something it isn't."

"Um, excuse me? He's here, isn't he?"

"To keep my family from having to plan my funeral."

"Right." This time, she's the one to make the dramatic face. "It's all about them and not at all because you two used to be crazy about each other."

"That was a long time ago."

"Says the woman who thought of him the second Special Agent Nolan suggested a fake boyfriend."

To be fair, he'd already been on my mind. "You know I didn't want to do this with just anyone."

"You could have asked a handful of other guys you know, but you only wanted him."

"He's a cop, Lena. He's the only one skilled enough to do it."

"Uh-huh. Keep telling yourself that." She picks up a peach sundress and carefully folds it before adding it to the suitcase. "You can't tell me that a little part of you didn't hope he'd say yes because a little part of *him* still has feelings for you."

Of course, I did, but I'm not foolish enough to think the chances of us having something more than this venture together are worth getting my hopes up. And I also need someone I can trust more than I need to rekindle an old flame.

"This is hard enough without going there." I add a few pairs of leggings to the pile, and she groans impatiently.

"What's the worst that could happen? If you went *there*."

Um, I could get my heart broken for a second time by the same man? "I'm not even sure I'm over Jake being gone, Len."

Her lips curve into a wry grin. "Oh, sweetie, you are so going to get your heart broken."

"Not if I'm careful." And surround myself with ten layers of Aiden-proof armor.

Her eyes sparkle knowingly but she doesn't say a word.

"Don't look at me like that."

"Would you rather I say what I'm thinking instead? That you're full of shit and we both know it?"

"Ugh." I get to my feet and go to my dresser for panties. "You're such a pain in the butt."

"Am I wrong?" she calls after me.

"Yes."

"Liar."

Dammit. I pause with my hand wrapped around a stack of silk and lace. "Would it make me a horrible person if I said no?"

"That I'm not wrong about you wanting more?"

My cheeks heat and I gulp. "I didn't say that…" But it *is* what I meant.

"He's only been around again for a few days, but let's be honest…" She stands and carries the suitcase to the bed. "You and Jake had a great friendship, and from time to time, it was more. But you never had the kind of feelings for him that I have for Wendell. And if we're being *really* honest... you never looked at Jake the way you still look at Aiden."

Shit. "I don't look at him *any* way, Len." Do I?

She laughs. "Sure, you don't."

"I don't!" And how would she know anyway? She saw us together for ten minutes before Special Agent Nolan called, and we came upstairs so they could talk alone.

"He told you to pack something nice *just in case*, and you blushed like you used to when he'd show up at our door in Madison."

"Because I don't have anything nice!"

She gestures to my closetful of dresses, pantsuits, and fancy shoes. "Right."

"Work clothes aren't *nice* clothes," I clarify, and she glares with knowing eyes.

"There's nothing wrong with admitting you're still attracted to him, O. And there's nothing wrong with admitting, even to yourself, that you'd love another chance with him either."

I open my mouth, but she holds up a hand.

"Don't you dare give me the new-widow excuse. We've already addressed the kind of marriage you were in. Besides, I'm not saying you have to jump headfirst into a real relationship. I just think you need to stop lying to yourself about what you want. You've done it for a decade already."

"I haven't been lying to myself." Not entirely, anyway. I'm well aware of how I feel, and my body hasn't let me forget how attracted I am to Aiden either. And the kiss last night at the Speakeasy? I'd spent half the night replaying it in my head, in rotation with his reaction to my assault. A simple kiss should not have been that powerful, but it had been. My surprise had only lasted a split second before instinct kicked in and my lips moved against his like old times. There'd been no hesitation. Not a single urge to pull back and stop either. Just the smoldering familiarity of all the stolen kisses we'd shared before.

I didn't even think about Jake, or the fact that I can still see the faint indention on my left hand from my wedding ring, until Troy showed up. And even then, the guilt for getting caught with another man was minimal. It hardly seems wrong to kiss a man I *actually* have feelings for.

"Letting my head go down that road right now would be dangerous. I need to think straight, and I won't be able to do that if I let my guard down." It's difficult enough being in the same room with Aiden most of the time, and it would be a hundred times harder if I let myself get distracted with *what-ifs*.

Lena's expression softens. "You're right. Staying safe has to be your first priority."

"Exactly."

"But that doesn't mean you can't keep an open mind. Aiden and Bren are going to bring down these creepy bastards, and this will all be over before you know it."

Tossing the handful of panties into the suitcase, I pull her in for a hug. "I hope you're right." Because I might talk a big game about keeping my head straight, but the truth is, my heart is already involved.

It has been since I was seventeen years old.

CHAPTER 17

AIDEN

*T*he Polish Exhibition House is now at the top of the list of places I want to take my mother. It's also the only place on the list since I just started it an hour ago, but she doesn't need to know that. One look at this place, and she'll think I flew her to the moon.

I snap a few pictures of the pre–World War I immigrant images despite the *no photos or videos* signs plastered everywhere and shove my phone back into my pocket before I get caught and kicked out.

The museum greeter at the front door had offered to give me a personal tour, since the official tour guide was busy with a family who'd apparently come down from Canada, but I'd declined in hopes of finding Eli Nowak and casually starting a conversation.

Unfortunately, he's been stuck in an office overlooking the main lobby since I arrived, showing an elderly couple a bunch of books.

"How's your browsing going?" the young blonde greeter asks, coming around the corner while I flip through a registry of Polish citizens who'd arrived in the US in 1902. That's the year my great-grandparents on my mother's side came over.

"It's going great. There's so much to see." Not that I've paid attention to much more than this display with my focus continually wandering back to Nowak. "It's overwhelming. I just found out I'm thirty percent Polish, and I thought the museum would be a good place to start looking into things. I probably should've started smaller."

She laughs. "Did you take a mail-in DNA test?"

"Yeah. I'm adopted and wasn't sure what my background was."

"Ah, I see. Did you subscribe to the research and records part of the DNA database, as well?"

"No. I didn't think it'd be helpful since I didn't have any close relatives to look into."

"Ah." She nods sympathetically. "I'm sorry to hear that. You should talk to Eli. He might be able to help you find the regions of Poland your family came from. It'd be a less daunting place to start."

"Eli?" I frown like I haven't been stalking the guy since I walked through the door.

"He's one of our volunteers who happens to be a genealogy buff." She glances at her watch. "He's in a meeting right now, but he should be finishing up any minute now. I'm sure he'd be happy to help you."

"Really? That'd be great. If he has the time."

She waves off my hesitation with a small scoff. "He lives for this kind of stuff, believe me. I'll go tell him you're here, and he'll come find you when he's free if you don't mind waiting?"

"Not at all. Thank you." Now to come up with my bullshit DNA story.

She smiles again before she hurries off toward the front of the museum, and I resume my search for Stanislaw and Serafina Kowalcyzk. Less than ten minutes pass when a friendly voice sounds behind me.

"I hear we have a new Polish relative to befriend."

Relative? I look up to see Eli Nowak standing back with his hands in the pockets of his khakis and a friendly smile on his face. He chuckles at my confused expression.

"We're all related in one way or another," he clarifies, but that doesn't make me feel any better, considering I've dated my fair share of Polish women in my primarily Polish town.

I tip my head toward the registry. "I suppose we are."

He extends a hand and I do the same. "Eli Nowak. My great-grandparents came to America in 1900. They were goat farmers from Zakopane."

Shit, maybe we *are* related. I'm pretty sure Zakopane is listed on my actual DNA tree.

"Aiden... Alexander," I finally say. "And I can't pronounce the region my ancestors are supposedly from. Sorry."

He chuckles. "I can help you with that. Let's grab a cup of coffee in my office."

Yeah, let's. Because the sooner I can figure out what the hell else he's up to, the sooner I can put him in cuffs.

"Amanda said you were adopted?" Nowak grabs a couple of paper cups from beside the communal coffeepot outside his office and fills them up. "Cream, sugar?"

"No thanks, black is good. And yes. I knew I didn't have any siblings but wasn't sure what my ancestry was." The lie rolls off my tongue with ease as I survey him. I'd found his picture online, so I knew he'd be a fairly nondescript guy. Tall, blond, and preppy like I'd expect a college history professor to be in contrast to Jakub Jelanovich's edgy, Beckham look.

"Do you live in the area?"

"No, I'm actually from Wisconsin."

"Which part?" He hands me one of the cups.

"North. A town called Copper Crossing," I lie. "It's close to Cole Creek, which you might be familiar with? It's a predominantly Polish town with a big festival every year."

"Hmm, can't say that I have." He shakes his head, no disguised recognition in his expression. "Come in and have a seat." He gestures to his office, and I follow, claiming one of the leather chairs recently vacated by the older couple.

"Thanks for this, by the way. I wasn't expecting to actually talk to anyone today." While he shuffles papers around on his desk, I scan the office. The pictures on the walls are historic, but the ones on his desk are personal, of him and a handful of various people. "Your family?" I lift my chin toward the frames.

"Yep. My mom and my sisters are in this one, then my grandparents, and here's me and a few of my cousins." He picks up the last picture and points to one of the men. "He's our family's only claim to fame; he's a footballer for the Polish national team."

"Ah, a soccer player."

He chuckles. "Don't let him hear you say that."

"I mean no offense. Those guys are some pretty badass dudes."

Nowak finally drops into his chair with a wry laugh. "I'd hate to piss 'em off in a bar fight, that's for sure. Anyway, let's talk about you. Do you know anything about your birth parents?"

"No. Unfortunately, my mom passed away a few years ago, and my dad, well, he's not a big talker." I cringe at the lie about my mother, who would smack me upside the head with a frying pan if she'd heard me say she was dead. Bad juju and all that. "I'm more interested in finding out about my heritage, not who my birth parents were. I want to be able to pass some culture down to my kids."

He lifts his coffee. "You have children?"

"Not yet." Or ever at the rate I'm going. "How about you?"

He eyes me for a moment, like he holds that particular hand close to his chest before he clears his throat. "I have two boys, and my wife is due in a few months with our first daughter."

"Ah, congratulations."

"Thank you. We're excited. So, what part of Poland is your family from according to your DNA profile?"

I pull my phone from my jeans and open up a screenshot from some random internet person's ancestry results. "This says my family came from… Swee-ot-nicky—"

"*Świątniki Górne*," he finishes with a proper accent and a chuckle. "It's just south of Kraków. Are you also Jewish?"

"Yes, that was my second largest percentage." It's actually German from my dad's side of the family, but not today.

"Makes sense. *Świątniki Górne* has a large Jewish population, as well. Let me bring up some information…" He turns to his computer and begins typing, giving me another opportunity to look around, though I'm not sure what I'm looking for. There was nothing in Jake's office to give me mobster vibes and there's nothing here, either.

Might as well get to the point.

"My friend offered to help me research when I got my results, but then her husband died, and now I feel bad asking."

He cocks an eyebrow but keeps his focus on the screen. "I'm sorry to hear that."

"Yeah, me too. Olivia would love knowing that we're both

Polish, but again, I'm not sure now is the right time to bring it up. Then again, I did hear she's going back to Cole Creek for a while, so maybe we'll connect."

He nods, and turns his monitor to me, where one half of the screen is filled with images of a vibrant town and the other shows a list of names. Surnames, specifically. "This is *Świątniki Górne*, and these are the most common family names in the area."

What are the chances that Zieliński—Liv's Uncle Joe's last name—would be right at the top?

"That's interesting." I chuckle and point to the name. "That's Olivia's mother's maiden name."

"It's a very popular Polish surname." Again, his only reaction is a polite smile. I need to up my game, so I put on a concerned face.

"You know, it just occurred to me that maybe I need to dig into this even deeper."

"I'm happy to help in any way I can."

Rubbing a hand around the back of my neck, I hesitate. "That friend of mine... Olivia? We're just friends now, but we were more in college, if you know what I mean. It'd be hella awkward to find out we're related."

He chuckles, leans back in his chair, and folds his hands. "Unless you were adopted locally, the chances are slim. And your parents probably would have steered you away from her if they were concerned, don't you think?"

"Right. Except we snuck around, because her dad told me to stay away from her."

His brows lift before he sits forward and starts tapping on the keyboard again. "What's her last name?"

"Bishop."

At that, he stops cold. "Olivia Bishop?"

"Yep, that's her."

His eyes cut to mine. "You're not talking about *Dr.* Olivia Bishop…"

My jaw slacks open like the good little actor I am. "You know her? She's a professor at UW-Milwaukee."

He spins away from the computer and busts out laughing. "Yeah, I know her. Her husband was a board member and a volunteer here." He shakes his head in disbelief as he openly looks me over, his focus lingering on my inked arms before he chuckles again. "So, you and Olivia, huh? I guess you do kinda remind me of Jake."

The fuck I do. I'm nothing like that son of a bitch.

"I never got the chance to meet him," I say dryly. "She didn't come home much after she got married."

"She's involved in a lot at the college. Or she was anyway. I think the feds have her locked down pretty tight right now."

I frown. "What do you mean?"

He blinks. "You don't know?"

"Know what?"

He blows out a breath and glances up to the ceiling, like he's debating whether or not he should say any more. "I hate to be the one to tell you this, but Jake didn't just die—he was murdered."

"You're shittin' me." I fall back in my seat with a huff. "What happened?"

He lifts a hand. "Not sure. Just that there was some threat against her, too, so the feds put her under their protection. I haven't talked to her since the funeral, so I'm not sure if there have been any new developments."

The funeral was a week before the mob showed up at her work with the target on her head. How would he know about any of that if he hadn't talked to her?

"Holy shit. I had no idea," I lie. "Like I said, I didn't want to bother her. I figured she needed some space right now."

He nods, his brow creasing. "Yeah, it's a crazy situation."

He opens his mouth and then shuts it again, hesitating. "If you do talk to her, could you do me a favor and tell her not to be a stranger? My wife has reached out to her a couple of times to check in, and I feel bad that we haven't been able to do more."

Like take her out in a dark alley, too? "If the rumors are true and she does come back home, I'll mention it. She'll probably get a kick out of us meeting like this."

He cracks a small smile. "Right? What are the chances?"

Pretty damn good, asshole.

Before I can respond, a knock sounds on the door, and Amanda, the greeter, pokes her head in. "I'm sorry to interrupt, but Vice Chairman Krol is here. He said there's a problem with one of the exhibit contracts. A financial discrepancy."

Nowak sighs. "Thanks, Amanda. Can you tell him I'll be there in a minute?"

She nods politely. "Sure thing."

"Thank you."

She closes the door quietly, and I push out of the chair. "I guess that's my cue to get moving."

He stands and offers his hand across the desk. "I'm sorry to cut this short before I could give you any useful information."

Oh, he was plenty informative. "That's all right. I'll have to come down again, that's all."

He smiles and picks up a card. "Call me or shoot me an email if you have any questions. And please do let Olivia know that we're thinking about her."

"I'll do that." I take the card and follow him to the door, my attention snagging on the man talking with Amanda across the lobby. He's dressed in a black suit and something about him seems familiar, but then he was probably in some of the pictures I'd seen online when I'd looked into the

161

museum. "Thanks again," I tell Nowak, and the guy in the suit glances over at us.

Our eyes meet and the hair on the back of my neck rises. I still can't place him, but the niggling in my gut says I've definitely seen him before. In person.

But where?

CHAPTER 18

OLIVIA

I've been back to Cole Creek exactly twice since Aiden and I broke up in college. Both visits were for funerals, and that has my stomach twisting into knots as we enter the outskirts of town where the familiar—and now eerie— Cole Creek Cemetery comes into view.

Aiden knows what he's doing bringing me back here, and I trust that my brother will do his damnedest to keep me safe, too. But there's an ominous *third time's a charm* feeling about coming home when someone wants to put me in that cemetery, too. It's like I'm tempting fate, or worse, throwing myself in front of it.

"You're either gonna throw up or bolt. Which is it so I know whether to slow down or speed up?" Aiden shoots me a sidelong glance from the driver's seat, and I tighten my grip on the passenger side door.

"I'm not bolting anywhere near the cemetery, believe me."

His frown turns into a grin. "Superstitious?"

"Ha ha, you're funny." I glare at him, and he gives a light-hearted laugh.

"Just trying to lighten the mood." He reaches over and pats my hand. "Anyway, I was thinking we'd drop your stuff off at my place and then head over to see your parents so we can let them know what's going on. You okay with that?"

My excitement at seeing Mom and Dad is drowned out by the wave of nausea in my stomach. My parents know that Jake was murdered, but they don't know the full story about the threats made against me. Uncle Joe told them the security was just a precaution because we didn't know what Jake might've been messed up in, and I'd hoped to keep it that way. I guess time is up on that front.

"How much do we have to tell them? About Jake, I mean."

Aiden taps his thumb against the steering wheel as we slow to a stop at the first intersection in town. There's no stoplight, of course, because even during the summer, there aren't enough people in Cole Creek to warrant one.

"We should tell them everything."

"I was afraid you'd say that."

He gives me a compassionate glance while a tractor with a trailer full of hay crosses the road in front of us. "Liv, we can't keep them in the dark. It's not safe."

"Can we leave out the part with my head in the middle of a bull's-eye? And the cat?"

He nods thoughtfully. "I suppose they don't need those details."

Thank god, because telling them that Aiden and I are seeing each other is going to be awkward enough. I don't need them imagining all the ways I might die, too.

"Are you ready for the wrath of my father?" I ask as Aiden maneuvers his truck through town, past the Cole Stop and Tulah's Diner, the library, the post office, Bobbie Jean's bookstore, and Kaminski's Auto, all of which are situated on Main

Street behind clean sidewalks and black lamp posts with hanging baskets overflowing with colorful flowers.

"I can handle your old man, Liv. The question is are *you* ready?"

Yes... but also no. My dad isn't going to be happy to hear about my history with Aiden, but he'll deal with it because my mother will make him. My real concern is telling my parents the truth before Aiden has a chance to talk to my brother.

"Honestly, Bren is the only one I'm worried about. And your mom."

"My mom?" His brow furrows even as he laughs. "Why the hell would you be worried about her?"

"Uh, because I adore her, and I'm pretty sure she's going to think I'm using you as a rebound. I don't want her to hate me for that."

He gives a soft snort. "She's not going to think that, trust me."

"How do you know that?"

"Because she's been on my ass about settling down for years now. At this point, I don't think she cares who I bring home as long as it gives her hope she might get a couple grandkids out of me someday."

Another wave of unease rolls through my stomach, and I swallow against it. "I heard Jesse and his son's mother got back together."

Aiden nods. "Yep. Her name is Hayden. She's great. So is Jett."

I bet. The perfect little family. "I'm happy for him." Even if I am envious.

"He had it rough for a few years, only seeing his boy every other weekend. But he never gave up hope, you know?"

I wish I could say I hadn't. But I gave up hoping for certain things a long time ago.

I paste on a smile and change the subject. "So, back to my parents. Don't you think we should talk to Bren first?"

"I called him last night and told him I was bringing you back with me today."

"And?" I hold my breath and wait.

"I told him we need to make this look natural and us showing up at his office definitely wouldn't qualify. Not to mention I don't want to have to cuff him in front of everyone when he tries to knock out my teeth."

I almost laugh. Almost. Because the thought of my big, bad, tough-as-nails brother in a pair of his own cuffs would be a sight to see. But I don't want anyone blowing up over me, especially not when there's already enough drama in my life.

"So, what's the plan?" I ask instead.

"He's going to come over later."

All right. Sounds low key enough. And if there is drama, no one will be around to witness it. "Speaking of later, what would you like to do for dinner? I assume you live like a consummate bachelor with a fridge that holds nothing but beer and frozen pizza."

He shoots me a crooked grin. "Are you stereotyping me?"

"Am I wrong?"

"Let's just say a stop at the grocery store is at the top of my to-do list."

Uh-huh. I can only imagine what his house looks like. Nothing but paper plates, mismatched cups, and the requisite oversized leather furniture with an enormous, ego-sized TV. He probably has a black comforter, too. And gray sheets that haven't been washed in weeks.

"I assume I'll be sleeping on the couch?"

He runs a hand around the back of his neck "Ah, no. I probably should have mentioned that Craig has been crashing at my place for the past couple of months. I asked him to find somewhere else to go, but unless he's found a place since we talked the other day, he may be around for a little while."

"Craig Perry? Did something happen with him and Rachel?"

"They're in the middle of a divorce."

"No way!"

"Yep. And he's been seeing Cady."

"Cady Reynolds?" I lurch forward, nearly choking myself with the seat belt. "You're kidding me."

He gives his head a single shake. "Afraid not."

"Tell me he didn't cheat." Rachel was a year older than me in high school, but we were good friends once upon a time. She'd confided in me that Craig's past relationship with Cady, even though they'd been teenagers, had been difficult for her to deal with. I can't imagine what she must be feeling now.

"Not that I'm aware of. I think—and hope—it's just a rebound."

"Like people are going to think you are to me." I glance out the window with a sigh. Maybe I do care what others think, after all.

"Not our business what other people think, just like it doesn't matter what anyone thinks about Craig and Cady. Or Craig and Rachel, for that matter."

True enough, but it's a bit more difficult to accept when *your* relationship is the one in question. Even if it *is* a fake one.

"This is me." Aiden slows at a dirt driveway a block out of town near the creek. Trees of all kinds line the short drive before the property opens up to a small lot that's probably three or four acres. The cute, one-story, cottage-style home is neat and cozy looking with brown siding, white-trimmed windows, and a front door painted my favorite cranberry red. There's even a big pot of marigolds on the front porch.

"Did you pot the flowers yourself?" I flash a cheeky grin as we unbuckle.

"Fuck no," he scoffs. "I came home from work one day and they were there. I didn't ask questions."

"Your mom?"

"Jinx."

"Jinx? Yeah right." The only thing I can imagine Aiden's youngest brother planting is his own seed in any willing woman. From what I've heard, anyway.

"I'm serious. He runs the landscaping part of Enders Excavating. He plants all kinds of shit and is pretty good at it, too."

"Wow." I clearly have a lot of catching up to do.

"Anyway, like I said, Craig's been staying here, and I haven't been home since Friday morning. I have no idea what we're walking into."

I wrinkle my nose playfully. "Or maybe you do know, and you're going to blame it on poor Craig because he's not here to defend himself."

He snorts and opens his truck door. "Ain't nothing poor about Craig, babe."

Babe. I suppose I'm going to have to get used to him calling me that again. At least for a little while.

I hop out, as well, and grab my laptop and messenger bags from the back seat while Aiden grabs my suitcase and overnight bag from the other side. We meet at the porch and clamber up the wide, wooden steps, side by side.

"This isn't what I expected," I admit, taking another look around the tidy yard. We're close enough to town to hear the late afternoon traffic, but far enough away to enjoy the privacy.

"It's not? What did you think? I'd have a tent pitched?"

"*Noo.*" I laugh softly and bump my shoulder into his arm. "I guess I still picture you living in your old apartment. There should be a keg on this porch."

He shoves a key into the lock and opens the door before giving me a serious look. "I keep it inside now."

I blink for a moment before I realize he's kidding. "You're just full of the jokes today, aren't you?"

Flashing a grin, he leads the way inside and then groans. "Fucking Craig."

Ah, he must be referring to the mess of blankets on the couch and the lineup of empty beer bottles on the coffee table, because the rest of the room is relatively clean, if not almost exactly like I pictured. The brown leather recliner is nearly half the size of the matching couch, and the TV is as big as my fireplace. The rug beneath the coffee table, however, is a soft, fluffy cream that gives the room an almost feminine touch, along with the cream-framed pictures on the side table.

"Is this your nephew?" I ask, picking up a picture of a little boy that's identical to Jesse aside from the blond hair.

"Yep, that's Jett. He turned four a couple months ago."

"He's cute."

"And he knows it." Aiden tips his head down toward the hall. "Bedroom is in the back."

"Oh. Right." The bedroom. Which I'm assuming is the only one if Craig has been sleeping on the couch.

"Don't tell Craig, but the sofa in my office pulls out into a bed. I'll sleep there and you can take my room, but we're going to have to be careful when Craig is here."

"That's fine." I'm down for whatever, as long as it doesn't involve sharing a bed, because there's no way I'd get a single wink of sleep with a half-naked Aiden next to me.

"The guest bathroom is here..." Hands full of my luggage, he lifts his chin toward a door on the left before tipping his head to the one on the right. "And that's my office. My room is around the corner."

Oh. Now I see his concern about Craig. There's no way he'll be able to use the bathroom and not realize Aiden and I aren't sleeping together. Which probably means we're going to *have* to sleep together at least occasionally. Great.

Aiden pushes open the last door on the L-shaped hallway and blindly tosses my overnight bag onto the king-size bed, which, much to my surprise, is not only made, but covered in a rather pretty old-fashioned quilt.

The closet doors are a golden oak like the rest of the doors in the house, and the walls are the same soft blue as his eyes. There are no pictures, but then there aren't any deer antlers or mounted fish, either. But what surprises me the most is The Lord of the Rings trilogy on the bedside table.

"Wow." I drop my workbags into an antique claw-footed chair in the corner and gape at him. "I take back the keg comment."

He wheels my suitcase to the closet and chuckles. "What assumptions did you make about me this time?"

"Are you really reading these, or did you put them here to impress the women you bring home?" I pick up the worn paperback copy of *The Fellowship of the Ring*, its cover tattered and pages dog-eared.

"You're not saying I have it in me to be shallow, are you?"

"You always hated reading, and you poked fun of me for loving it so much."

"I wasn't poking fun—I was trying to get you to pay more attention to me," he clarifies, and I glance up with a small smile.

"Oh, is that what it was?"

"Yes, and for the record, I've read that series three times, because some crazy person once told me that books are always better than the movies." His gaze is playful but pointed, and I can't help but giggle.

"Was she right?"

"You know she was."

"Dang right." I set the book back down and glance around when a sudden wave of emotion hits me out of nowhere. For such a long time, I'd allowed myself to believe he hated me. That I'd done irreconcilable damage to not only our relationship, but our friendship, too. Yet, over the course of the past week, he's proven that untrue. More than that, he's shown me that he might've even held on.

My eyes burn and my throat begins to constrict, and I blink fast to keep the sudden tears at bay.

"Liv?" Aiden's hands are on my shoulders, turning me to him as I sniff. "Hey, what's going on?"

"I-I don't know. I think being home after all this time is starting to hit me."

His thumbs stroke my shoulders gently. "I get it. Maybe we should hold off on seeing your folks. Let you get your bearings first."

"No, I'll be fine." The less time I spend alone with him right now, the better. "I'd rather people see us together sooner than later, so they can gossip and get it out of their systems."

He smiles softly. "We're gonna turn some heads, that's for sure."

"I know." And god help me, but I'm starting to begrudge that it won't be for real like it might've been all those years ago. "And you're sure you want to do this? Here, I mean?"

"I'm not worried about a few rumors, Liv. We're grown-ass adults, remember?"

I give a soft laugh. "Yes, but your reputation might take a few hits over something that isn't even real. That doesn't bother you?"

His laugh is harsher than mine. "Babe, I'm a cop in a small town. If I let the opinions of others bother me, I'd have resigned a long time ago."

His phone beeps with a message before I can respond, and he frowns when he reads it.

"Everything okay?"

"Uh, yeah, it's just Bren. Something came up and he won't be able to come over tonight. He has a few minutes now, though, so he said he'll meet us at your parents."

"Now?" Heat fills my cheeks where my tears have barely dried.

"Now." Aiden nods, tucking his phone back into his jeans. "You sure you're ready for this?"

"No, but I will be." As long as I keep my head away from all the memories I have with Aiden in my childhood home, I should be just fine.

CHAPTER 19

THIRTEEN & A HALF YEARS EARLIER...

OLIVIA

"*D*on't tell my mom, but these mashed potatoes are the bomb, Mrs. Bishop. And that green bean casserole..." Aiden gives an almost indecent moan on the other side of the dining room table, and I bite my lips together to keep from giggling.

Even though he'd had Thanksgiving dinner with his own family a couple hours earlier, he accepted my mother's invitation to eat with us, too. I'd like to think it's because he wanted to see me, as well, since he and Bren have spent all of their break at the Enders' hunting camp, but I know better than to get my hopes up. We snuck out a few times over the summer, but he's been off at college since the end of August, and aside from homecoming weekend in October, we've barely talked let alone shared any stolen kisses.

"Mom, you don't mind if Aiden crashes here tonight, do

you? We're heading back to camp right before sunup anyway."

Mom shakes her head, and while she and Bren hash out the sleeping arrangements, Aiden's devious blue eyes lock on mine. Beneath the table, his sock-clad toes tease up the inside of my bare calf, and I squirm in my seat at the promise of what that might mean.

I'm not naive to the fact that he's been living college life to the fullest like any hot-blooded eighteen-year-old male with newfound freedom would do. But I won't let that knowledge keep me from having a little fun of my own, too. Especially when the boy in question is the one I've crushed on for almost half of my seventeen years.

After the turkey and leftover fixings are cleaned up and put away, Mom and Dad take a ride over to Uncle Joe and Aunt Candy's for another round of dessert while I hang back with the boys. They break out Bren's old PlayStation and play *Madden*, and I curl up in a recliner and pretend to do homework instead of drooling over Aiden's biceps and forearms. He's bulked up quite nicely in the few months he's been away at the academy, and my hands itch to reach out and see if he's as hard and as hot as he looks.

"Olivia!" Bren's bark breaks into my naughty thoughts, and I scowl across the living room.

"Must you yell? Jeez."

He rolls his eyes. "Apparently, I do. I've asked you to get us something to drink three times already."

To that, I snort. "I'm not sure what kind of *service* you've been getting in college, but it's not available here. You want something to drink, get it yourself."

Aiden laughs. "The only service he's been getting is from his right hand."

Bren drives a backward fist into the center of Aiden's

chest, and he falls against the back of the couch, groaning and laughing at the same time.

"That's what my right hand has to say about that, asshole."

"There's no need for violence, *Brendan*." I enunciate his full name like our mom does just to piss him off, and it works. He glowers as he gets to his feet, blindly tossing his controller onto the couch.

"Who does homework on Thanksgiving anyway?" he grumbles on his way to the kitchen.

"Uh, people who actually take their education seriously, that's who."

"Are you saying I don't?" he calls from the other room at the same time Aiden jackknifes up from the couch and sprints over to my chair. One of his hands slides around my throat to lift my chin as the other pushes back into my hair, so he can press his lips against mine in a hurried but intense kiss that ends just as quickly as it started.

He's already back in his seat, cueing up a new game before Bren returns, leaving me to process what the heck just happened.

"So?" my brother asks as he pads back into the living room with two cans of Pepsi. "You don't think I take school seriously?"

I wet my lips, tasting Aiden for a second time, and smile to myself. "I mean, you're going to school to be a cop. It's not like that's hard."

Both of the guys scoff at the same time, and I giggle. The only thing I love doing more than antagonizing my brother is kissing his best friend, both of which have now happened in the same minute. I'm a lucky girl.

"And to think I was going to let you play," Aiden mutters from the other side of Bren, and the potential double meaning of his words makes me grin even harder. He's never tried anything with my brother so close before, but something tells me he might be up for it tonight, and I wouldn't mind pushing our luck a little either.

My parents come home an hour later, but instead of hanging out with us in the living room, they go upstairs to watch TV in their own room. It's early yet, barely after eight o'clock, but I follow after them and get changed into my pajamas. I also grab a blanket and a pillow from the closet for Aiden, and head back downstairs just as Bren stands and stretches.

"I'm gonna grab a quick shower and then we're gonna watch a movie. Olivia, do you think you could refrain from being a smart-ass for once in your life and make popcorn without complaining?"

I toss Aiden the blanket and pillow and press a hand to my chest in mock offense. "Me, a smart-ass? Whatever do you mean?"

My brother shakes his head as he strolls to the stairs. "Just make the fucking popcorn."

I bat my eyelashes and then giggle when he raises a single-finger salute.

The second he's out of sight, Aiden grins. "You want some help?"

"I suppose. Otherwise, we'll have to listen to him pout all night." I tip my head toward the kitchen, and he follows. While I grab the box of microwave popcorn from the cupboard, he takes out two bowls from another.

"You should swap spots with him before he comes back down. Sit on the couch by me."

I smile up at him as I tear the plastic off of a package of popcorn. "Yeah? Why would I want to do that?"

He shuffles closer and dips his lips to my ear. "So I can hold your hand under the blanket."

"Just hold my hand?"

"Maybe cop a feel." One of his hands lifts to my hip while

the other curls boldly around one of my boobs. "You're not wearing a bra?"

I shake my head. "I don't wear one to bed."

A low groan rolls in his chest as his thumb circles around my hardening nipple. "Show me."

"Right here?"

He nods, his fingers already reaching for the hem of my tank top.

I sigh, and while he tugs up my shirt, I reach around him to put the popcorn in the microwave. As I press buttons, he lowers his mouth and laves a tongue around one peak.

"Fuck, you're pretty," he murmurs, his mouth going back and forth from one breast to the other until my entire body shakes.

"You're killing me," I whimper, greedy heat already building between my legs.

"You want more?" He grazes his teeth over one bud and I shiver.

"More?" There's no time for more. Bren will be back in a matter of minutes, and my parents could come down at any time.

"You'll have to be quiet." He stands upright again, his gaze dark and devious as he backs me up against the counter.

"We can't... *ohhh.*" My protest melts into a moan as he pushes a hand into my shorts and panties, not stopping until one long finger is buried inside of me.

"Already so wet." His voice is low and raspy as his lips find the shell of my ear. "Your pussy is always ready for me, isn't it, Liv?" he whispers. "Always hot and wet, waiting for my fingers."

"*Unngh,*" is my only response as my eyes slam shut and I get lost in the sensation of his hand working between my legs. He thrusts his finger in and out at least a dozen times before he adds another and presses his thumb against my clit, making my ears ring.

"If we had more time, I'd put you on this counter, spread your legs wide, and tongue you until you come all over my face. Fuck, I can already taste you, Livi. So sweet and so innocent. But not with me. You're a dirty girl with me, aren't you?"

"Aiden, oh god." My hand clamps around his wrist as he continues to fuck me with his fingers. "I'm going to come."

"Of course you are." He chuckles in my ear. "Because you love when I touch you... when I do things to you that no one else knows about."

My fingers dig into his skin as everything in me tightens, ready to snap.

"One of these times it's gonna be my dick you come on. You're gonna let me fill you up and make you—"

"Ahhh!" I cry out as I come, but his mouth is on mine before the sound escapes my lips. He kisses me hard and deep while my body pulses around his fingers until every last flutter is set free. Only then does he pull back and carefully remove his hand from my shorts.

"That's my girl," he praises with a wicked smile just as the microwave goes off beside us. "And just in time, too."

I give a breathless laugh as I sag back against the counter, not quite believing he could make me lose my mind in three minutes flat.

He holds up his hand and waggles his damp fingers. "The popcorn smells good, but I bet these taste better."

My frown of confusion morphs into an O of lust as he sticks his fingers into his mouth and licks them clean.

"Mmm, I was right." He moans and all I can do is stand there and pant. "So, I take it you'll be sitting next to me on the couch?"

I gulp hard and nod, and he winks.

"Damn right you are. Now, let's get the rest of this popcorn made."

――――――――

Two hours later, the credits begin to roll on the TV and Bren yawns from the recliner. Despite his big talk about copping a feel, Aiden didn't try to touch me even once during the movie, which is just as well. After what happened in the kitchen earlier, the last thing I want to do is get caught and put a premature end to whatever the heck is going on with me and Aiden.

"I'm hitting the hay," my brother announces. "Five o'clock is going to come too damn early."

"You're telling me." Aiden covers a yawn of his own as I get up and collect the empty popcorn bowls and soda cans.

"You good here, sis?" Bren asks, and I nod.

"Yep, I'll clean up. Lord knows you need your beauty sleep."

He snorts and nudges me with a shoulder as I pass by on the way to the kitchen. "Love you, too."

"Uh-huh." As I dump out the unpopped kernels and toss the empty cans into the recycling bin, he and Aiden hash over their plans for the morning and say good night. By the time I've washed and put away the bowls, a shirtless Aiden is stretched out on the couch with an arm tucked behind his head as he channel surfs.

"You going to bed, too?" he asks as I organize my homework and set it aside for tomorrow.

"I should." But I don't want to. We don't get to talk that much now that he's gone off to school, and when we do, my brother is always around.

He crooks a finger at me, and my cheeks instantly heat. "He's going to figure out I haven't gone upstairs."

179

"No, he won't. He could barely keep his eyes open during the movie. Come and talk to me." He shifts back on the couch and lifts the blanket, inviting me into his cocoon.

"I definitely can't do that."

His lips turn down into a pout just as I click off the lamp and the room goes dark other than the TV glow. "But I've missed you," he whispers, and my insides turn to goo.

"You're going to get us in trouble."

"Cuddling with you will be worth it."

Ugh. How does he always know what to say? "Fine, but if someone comes down, I'm ducking and you're going to look really fat."

His body shakes with laughter as I lie down in front of him, my butt nestled in his lap. His very unobstructed lap.

I stiffen. "Where are your pants?"

"On the chair."

"Uh, why?"

"Uh, because eventually I'm going to sleep?"

Right. Now, every time I sit on the couch, I'm going to think about him sleeping here in his boxer briefs. Great.

"And maybe because I just want to be close to you like this. Is that alright with you?"

Goose bumps wash over my skin as he leans down and kisses my temple. "Yeah, I guess."

"You guess?"

"Is that all you want? To be close?"

He's quiet for a moment while he picks a channel, drops the remote, and then laces his fingers with mine on top of the blanket. "I had plans to get into your shorts again during the movie, but then it occurred to me that you might think that's all I want from you."

I scrape my teeth along my lips and swallow. "It's not?"

"Fuck, no." He turns me quickly to face him. "Do I like making out with you? Yeah. A fuck lot. But I like *you*, too,

Liv. And I don't want you to think we have to fuck around every time we see each other. That's not what this is about."

I press my hand to his bare chest, letting my fingers tease lightly through the dusting of dark hair down the center. "Then what is it about?"

"Us," he says without hesitation. "I don't know what it is about you, but it's just… it's so fucking different with you. Don't get me wrong—I love kissing you and touching you and making you come—but sometimes I just want to call and talk to you, too."

My lips curl into a giddy smile as warmth fills my chest. "You do?"

He brushes the hair back from my face and nods. "Would that be okay?"

It would be more than okay. As much as I've enjoyed all the physical stuff we sneak in whenever we see each other, I've missed just hanging out with him, too. And the number of times I've wanted to call him just to tell him about something exciting that happened is endless.

"I'd like that." I lean up and brush the tip of my nose against his. "In fact, I kinda like you, too."

One corner of his mouth lifts. "Yeah? I bet you tell all the guys that."

"Nope. Just the ones with pretty blue eyes and big, strong arms."

He chuckles and pulls one of my legs up to his hip. With one simple shift, we could be touching a lot more intimately, but he doesn't make that move, and it's nice, just lying here with him like this.

"So, what's your plan for next year? Have you decided on a college yet?"

"I'm holding out hope for Madison, but I won't hear from them for a couple more months."

"Ah, you'll get in, no problem. You still got a perfect GPA?"

"I do." And I'm not sure why admitting that to him makes me feel silly and juvenile.

"That's friggin' awesome, Liv. I'm so proud of you." He presses a kiss to my forehead, and I shrug.

"It's not a big deal."

"The hell it isn't." He pulls back, his eyes searching mine. "What's going through that pretty head of yours?"

I trace a line between two tiny moles on his chest while I contemplate my response. I'm not sure how to explain that my grades have never been as important to me as they have been to my parents. I don't need to be at the top of my class or get into my dream school to be happy. But my parents and even Bren... they hold me to a higher standard, and for as long as I can remember, I've gone above and beyond to make sure I meet their expectations.

"What if I told you it doesn't matter to me if I get into Madison?"

He arches an eyebrow. "You just said you were hoping to get in."

"I am, but if I don't, I'm not going to be crushed. I've already been accepted at every other state school I've applied to. I'd be content at any of them." And if I ended up enrolling somewhere closer to him, even better. But we're not even seeing each other, let alone in a relationship that would justify that decision. It would be completely out of line to say those words out loud let alone let them take root in my mind.

"But what is it you want to do after school, Liv? Which school will set you up best for that?" His hand slides up the back of my thigh, squeezing gently.

"I still want to teach. Preferably at the college level."

He grins. "Professor Bishop. I like it."

"Dr. Bishop," I correct him, and his grin widens.

"Fuck yes. That's what I'm talking about."

"I know it's silly, but I couldn't care less about the rest of it. It doesn't matter if I'm valedictorian or where I get my degree, as long as I get that title someday."

"Baby, I don't think it's silly at all." He shakes his head and glances down, almost shyly. "Do you think it's silly that I want to be a federal agent?"

"No!" I shove at his chest. "I can't wait to see you with an FBI badge."

"Yeah, well, let's see if I can get through cop school first. I've heard it's easy, but it's been kicking my ass so far."

I purse my lips. "I was kidding about that, you know. I know it isn't easy. But there isn't a doubt in my mind that you'll come out on top *and* be an amazing agent someday."

"I appreciate your faith in me," he says softly, and there's a vulnerability in his voice that tugs at my heart.

"Can I tell you a secret?"

He nods and I lean up to brush my lips against his.

"You're crazy talented with your hands and your mouth, but your heart is what I love most about you."

"My heart, huh?"

I steal another kiss. "Especially when you share it with me."

CHAPTER 20

PRESENT...

AIDEN

"Why does this feel like coming home after breaking curfew? Like I've done something wrong and am about to be punished?" Olivia wrings her hands together in her lap as I pull into her parents' driveway on the opposite side of Cole Creek.

"Maybe because we're about to confess all the times you snuck out with me so we could fuck like rabbits behind everyone's back?"

She shoots me a scathing look that quickly morphs into a fit of giggles. "Oh god, we were awful!"

I shrug. "I thought we were pretty good."

She swats my arm with one hand and holds her stomach with the other as she continues to roll with laughter. "We had so much sex the summer after I graduated high school, and not a single person caught on to us. How is that possible?"

"They were too busy getting into their own trouble to

184

pay attention to what we were doing." I park next to her dad's truck and silently note the location of the security cameras. "Looks like your mom's been keeping your old man busy."

"No kidding." She unbuckles, and with wide eyes, takes in the gardens upon gardens of flowers and vegetables. "They were serious when they said they expanded."

I chuckle and hop out. Like my mom, Liv and Bren's mom is a second-generation Polish American. Their grandparents both came from Poland in the early 1900s hoping for a better life. My mother inherited her grandmother's love of cooking, and Olivia's carried on her grandfather's green thumb.

"They have enough vegetables here to keep the entire town fed."

"They're the highlight of the farmers' markets every Saturday morning."

Liv's face lights up with pride. "Oh, I've heard. It's Mom's favorite day of the week. I'd love to go with them this weekend. Do you think that's possible?"

"Yeah, I think so. Let's get this part over with, and then we'll figure out the logistics."

"Okay." She nods and then pulls in a deep breath. "And Bren's on his way?"

"Yep. He should be here any minute." I would have preferred we talk separately, so he could get pissed off and get it out of his system, but if this is how we have to do it, so be it.

"All right." Liv pulls her shoulders back with determination as the front door to the house opens and her old man steps out. "Let's do this."

She climbs out of the truck and a huge grin slashes through her dad's thick red beard. "Olivia Rae?"

"Surprise!" She sprints up the cobblestone walk and

throws her arms around his neck. "Oh my gosh, I've missed you so much!"

He chuckles and squeezes her tight, all the while watching me approach with curious eyes. "I've missed you, too, sugar bean, but what the heck are you doing here? With this guy, no less?"

"We'll get to that, but right now, I need all the hugs I can get. Where's Mom?"

Just then, Joanna Bishop bounds out of the house with wide brown eyes already swimming with tears.

"What on earth!" She throws her arms in the air and the three of them hug it out like they haven't seen each other in years instead of the couple of months it's been since Jake's funeral.

I stand back, hands tucked in my pockets, and let them do their thing. As nervous as Liv had been about the prospect of coming home, there'd been a longing in her eyes, too. An unspoken need for the kind of fulfillment only family can give, particularly after having someone she'd cared about taken from her so horrifically.

Ten minutes and a hundred hugs later, we're all seated around the Bishop's dining room table with glasses of freshly brewed iced tea.

"I just can't believe you're here," Joanna says for the fifth time from the chair beside Liv, where she fusses with her hair like the busybody mother she is. "It's been, what, four years?"

"Five," Cal—short for Callum—corrects from the head of the table. While Olivia could pass for her mother's twin with long dark hair, dark eyes, and a petite frame, Cal and Bren share the same Scottish genes with thick red hair and a stocky build. Liv got a few of her dad's freckles, too, but in places I'm not supposed to know about.

"It's been too long, that's for sure." Olivia takes her mother's hand into her own. "But all things considered, it felt like it was time."

Joanna's brow creases as she bites her lip. "How are you holding up, sweetie?"

"I'm okay." She glances to me and smiles. "Lena and Aiden have kept me from going too stir-crazy."

Cal arches an eyebrow as he kicks back in his chair, crossing one boot-clad ankle over the other. "Is that so?"

Bren had been the one to lay down the law where Liv was concerned back when we were in high school, but her old man had given his fair share of subtle warnings over the years, too. It wasn't that he didn't like me—hell, I was like another one of their kids—but Olivia was and still is his only daughter. The one who had a future outside of Cole Creek, not here with a roughneck country kid like me.

"Just figured she needed a friend," I say, lifting a shoulder. "She's been through a lot."

"Right." Her old man narrows his eyes as the front door opens and Bren appears.

"Sorry I'm late. It's been a hell of a day. Probably because someone decided to take vacation at the last minute." He juts his chin at me before he silences his phone and joins us in the dining room. "Hey, sis."

"Hey yourself." Liv gets to her feet to hug her brother. "And technically he's working, so don't you dare give him a hard time."

"Working?" Cal asks with suspicious irritation. "Who's going to tell me what's going on here?"

I open my mouth at the same time Bren does, but Liv beats us both to the punch. "I'm in trouble, Daddy. Have been since Jake was killed."

Joanna sucks in a breath and Cal scowls, but neither seem all that surprised when Liv tells them Jake's murder had been a mob hit, hence her uncle's insistence on the surveillance.

But when she tells them about the guy who showed up at the end of her lecture—minus the target picture—and about Jake's involvement with the rogue group, her mother does a quick sign of the cross.

"What the hell did he get himself into?" Cal demands, and Bren sighs as he takes a seat.

"We're not sure. The SSP will only tell the feds that he was an associate that went rogue and ended up taking a few million with him."

"For fuck's sake." Cal shoves away from the table and begins to pace. "I knew that guy was up to something. It's probably the reason he wanted to marry Olivia in the first place. So he could come over here and cause trouble."

Across the table, Liv's lips begin to tremble. She has more secrets than her family may ever know, and I'm pretty sure she's beaten herself up about them plenty without her dad adding more punches.

"We have no proof he was involved with the Polish Mafia before he came to the States, and believe me, I wish more than anyone that we could pin this guy as a complete asshole who had ill intentions from the start. But we can't, so let's not assume the worst."

Cal turns to me with a frown. "If this is a federal case, how do the two of you know so much?"

Bren glances to me as if to say, 'All yours, man,' and I give a single nod. "I was sworn in as a federal agent last week."

Joanna glances between Bren and me. "I don't understand."

"Olivia is under my direct protection right now. I guess you could say I'm her bodyguard."

Cal grips the back of the chair he'd vacated, his jaw ticking. "Why you?"

Liv's panicked eyes dart to mine but her father's irritation doesn't faze me.

"Because I did what any old friend would do, and I went down to Milwaukee after Jake died to make sure Liv was holding up okay. Neither of us expected it, but we rekindled an old flame."

Bren's eyes narrow in my peripheral just like his old man's do on the other side of the table. "You what?" the older Bishop snaps.

"It's a ruse, Daddy." Liv pulls her shoulders back even as she swallows anxiously. "Aiden's pretending to be my boyfriend, but what he's actually doing is protecting me."

Cal homes in on me. "I'll ask again… why you?"

"Callum," Joanna says softly. "It doesn't matter why. The point is he's helping her."

"It does matter," he argues. "You can't tell me there aren't federal agents who could have done this."

Heat creeps up the back of my neck and I ball my hands into fists beneath the table. His insinuation that I'm not a good enough cop feels like high school all over again when I hadn't been good enough to date her.

I clear my throat. "With all due respect, I'm the best guy for the job."

"How are you—"

"Daddy, I asked for him." Liv gets to her feet and rounds the table to stand behind me, reassuring hands curling around my shoulders. "I needed someone I knew and could trust. Someone I'm comfortable with."

Her father's steely gaze shifts from me to her and back again. "Comfortable…" he mutters like the word tastes bad in his mouth, and this time, Bren is the one to interrupt.

"Look, it's weird to me, too. But there's no one I trust more with my sister's well-being."

I crane my head from side to side, trying my damnedest not to let the belatedness of that statement bother me, when

Liv's soft fingers stroke against my neck knowingly. If only he'd thought that ten years ago.

"No one else can know that we're not really together," Liv says. "We can't risk someone saying something they shouldn't and that information getting into the hands of the wrong people."

"I'm not sure I understand…" Joanna frowns.

"The feds want the guys that killed Jake to think that they're not protecting Olivia like they were. That she's an easier target now."

Her mother gasps. "Why would they do that?"

"Because it's the only way to catch them once and for all."

"They're using her as bait," Cal snarls, his face turning red. "Fucking cowards."

"Callum Bishop!" his wife scolds, then glances to me. "That's not what they're doing, is it?"

I nod slowly, hating that it's the truth. "They had their mind made up before I agreed to help, which is why I said yes. It was either me alongside her or someone else, and I couldn't take that chance. It's also why I insisted they let me bring her back home. I need people I can trust, too." I glance to Bren, who dips his head in acknowledgment.

"We're gonna bring these assholes down," he says confidently. "But things might get messy in the process, which is why we're telling you the truth. We don't know what these guys might do to get to her, and we need you to be fully aware of that. It's possible they may come here."

Joanna swallows hard, and Cal's shoulders snap back with determination. "Let them try," he seethes, his hand going to the pistol that's no doubt loaded at his hip.

"Dad, I don't need you shooting anyone, okay? I'm going to have someone nearby at all times, and the feed from your surveillance will be fed to the sheriff's office."

Cal scoffs while Joanna's shoulders sag in relief. Olivia's

fingers, on the other hand, begin to knead into the sides of my neck so gently, I wonder if she realizes she's even doing it.

"So, everyone else is going to think you're dating." Her mom bites her lip. "What about your family, Aiden?"

"These guys want money they think Olivia has access to. My family isn't going to give them that." I'm not thrilled about lying to them, my own mother specifically, but it's part of the job and certainly not the first time I've had to fib a little about my involvement in a case.

"What are you going to tell them?"

Bren looks my way, also curious about the answer to his mother's question, but his focus snags on Olivia's fingers still working their magic on the tendons in my neck. He clears his throat and Liv drops her hands like he busted her jerking me off.

"We're, um, going to tell the others that we used to date," she says quickly and maybe a little guiltily. "Like Aiden said, he offered me support and one thing led to another."

"He's basically her rebound," Bren adds dryly, as if to remind me of my place. "So, no one will be surprised when it doesn't last."

Oh, what I wouldn't give for one of our old police academy sparring sessions right now, so I could kick his ass and not have to explain myself.

"And how long is this charade going to last?" her dad asks, and I respond without hesitation.

"As long as it takes."

CHAPTER 21

AIDEN

The visit to Liv's parents went as well as I'd expected it to go, with the exception of Bren getting called out to a boating accident on Amber Lake before I could talk to him alone and tell him the truth.

Like Liv, I'm not thrilled about asking him to help keep an eye on her, knowing I haven't been honest with him. It won't change his commitment to her, but it's damn sure going to change how he feels about me and that only adds to the guilt I'm already dealing with where she's concerned.

"Earth to Aiden." Liv nudges my arm as we stand in front of the meat counter at the grocery store.

"Shit, sorry." I blink out of my trance. "Did you say something?"

Lorelei Kaminski grins from behind the glass case. "Thinking about something other than that frozen junk he usually buys has short-circuited his brain."

"I guess so." Liv laughs. "I asked if you wanted steak kabobs or chicken. Or maybe some of each?"

"Uh, steak. Always steak."

She gives her eyes a half roll and adjusts the shopping basket looped around her arm. "Can we please have three of the steak kabobs, Lorelei?"

"Just three?" I have no idea what comes over me, but I lean down to her ear. "Gotta have at least four, babe. I need my energy, remember?"

Her eyes go wide, and Lorelei bursts out laughing. "How about I give you five, just in case?"

"Perfect." I wink at the older lady while Liv elbows me in the ribs.

"Jerk," she mutters under her breath.

"What? I could have said I'm a growing boy," I mutter back.

Her face immediately sours, and she makes a gagging sound. "Eww. Do me a favor and never say that again."

"You used to like my growing—"

"Olivia Bishop?" A familiar female voice gasps behind us, and I don't need to turn to know who it is or what's going to come out of her mouth next. "What in the hell are you doing with *my brother?*"

"Amelia!" Liv shoves the basket at me and sprints to my sister for a hug. "Oh my gosh, it's been forever!"

Amelia welcomes Liv with a bright smile, but over her shoulder mouths, *"You have so much explaining to do."*

"How have you been?" Liv steps back, surveying my youngest sibling with the sincerest smile I've seen since we started this ruse. "You look amazing!"

"Oh, jeez. Thanks. You look pretty fabulous yourself." Amelia's grin flips to a frown. "I'm so sorry to hear about your husband. Are you doing okay?"

Liv tucks a strand of her hair behind her ear with a sigh. "Thank you. I'm doing fine, thanks in part to your brother." She glances my way. "He's been a big help."

"Has he now?" Amelia inclines her head curiously, her blonde ponytail swinging to the side. "He's usually a pain in the ass."

Liv laughs. "Yes, well, he's been that plenty of times, too. But mostly, he's been amazing."

Amelia's brows lift, and I can only imagine the barrage of text messages I'm going to get as soon as she walks away. "So, are you in town visiting your parents?" she asks Liv.

"I'm in town visiting everyone, since this one here reminded me that it had been a while since I came home." Liv reaches out and runs her hand down my arm until her fingers tangle with mine. "So, I'm here for a couple of weeks. We should get together. I heard you're a graphic designer now. I'd love to hear all about that."

My sister nods eagerly and they exchange phone numbers while I stand back and wonder what the hell I've gotten myself into. Not that this is really about me at all—Liv and I are six and seven years older than my baby sister, and if I remember correctly, Liv used to mentor Amelia in an after-school arts program when we were younger. It's natural they'd want to catch up, and for Liv's sake, I'm glad. She needs more friends in her life right now, though I'm not exactly thrilled about my sister being one of them.

"Anyway, I need to get going. I'm shopping for Mom. She's in the middle of baking—big surprise, right?—and she ran out of sugar and baking soda. You should stop by and see her while you're in town, Olivia. She always has cake or pie, and don't tell her I said this, but it really is the best in town."

Liv reclaims my hand. "I'm sure we'll visit soon, right, babe?"

"Uh, yeah." I clear my throat and shift from one boot to the other like I'm suddenly standing on hot coals. "I'm sure we will."

Amelia laughs, clearly enjoying my discomfort and probably coming up with a hundred more questions for her text attack. "I'll let you two get back to shopping. Don't forget to call me, Olivia." She gestures to our enjoined hands. "We clearly need to catch up."

She hurries off toward the checkout lines at the front of the store, and Liv and I exhale in unison.

"That was..." Liv begins, and I nod.

"Yeah." It's just the beginning.

"Here you go, folks." Lorelei hands the wrapped kabobs over the counter with a wink. "I hope it's enough sustenance for you, Detective."

Liv giggles, and I groan, though I can't blame the lady for that one.

I brought this all on myself.

OLIVIA

"How's it going in here?" Aiden saunters in the living room later that evening where I've been replying to more discussion board posts and prepping for finals next week. After dinner, I used his office for my evening lecture, and when I was finished, we swapped rooms so he could get the pullout sofa ready for bed.

"Better than earlier. Most of the students really upped their game this week in our online chat. I think some of them might've even learned a thing or two this semester." I set my laptop aside and stretch my arms above my head. It's getting late, and the excitement of coming home and seeing so many familiar faces is catching up to me.

"I'm sure whoever is paying their tuition will be happy about that." He smiles and takes a seat in the recliner. At some point, he changed into a pair of gray sweatpants instead of his jeans, and his feet are bare on the fluffy rug. Why the sight of him dressed down is so attractive, I'm not sure. But I like it. A lot. "Why are you looking at me like that?" he asks, and I blink fast.

"Hmm?" Was I staring? Shoot, I was. "Oh, um, I was just noticing how tanned you are. I'm jealous."

He leans forward, elbows on his knees, and chuckles. "Uh-huh."

"What? Did you think I was checking you out? *Ppsshh.*" I wave him off, hoping the heat in my cheeks isn't visible in the dim light from the lamp. "I've been cooped up all summer. I have tan envy, that's all."

He sticks his tongue in his cheek and arches a dark eyebrow. "You saying you want to hit up the lake tomorrow?"

I gasp. "Could we?"

He lifts a shoulder. "Why not? Shouldn't be too busy during the middle of the week."

Excitement blooms in my chest and I do a seated happy dance on his couch. "If you're serious, I would love that. I didn't bring a suit though. I'd have to borrow something from Amelia or buy one in town. Does Brenda Sue still have that little boutique behind the Cole Stop?"

"The boutique is still there, but Brenda Sue retired. Bailey runs it now."

"Really?" This keeps getting better and better. Bailey Janikowski and I were friends in high school, but we haven't talked since we graduated. "If you don't think it'd be too risky, I would love to take you up on that."

"It'll be fine. Hayden, Jesse's fiancée, has a cabin over there. I'm sure she won't mind us using the beach if the main one is too crowded. The feds would probably appreciate that, too."

Ugh. "I almost forgot about them. They'll be here tomorrow?"

"Yep. Nolan called while you were in your lecture. Special Agent Bolinger volunteered to take the assignment provided he could bring his wife along. They found a cabin to rent a few miles out of town. I'll keep him updated, but he'll maintain his distance. He's more or less here in case shit hits the fan."

"That's a relief." In fact, if I never see another federal agent parked outside my house again, it'll be too soon. "Hey, Aiden?"

"Yeah?" He gives me a sideline glance, the play of shadows and lamplight making him look younger. More like the boy I fell in love with all those years ago instead of the man I owe so much to now.

"Thank you. I know I've said it before, and I'll say it a thousand more times, because I really need you to understand how much I appreciate this."

"Liv, you don't have to thank me. It's—"

"Please don't tell me it's your job." Yes, it's the truth, but I really want it to be more, too.

He eyes me for a long beat before he looks to the floor with a sigh. "What do you want me to say, Liv?"

"I don't know. I…" I push a hand through my hair and let it drop to my lap. "Maybe I want a small part of you to be doing this because we used to be friends."

His jaw tics, and he swallows. "You can check that box off, too, if it makes you feel better."

A surge of warmth floods my veins. "It does."

"Good. Is that all?"

Not in the least, but I'll bide my time as far as questions about us are concerned.

"You haven't said much today about last night. Are you... okay?" I bite my lip. I don't want him to hold back his feelings because he has a job to do. That's not fair to him.

"I don't have a lot to say that doesn't involve how I would

have killed the bastard if he wasn't already dead," he says gruffly, stretching out his hand with the red, swollen knuckles.

"Somehow, I don't believe that."

He continues to focus on his hand, clenching and unclenching it, before he speaks again. "I should have been there, Liv. Fuck, I should have made sure it never happened at all, and that's a load I'm going to carry for the rest of my life. But I can't think about that right now or it'll distract me from what I have to do now."

"Aiden…" I move to the edge of the couch, but stop short of going to him, because he'll just push me away. "It's not your fault. You know as well as I do that those kinds of men always find an excuse. If it hadn't been our relationship, he would have come up with another reason to justify his actions."

"He wasn't a man." His voice is so low that I shiver. "Men don't violate women like that. They don't put their hands on them, and they sure as fuck don't take what's not theirs. He was a coward. A sick, spineless fucking coward."

I wrap my arms around myself, the chill from his words palpable. "I know."

He shakes his head and then pushes to his feet, his gaze averting mine. "I'm gonna hit the hay. It's been a long day, and we could both use some sleep. The doors are locked, and the alarm system is on. If you need anything, you know where to find me."

"Aiden, wait—"

"Good night, Liv."

Moments later, his office door shuts behind him, and I bury my face in my hands.

I hate that he's shouldering the blame like he is. He's a cop —he knows that perpetrators of violent sexual crimes are usually narcissists who will use any excuse possible to put the blame on someone else. But he's made this personal, and if he doesn't deal with his feelings now, they'll take root and be even harder to break free from later.

God knows, I blamed myself for a long time, too. And the shame… it felt like a sinister witch living in my head, spewing lies about everything I'd once believed to be true. She'd even convinced me that love wasn't something I was capable of anymore because so much hatred lived inside of me. There was no room for all of my emotions to coexist.

Her lies dug deep into my soul and convinced me that marrying a man I cared about but didn't love was the best chance I'd have at being somewhat happy again. And for a little while, I was. At least, until the lies began to unravel, and the pain I'd buried for so long began to break free, reminding me what it felt like to truly feel again.

Jake's death knocked the wind out of me. I'd loved him like I love Lena, and I will grieve the loss of that relationship for a long time. But finding out he'd taken money that could have helped countless children and families… it angered me at the same time it gave me relief. For the first time in nine years, I was finally free from the chains I'd shackled to my own wrists as a desperate means to protect myself.

Aiden's guilt may not be the same kind of desperate pain that I'd run from, but it will slowly burrow its way into his bones and hold on tight.

I can't let him do that to himself.

I can't go back and change my past, but I can help him from making the same mistakes. It's the least I can do for him with all he's doing for me.

CHAPTER 22

OLIVIA

"*S*o, no Craig last night?" I ask from the kitchen table, my laptop and a cup of coffee already keeping me company, when Aiden pads into the room with sleep-tousled hair bright and early the next morning. He's dressed in the same gray sweatpants from last night, and the morning look takes me right back to my college days when he'd visit for the weekend.

"Nope." He goes to the cupboard for a coffee mug, and such a simple movement shouldn't look so sexy, but without a shirt, the stretch and flex of his arms and the way his sweats slip a couple millimeters down his hips makes me glad I'm already seated with my legs crossed. "He texted to say he's going to stay at Cady's for a while."

My heart sinks. "Because of me?"

He fills the mug and replaces the pot on the warmer before he leans a hip against the counter and faces me. "I told him last week he needed to find another place."

"Last week *after* you took this job?"

He lifts a shoulder. "Maybe."

"Aiden, you didn't have to do that. I already feel bad enough about staying here."

"Believe me, it was well past time he left. Besides, he needs to find a place of his own for visitation with the kids. It's been five months since he and Rachel separated."

"It's only been five months? And he's already seeing someone?" Says the woman who's allegedly in a new relationship a whopping two months after her husband died. "And you're sure he wasn't cheating?"

"He swears he wasn't, and I haven't pushed him for more. Not something I want to involve myself in." He takes a sip and lifts his chin toward my laptop. "Already working?"

"Yep, I still have a bunch of final projects to read through. Oh, and I have a lecture tonight, several tomorrow, and then two Thursday." I bite my lip, because I'm sure the last thing he wants to do is be cooped up in this house with me any more than he has to. "I promise next week will be lighter because it's finals week."

"Liv, it's not a problem. In fact, you're welcome to use my office if you want. It's clean, I promise." He holds up a hand and I smile at his defensiveness.

"Hey, I'm not judging. And that would be great. Thank you."

"I'll even put the pullout away for you." He grins behind his coffee, and I press a hand to my chest dramatically.

"My hero."

He rolls his eyes. "You still up for the lake today?"

"I've been looking forward to it since you mentioned it. But Amelia doesn't have a suit that will fit me. I'll need to go shopping if you don't mind being my escort in town."

"We can do that. We'll need to grab some snacks and drinks anyway."

He's trying so hard to be accommodating, which I appreciate, but I also know that the more we go out in public, the more stress I'm causing him. Hmm. Maybe I should plan something relaxing for us to do here.

I get to my feet for a coffee refill when my cell phone rings next to my laptop. It's barely after seven o'clock in the morning, so my first guess is that it's Lena calling to check in. But it's not. In fact, I don't recognize the number and there's no caller ID.

"I don't know who this is." I show Aiden the screen. "It could be a student, but I doubt any of them would be calling this early."

"Your students shouldn't have your personal number." He gives me a pointed look before he takes the phone and snaps a pic of the screen with his phone. "You have your voice mail set up?"

I nod.

"Let's see if they leave a message." When the ringing stops, he hands it back to me, and I sit down again, no longer in the mood for another cup of coffee.

We sit in silence for several minutes, waiting for a message to pop up, but nothing comes. The caller didn't leave a message, which for some reason, makes me queasy.

"I'll do some digging and see if I can figure out who the number belongs to. There's a chance it could have been a wrong number, too." Aiden's voice is gentle enough, but something in my gut says otherwise.

Who the heck could it have been?

AIDEN

GRANDPA KOWALCYZK'S TOENAILS.

The guy I busted a couple months back with coke up his ass.

That time Mrs. Janikowski tried to slip her tongue into my ear.

I've spent the last half hour recalling every disgusting thing I've ever encountered in my thirty-two years to keep from thinking about the sexy-as-hell woman lying on the beach towel next to me in her new emerald bikini.

"I'm not burning, am I?" Liv glances up from her paperback, her dark hair twisted up on top of her head and a pair of oversized white sunglasses on her nose. "I already feel crispy, and we just got here."

Grinding my teeth together, I flick a quick look at her curvy backside glistening beneath the sun. "Your sunscreen isn't even absorbed yet. You're fine."

"Really?" She stretches back, trying to reach a spot on her ass. "I think I missed a spot... right... here."

For the love of friggin' god. "Nope, pretty sure you got it all."

"Hmm. All right. But if I end up with a burned spot on my butt, it's your fault."

Well, that's a chance I'm willing to take, because I'm sure as hell not going to take a closer look or—god help me—rub lotion into her ass.

What had I been thinking suggesting we come to the lake anyway? It seemed like a less dangerous alternative to her sunbathing in my backyard, now I realize that it doesn't matter where she does it. Anywhere I have to be in close proximity to Olivia Bishop in a bikini is a dangerous place to be.

I had lain on the pullout last night trying not to imagine her in my bed. Her bare skin against my sheets. Her hair spread across my pillow. The way her ass might've pressed back into my lap if I'd been lying beside her.

I was hard in minutes, fighting off the urge to wrap my hand around my dick and satisfy the craving I've had for her since I saw her outside my hotel room door. Hell, the craving I've had for her since we shared our first kiss fourteen years ago.

And I'd almost given in to the temptation, too, until the image of her face, battered and bruised, flashed through my head, and my dick shriveled up like a friggin' raisin.

The last damn thing I should be doing is getting off to thoughts of Liv when she went through what she went through *because of me*. Doing so would make me no better than the asshole who took without her permission ten years ago.

"I was thinking we should visit your parents today." Liv flips a page in her paperback. "You know, before they start hearing rumors."

I take a drink from a bottle of water and watch a Jet Ski make waves on the lake. "Sure. If you're up for it."

"I'm as up for it as I'm ever going to be." She sighs. "It's starting to bother me that we're going to get your mom's hopes up."

Welcome to the club. "She'll get over it." Just like I will.

"That doesn't make me feel any better."

"We've gotta do what we gotta do, Liv." Recapping the water, I set it aside and turn my ball cap around, catching Liv's teeth clasp around her lip in my peripheral. She flips over and quickly sits up while I dig my fingers into my towel at the sight of all that new, pale but fucking gorgeous skin.

"You have to be careful." She reaches over and adjusts the cap, so it rests on my hair instead of my forehead. "You'll get a tan line if you keep it too low, and that'll look silly."

I snort. "You worried about having an ugly fake boyfriend?"

A small smile curves her lips as she smooths one of my

eyebrows down with her thumb. "*Noo*. In fact, maybe I should have left it alone so you'd look ridiculous, and I wouldn't have to worry about other women checking you out."

"Uh-huh."

"Don't *uh-huh* me. I saw Bailey eyeing you up earlier at the boutique."

Yeah, she probably did. "So?"

She lifts a shoulder. "She seemed disappointed that you came in with me."

"Are you fishing for something?"

"I'm not infringing on your dating life or anything, am I? Bren said you weren't seeing anyone, but who knows, maybe you had something going on that he didn't know about."

I stretch my legs out in front of me and lean back on my hands. "You've got nothing to worry about."

"That doesn't answer my question."

I give a low laugh. "So, you are fishing."

"I just want to know how many dirty looks I'm going to get now that I've taken Cole Creek's hottest cop off of the market."

Jesus Christ, when she says shit like that...

"I just mean I can't afford any more enemies. So, if there's someone I need to be extra nice to, like Bailey..."

"There isn't." I'm no monk, but I haven't dated anyone seriously in almost three years, much to Bailey Janikowski's dismay.

"But you do date, right?" She frowns like she's genuinely concerned, which I'm not going to lie, is a little weird. We haven't been together in ten years, but I'm pretty sure there will never be a time when talking about other women with Liv isn't awkward.

"My love life is just fine, I promise. Now, can we change the subject?"

"One more question."

I groan.

"You've been happy, right?"

Dammit, I should have seen that coming.

"It would make me feel a little better knowing that there's been someone or maybe even a couple someones who've made you happy and given your mom hope before this... thing we're doing."

It'd make me feel better, too, but I can't tell her that. Thankfully, the muffled sound of a phone ringing interrupts before I can tell her that.

"That's me... somewhere." She reaches into her beach bag and digs around for her phone, all the while holding her breath. I came up empty on the phone number this morning, other than it was a prepaid phone, and no doubt Liv is worried she'll see that same number again this time.

Her shoulders sag in relief when she finally finds the phone. "It's Elena, Victor's wife."

Victor, the immigrant neighbor. "Put it on speaker."

Liv accepts the call with a tentative smile. "Hey, lady. Long time, no talk."

"Olivia!" The other woman's reaction is far from reluctant. "It's been too long indeed. How are you?"

"Pretty good. I was actually going to call you but got busy. Agent Morales said Victor stopped by when he was walking Chewy. He saw I had a visitor and was worried."

"He mentioned that. Is everything okay?" If her husband is up to something and she's aware, she's good at hiding it, because she seems genuinely concerned, though I'd get a better read if I could see her face.

"Better than okay." Liv pushes her sunglasses to the top of her head and mouths, *"Should I tell her I'm here with you?"*

I nod. I didn't find much on this guy online, so anything additional would be helpful.

"I'm actually in my hometown right now. An old friend came to pick me up."

"Up north? Oh, that's wonderful! I'm so happy you finally got out of the house."

"Me too." Liv's smile is soft and sincere, reassuring me that bringing her back here was the right decision. "Please tell Victor that all is well, and I'm enjoying some much-needed time away."

"Hey, babe, you want some more sunscreen?" I ask loud enough for the other woman to hear, and Liv's eyes go wide as her friend gasps.

"Who is that?"

"Um, that would be the old friend I mentioned."

"Shut the front door! A man? Get it, girl!"

Liv laughs nervously. "I know it's kinda soon…"

"Oh stop. After the ordeal Jake put you through, you deserve a little happiness."

Liv's cheeks turn pink as her eyes meet mine, and then something passes over her gaze that makes her blush deepen. "I can't argue with that."

"Anyway, now that I know everything is okay, I'll let you get back to your *old friend*." The other woman enunciates the words like she knows better than to believe there's anything friendly about me. "Let's have coffee when you get back home so you can tell me everything."

"I would love that." After a quick goodbye, Liv ends the call and sighs. "See what I mean? Elena and Victor are the sweetest people ever."

Maybe, maybe not. But one thing is for sure…

If Liv keeps blushing and looking at me like maybe she wishes this arrangement was more real than ruse, I'm going to have one helluva case of blue balls by the time this case is over.

"OLIVIA RAE BISHOP!" Ma throws her hands in the air and sprints around the kitchen island as fast as a middle-aged woman in cheap flip-flops can sprint. "It's still Bishop, right? Oh my gosh, I should be calling you doctor!"

Olivia barely has time to brace herself before Ma pounces, rocking her from side to side in a bear hug that's probably registering on the Richter scale somewhere. "It's still Bishop, and only my students are allowed to call me doctor, Mrs. Enders."

Ma pulls back and swats Olivia's shoulder. "Well, then you're only allowed to call me Janice, or I'll feel older than I already do, seeing you all grown up and as gorgeous as ever!"

"Oh my gosh, thank you." Olivia turns as pink as the sundress she's wearing, which I hate even more than her damn bikini. She wore dresses just like this one in college for one reason and one reason only—easy access.

"Anyway, come and sit." Ma drags Olivia to a chair at the kitchen table, where I can guarantee a piece of pie will materialize with a snap of her fingers. "I have a fresh strawberry rhubarb pie or one small piece of peach cake left. Which will it be?"

"You made peach cake and didn't tell me?" What the hell?

Ma pins me with a tight smirk. "If you would have come to visit this weekend, you would have known. Your brothers ate your share instead."

Those friggin' traitors.

"Anyway, which would you like, Olivia?"

"Um... the cake sounds lovely, but I'll take the pie, so Aiden can have the other."

Ma huffs. "Oh, no. He lost his chance. Peach cake for you, my dear."

"Seriously?" I scoff.

"Seriously." Ma doesn't bother looking at me again as she moves about the kitchen, quickly dishing up the cake and grabbing a fork before she joins Olivia at the table. "So, how long have you been in town, sweetie? Gosh, it's good to see you."

"I've only been here since yesterday." Olivia takes the cake and glances up at me apologetically.

"Oh, I bet your parents are happy to have you back at home. It's been a while, hasn't it?"

"It has, and they're definitely glad I'm here. But I'm actually staying with Aiden."

Ma's eyes widen. "You are?"

I rub at my jaw and nod. "Yeah. That's kinda why I haven't been over to visit."

Ma blinks as the pieces start to snap together, a mix of optimistic curiosity and guarded anticipation playing across her face. "Are you two...?"

"We are." Might as well cut to the chase.

Ma bites her lips together but fails to contain her giddy smile. "In that case, you're forgiven for not dropping by this weekend."

Olivia's cheeks flush again like they had at the lake. "Am I allowed to share this with him now?"

"Oh, I suppose." My mother laughs before she rests her chin on her hand with a wistful sigh. "I always hoped you two would get together."

Olivia smiles, but my gut tightens. At my age, I shouldn't give a shit what my mother thinks, but it bugs the hell out of me that I can't give her the same peace of mind that Jesse has.

I'm not jealous of my brother, because he went through hell before he and Hayden got back together. But I'd love to give my mother the same kind of bone-deep sense of satisfaction that's so obvious every time she looks at my nephew.

"We appreciate that, Mrs. Enders. And this tart is

phenomenal." Liv takes another bite and then hands me the plate and fork. "I'd love the recipe if you're willing to share."

And here we go. As if the two of us *dating* isn't enough, she has to go and kiss my mother's ass about her baking.

"Oh, I'd be happy to share, honey." Ma beams. There is nothing—and I mean nothing—Ma feeds off of more than compliments on her cooking. "Do you like to bake?"

"I love it. Mostly my friend Lena's recipes. Or rather, her grandmother's. My grandma liked to can vegetables more than she baked."

The two women dive into a conversation about their favorite recipes, and I sneak away to the backyard where my dad stands in front of his tool shed, sucking his teeth.

"I think it's time to replace this old relic," he says without looking back when I approach. "Wood's looking a little shoddy."

"It's not so bad. New eaves should do the trick."

"Eh, but what fun is that?" He winks and then trots inside to tinker with the weed whacker that's torn apart on a table. There's probably nothing wrong with it, just like there's nothing wrong with the shed, but retirement boredom says otherwise. "Was that the Bishop girl I saw getting out of your truck?"

"Uh, yeah. She's visiting for a while." I tuck my hands into my pockets and watch him work.

"Right," he says distractedly as he inspects the carburetor. "Heard she's staying at your place."

And that's the thing about dads. They act like they're off in another world, but they miss nothing.

"You did, did you? From who?"

His eyes dart to mine over the top of the glasses perched on the end of his nose. "I ran into Cal Bishop at the Cole Stop this morning."

Hopefully Cal wasn't too chatty. "What'd he have to say?"

"Not much, other than you've apparently been taking advantage of his daughter while she's grieving."

What the fuck? "He said that?"

Dad lifts a shoulder. "No, but I'm a father. I know it's what he's thinking. You sure she's ready for whatever you two are doing, seeing as her husband just died?"

No, but I can't tell him it's not real to reassure him. "I'm just helping her out, Dad."

"Like you did when you were kids?"

My gaze snaps to his, and he gives a single nod.

"You might've kept everyone else in the dark, but you and I are a lot alike in that we both notice things that others don't." He holds the carburetor up to the light again and sighs. "You couldn't keep your eyes off her anytime you were in the same room together."

Fuck. "How come you never said anything?"

"Not my place." He shrugs. "But that was a long time ago and now... well, I'm more worried about you than I am her, son."

Heat burns up the back of my neck. "I know what I'm doing."

He nods. "I'm sure you do. That's not going to stop me from worrying about you getting hurt again."

Again? Damn, he really did pay attention. "I'll be fine."

"Then forget I mentioned it." He smiles like we didn't just have the most awkward conversation we've ever had aside from the *cover your pecker* one we'd had when I was thirteen. "Grab that carb cleaner from the shelf, will you? You can help me get this thing running again before Jinx shows up and tries to do it for me."

Anything to pretend this conversation never happened.

CHAPTER 23

OLIVIA

*W*ednesday is my busiest day of teaching, so I spent the entire morning holed up in Aiden's office giving online lectures and answering emails from the handful of students who decided to finally take my classes seriously... a week before finals.

Hey, Dr. Bishop, any chance I can get some extra credit? I really need to pass this class so I can graduate.

Hi, Doc B, remember when you said I could submit my paper late? I know it's been three weeks, but...

Um, my neighbor's cousin's llama died, so I couldn't turn in my final project on time.

By the time noon rolls around, I force myself to take a break before I say something snarky that results in a phone call from the dean. He's already irritated with me because I can't teach in person, so I'd rather not piss him off again.

Pouring a glass of water at the sink, I catch a glimpse of Aiden outside... just as he strips his blue T-shirt over his head and uses the cotton to wipe sweat from his brow.

Holy hot.

I tried not to ogle his miles of muscle and golden skin yesterday at the lake, because it seemed like he was trying not to do the same to me, but since I'm inside and he's out there, there's no reason I can't look today, right?

I sigh and press the cool glass to my cheek as he tosses the shirt into the grass and picks up an axe.

I barely have time to notice the pile of wood at the edge of the yard before he whips the tool around, the broad muscles in his shoulders and back rippling just before the axe connects with a huge chunk of wood and splits it in half like a cookie.

"Good lord…" I used to help my dad and Bren with firewood for camping when I was younger, but they sure as heck never did it like that.

Across the yard, Aiden sits one of the halves upright again and repeats the movement until there are four pieces of wood instead of one… and my heart beats so hard I can feel it between my legs.

For Pete's sake, he's chopping wood, and I'm getting hot and bothered like he's doing a striptease. What is wrong with me?

I lower the glass to my chest, letting the perspiration cool my heated flesh, when Aiden suddenly glances to the window and I almost drop the glass in the sink.

He gives a small wave and then goes back to work on the woodpile. Rolling out a chunk of wood that's twice the size of the first, he sets it up and then proceeds to wield the axe like some kind of sexy, tattooed lumberjack until his back is covered in sweat and I'm in need of a fresh pair of panties… and apparently a little dignity.

Heat fills my face as he looks back once again, his brow furrowed and his nostrils flaring from the exertion. For a long beat, he simply stares, and I wonder if he knows what he's doing to me.

Maybe I'm not the only one struggling with the lingering pull between us. And would it be so bad to test those waters?

After all, he was my real boyfriend before he was my fake one. There has to be some leniency in the rules for that, right?

———

It's after eleven o'clock by the time I catch up on my work, and while I feel guilty for ignoring Aiden most of the day, I had to do it to keep myself focused on work and not this strange tension between us.

I knock on his office door after I get ready for bed and find him mulling over something on his laptop with an all too serious expression on his face.

"What do you know about Frank Krol?" he asks without looking up.

"Troy's brother-in-law?"

He nods and then leans back in his chair, locking his hands behind his head.

"Not much. I've only met him a couple of times at the Speakeasy."

"Did you know he's the vice chair at the Polish Exhibition House?"

"Frank? With four kids and a bar to run, I'm surprised he has time."

"I saw him at the museum when I went to visit Eli Nowak. He was at the Speakeasy the night we were there, too, talking to Agent Getty. You didn't point him out."

"I didn't realize I should have." I lean into the doorframe and frown. "Where are you going with this? Did you link the phone number to him?"

"No. I just can't shake the feeling that the museum and SSP are connected. I mean, it's almost too obvious, which could be why the feds didn't look any deeper than they did. Or maybe they do know, but their bargain with the SSP on this case has them turning a blind eye."

My stomach twists at the thought. The FBI and SSP do have some sort of morally gray agreement that I've tried not to think too much about, because Nolan assured me that the mob was on our side with this case. And I have to believe Uncle Joe would have come forward to say otherwise if it weren't true.

"Anyway, I've got some more digging to do before I can say for sure. You haven't heard from Victor's wife again, have you?"

"No, not since she called yesterday."

"How about Eli Nowak's wife? Did you text her like I suggested?"

I nod. "She sent me a picture of her and the boys at the park, and said she was crazy busy at the moment but would call sometime soon."

Aiden rocks back in the chair and looks up to the ceiling. "All right. Let me know if she does. I'd like to listen in if possible."

"Sure. Amelia also invited me to lunch tomorrow. I hope it's okay that I said yes."

He cocks his head to the side.

"Hey, you said if we came back here, I'd be able to have a life, so don't look at me like that."

"It's been three days."

"Yep, and people are going to wonder why we're always together."

One eyebrow lifts. "Maybe we're enjoying each other."

Warmth creeps up my neck just like it did when I watched him outside earlier. "Your mom said there's a street dance fundraiser on Saturday for new fire department equipment. Maybe we could *enjoy each other* there."

His eyes darken slightly before he shakes his head. "That might be a little too public."

"Oh, come on. Every cop in Pine County will be there and all of the firefighters, too. It's the safest public venue possible."

"Let's start with the lunch date."

"I'll take it!" In fact, I might've purposely mentioned the street dance to make the lunch date seem less threatening.

"Don't get too excited. I'll have eyes on you at all times."

"Maybe, but you'll be far enough away that Amelia and I can spill all the tea." A devious smile lifts my lips. Time to test those waters. "Like the fact that I enjoyed watching you split wood earlier."

His jaw pulses beneath his beard and the tendons in his arms flex as he stretches his hands. "Good," he says gruffly. "You can help me pile it tomorrow."

I bite back a laugh. It's not the flirty response I hoped for, but it's not rejection either. I'll take it.

DESPITE THE ROLLER coaster of emotions today, which should have left me exhausted, I'm still wide awake at nearly two in the morning, staring up at the ceiling in Aiden's bedroom.

So much has happened this past week, and my head still hasn't caught up. Seeing Aiden again, finally taking some action on this case, coming home, and not only seeing my parents, but stepping foot inside my childhood home. It's crazy and scary, yet it feels surprisingly right, too. A part of me always felt bad that I'd stayed away for so long, but it had been necessary to keep from getting too deep into my head about Aiden and the unfinished business between us. So, I'm not surprised that coming home again feels as good as it does; I just didn't expect to come home *with* the man who'd kept me away.

Now to get him on the same page about being with me. That's going to be the real challenge.

With a sigh, I roll over and curl my arms around a pillow when there's a sound in the hallway. I still and listen closely, realizing that the noise isn't actually in the hall but outside the back door. It's barely audible with the bedroom door only partly open, but it's definitely there, almost like a faint scratching. Or picking maybe.

Oh my god, is someone trying to pick the lock?

I sit up in bed and send a quick text to Aiden. I'd call but if someone is trying to break in, they might hear the ring and run off. When minutes go by and he doesn't reply, I slip out of bed and tiptoe to the door to listen closer just as there's a loud metallic crash that has me jumping out of my skin.

Heart racing, I hurry out of the room and down the hall to Aiden's office as quietly as possible to find him sprawled out on his back, thick arms above his head, and in nothing but a pair of black boxer briefs.

Gulping down the flash of lust, I shake his shoulder. "Aiden," I whisper. "Wake up. I hear something outside."

But he doesn't move. He simply keeps snoring like the dead.

"Aiden!" I pat his cheek a little harder than necessary, and he snaps awake, blinking up at me in confusion.

"What? What's wrong?" His voice is husky with sleep, and I press my finger to his lips in a panic.

"Shh! I heard something outside. I think someone might be out there."

He frowns and swings his legs over the side of the pull-out. "Did you see someone?"

"No, but it sounded like someone was trying to pick the

lock on the back door. Then something fell. Something metal."

He blinks at me for a moment before he sighs and gets to his feet, scratching a hand through his hair, almost in annoyance. "It's Gertie."

"Gertie?" Who the heck is Gertie?

"My cat." He pads out of the room, not bothering with pants, and flicks on the hall light. "Actually, no. I don't claim her. But she's apparently claimed me," he grumbles as he hoists open the cover of a wooden chest near the door and scoops up a cup of dry cat food.

I press my fingers to my lips to contain a giggle. Not his cat, but there's not only a current bag of food but a backup one, too. And the little toy mice? I'll pretend I don't see those either. Or Aiden–all big and brooding, covered in tattoos and oozing testosterone–feeding his noncat at two o'clock in the morning... in his underwear.

He unlocks and opens the back door, and a flash of black and white fur darts into the house and out of sight. "Goddammit, Gertie!"

I can't help it. I burst out laughing as he slams the door and marches toward the front of the house with the scoop of cat food.

"You are such a pain in my ass!" he yells before she meows loudly in response. "Hold your damn horses! I'm getting a bowl!"

I follow after and lean into the kitchen doorway as he pours the cup of food into a plastic bowl and sets it on the floor. The cat weaves a figure eight around his legs as thanks before she dives in like she hasn't eaten in days.

"Wait, who fed her this weekend?"

Aiden glances up with a frown. "Huh?"

"Did Craig feed her while you were gone? Or has she been without food?"

"What? Of course, she had food. That crash you heard? That was her knocking her big ass food bowl around to get my attention."

I bite my lips together to keep from laughing. Not his cat, my rear end.

"Look, I don't even like this cat. But I did her a solid once and now she won't go away."

"A solid?"

He flips his hand in the air, gesturing wildly toward the kitchen window. "I found her outside the garage one night getting tag teamed by two tom cats. So, I took her to the vet, and when they could verify she wasn't already knocked up, I had her fixed. Now she thinks she lives here. It's fucking annoying."

"Oh, Aiden." I give in to the grin and laugh. "I hate to break it to you, but you *do* have a cat." And his denial about it is the most adorable thing I've ever seen.

"No, I don't," he insists.

"Is this the first time she's been in the house?"

He blinks and then shakes his head. "I'm not going to stand here in my fucking boxers and argue with you about a damn cat."

"I'll take that as a no." My shoulders shake with amusement. "It's cute, you know. You with a cat. I mean, I always thought you'd end up with a dog, but a cat fits your personality, too."

His eyes narrow to slits. "Oh really?"

"You're both temperamental and stubborn. And you used to love when I'd pet you."

That irritated gaze turns from pale blue to midnight with a single blink before it sweeps slowly down the length of my body. My tank top and boy short panties cover plenty, but the way he takes me in like it's the first time he's truly seeing me in all these years makes me feel bared to him.

And I want him to see me.

"You're staring," I rasp.

"You're playing with fire."

I lick my lips in a futile attempt to maintain my composure and not melt into a puddle of lust on his kitchen floor. "I'm just calling it like I see it."

"It's not my cat."

"Fine." I lift a hand. "It's not your cat."

One corner of his mouth hitches up into a smirk. "Now you're playing games."

"I don't play games."

"Bullshit." He takes a single step forward and mocks me. "You used to love playing games."

Uh-huh. I sure did. Especially the kind that involved losing our clothing. "Who's playing now, Detective?"

He gives a low laugh and flexes his hands as if they itch to reach out and touch me. "You should go to bed, Livi."

"You keep telling me that. Why?" Now I am most definitely playing, and I don't care if I win, because breaking down his walls little by little is victory enough.

"You don't want me to answer that."

Oh yes I do. I want to hear him say he still wants me as badly as I want him. And that he forgives me for keeping the truth from him.

"You're my client right now," he says in a low, warning tone that matches the storm brewing in his eyes.

"I am. And you're supposed to be my boyfriend." *So, take another step, Aiden. We both know you want to.*

"Fake boyfriend," he corrects, his hands still flexing.

"Maybe we should practice."

Those dark eyes flash with fire before he takes another step and then another until his chest bumps mine and he glares down at me.

"I just like to do things right," I whisper. He's so close, and his lips are right there. Just a little push up on my toes and I could kiss him. Really kiss him, not like the kiss in the bar.

"I do, too." He trails the backs of his fingers against the side of my face, and then down my neck to the soft swell of flesh rising from my tank top. "And that's why I'm going to tell you one more time to go to bed."

"Aiden…" His name is a plea. Just one kiss. One real, *I feel it, too* kiss.

His nostrils flare and his breathing deepens, like it pains him to hold back. "Livi, I need you to walk away." His voice is like gravel. "For your sake and for mine."

"Why? There's nothing wrong with this. There never was." I lift my hands to his face and cup his jaw, and his eyes slam shut.

"I don't–" He breaks off, clenching his jaw so hard that I can feel it pulsing in my hands. "I don't want to fucking hurt you."

"You could never hurt me," I whisper, my nose brushing against his as I edge closer, hoping his lips will graze mine.

But his face pinches as he takes a purposeful step back. "I already did."

Then he spins and stalks back to his office, slamming the door behind him.

CHAPTER 24

AIDEN

Grandma Kowalcyzk's underwear hanging on the clothesline.

Bren's tibia sticking out of his leg after he crashed his dirt bike in seventh grade.

Catching Hayden with a mouthful of my brother the summer he got her pregnant with Jett.

Liv crying all alone in bed, her mind even more broken than her body the morning after she was assaulted.

Trimming my beard in front of the bathroom mirror, I replay the last scenario over and over in my head until it drowns out the image of her standing in the kitchen last night, practically begging for me to kiss her.

She has no idea how badly I wanted to do just that. Or how hard it is to keep my hands off her when I catch her watching me. And when she touches me like she had at her parents or in the grocery store, it's damn near impossible to keep the *what-ifs* from taking root in my idiotic head.

What if this shit with her husband happened for a reason?

What if her still being more comfortable with me than anyone else after all this time apart really does mean what I want it to mean?

What if there's still a chance for us?

Then she has to go and say shit like she did last night, and my dick thinks it should have some say in the matter, too. The truth is there will *never* be a day when I don't want Liv, but knowing she still wants me, too?

I'm in so much fucking trouble I can't even think straight.

I have a job to do, but more than that… my choices in the past cost her in the worst possible way. I can't take that chance again. I need to keep my head straight before I fuck up and she suffers even worse consequences a second time.

And I haven't talked to Bren yet either, which is eating away at my conscience, too. He's been tied up with work all week, partly because it's summer and more people are doing stupid shit and partly because he's doing my job right now, too.

The guilt keeps piling on, and there's no end in sight.

Liv and I pull into the side lot next to The Creek, Cole Creek's pub and grill, just as the lunch rush hits. It's busier than I expected for a Thursday, but the crowd could work to our benefit, too.

"Looks like Amelia is already here." I point to the red SUV in front of the old brownstone building. "I don't see Jesse's truck, though."

Liv shakes her head. "I can't believe you scheduled your own lunch date. Don't you think Jesse and Amelia are going to think this is weird? Us girls doing our thing while you boys do yours?"

I shrug. "I don't care if they do." Amelia accusing me of

being a stalker boyfriend is far from the worst thing she's called me, and Jesse's going to catch on to the truth a lot faster than our baby sister, so there's no point in even trying to fool him.

"Whatever." With a resigned sigh, Liv hops out of the truck and starts for the front door without waiting for me.

"Hey…" I catch up quickly, snagging her hand and pulling her to a stop. "Don't get pissy about this, okay?"

Her shoulders, left bare in a black sleeveless top, drop before she turns back to me. "I'm sorry. I'm just so tired of this."

"Tired of us?" I stroke my thumb over the top of her hand.

"No." Her dark eyes flit back and forth between mine before she shakes her head and the glossy curls from her updo tease her cheeks. "I appreciate this… *us*. But feeling like a prisoner in my own life is getting old."

"I know, babe." I tuck a lock of hair behind her ear and slide my fingers along her jaw to lift her chin. "It'll be over before you know it. I promise."

Faint worry lines form in her brow, and before I realize it, my lips brush against hers. I hate knowing how miserable she is, and I wish like hell I could end this all today, so she could get on with her life.

But I'm also not ready for it to end, because it feels like we've barely gotten started.

Even though it's the last thing I should be thinking—like kissing her is the last thing I should be doing—my hand slides into her hair so I can deepen the kiss anyway.

If I can help her relax and make her feel good for a little while, why not do it? We're in public, so it's not like we can take it further than a little kiss anyway.

Running her hands around my waist, she lightly fists my T-shirt. "Aiden…" she whispers, opening her mouth just enough for me to tease my tongue against hers.

She tastes so damn good and her body melts into mine just like it used to. I could get lost in her all over again if I let my—

"Well, well, what do we have here?" A deep voice sounds from behind Liv, and I pull her protectively into my chest even though there isn't a need.

"Fuck off, Jesse," I grumble as Liv hides her face in my shirt. It was a brief, relatively innocent kiss, but knowing her, she's blushing like we just got caught with our pants down.

"I heard the rumors, but now I see they weren't rumors at all." My younger brother grins as he looks us over in front of the pub. It's only noon and his jeans and Enders Excavating T-shirt are already filthy. "You joining us for lunch, Olivia?"

"Ah, no. She's with *me* today." Amelia appears out of nowhere, glancing between me and Jesse like we're the most annoying people she's ever met. "And don't even think about sitting with us. We have girl stuff to discuss."

She tugs Liv into the pub, and they reappear a second later in a booth on the other side of the glass right where Liv and I had been standing.

Great. Not only did Jesse catch us, but Amelia had a front-row seat the entire time.

I run a hand over my hair and sigh. "Too early for a beer?"

Jesse chuckles and holds the door open for me. A minute later, we claim two stools at the bar where I can keep an eye on Liv, but thankfully not hear a thing that comes from my sister's mouth.

"So, you want to tell me what's going on or should I make assumptions?" Jesse waves over Finn, the bartender, and we both order Cokes.

"Both of those options suck." But if I'm going to tell anyone else the truth, it's him. I'm close with all my siblings, but Jesse is the only one I'd trust with my life. Liv's, too.

"Does this have anything to do with that case you went

down to Milwaukee for?" my brother asks as Finn sets our drinks in front of us along with two menus.

"I don't know anything about a case," I mutter, tearing open a straw and sticking it in my glass.

"Right." Jesse gives a short laugh and browses the menu even though we're both going to order the same thing we always do—bacon cheeseburgers with fried onions and fries. "Bren know about this?"

"Yep."

"And you're not dead yet?"

"No, but once I've served my purpose, there's a good possibility that could change."

"Ah." Jesse nods and sets the menu aside. "I heard the mob took out her husband."

"I might've heard that, too."

"You sure this is a good idea, man?"

"As a cop, yes. As far as the other, not a fucking chance."

"And Bren knows about *the other*?"

I stretch my head from one side to the other until my neck pops. "Not exactly."

"Dude…"

"Look, I know. Everything happened so fast—"

"You've had fourteen years."

Fucking hell. He knew way back then, too?

"Is this for real or…?"

I shake my head.

"That kiss didn't look fake, man."

Yeah, no shit. "It's complicated."

"Obviously." He leans back in his seat as Finn returns a second time, and we both order our usual.

"I'm paying for the ladies, too, so if you could make sure I get their bill that'd be great," I tell the bartender as I gesture to Liv and Amelia. Finn nods and Jesse arches an eyebrow.

"Why the hell would you do this to yourself?" my brother asks when we're alone again.

"Bren's my best friend."

"Cut the shit, Aiden."

And that right there is why I usually want to punch him and hug him at the same time. "Maybe I still care about her."

"Now we're getting somewhere." He flashes a grin, and my gut drops like he dumped a load of rocks into it.

"I shouldn't have kissed her."

"Why not?"

"Because…" I hesitate, my thumb swiping at the condensation on my Coke. I don't want to breach Liv's trust, but if I don't get some of this shit off my chest, the damn thing might burst. "Because she told me why she broke it off all those years ago, and it's a million times worse than anything I came up with on my own."

Jesse frowns. "Okay…"

"Imagine the worst thing that could happen to a woman, man. And double it."

He studies me for a moment, and when his eyes glaze over and the hand resting on top of the bar becomes a fist, I know he's figured it out.

"He beat the hell out of her, too," I rasp, the words feeling like sand on my tongue. "And I didn't know. She wouldn't see me. I…" I break off as anger swells anew in my chest. "I should've been there, man."

Jesse sits forward again. "Let me get this straight," he says quietly so no one else hears. "You don't think you should've kissed her because of something that happened ten years ago?"

"I fucking failed her." And saying those words out loud isn't nearly as cathartic as I'd hoped. If anything, hearing them only makes the disgust I feel toward myself stronger. "I have no right to touch her now."

Jesse shakes his head, his jaw clenched tight. "Did you ask her how she felt, Aiden? Or are you making assumptions?"

"What?" I pull back. "I think it's pretty obvious how she felt, don't you think?"

"*Now,* asshole, not back then."

"What's the fucking difference?"

My brother scrubs a hand over his face and sighs. "You do realize it's been ten years, right? You just found out what happened, but she's had a long time to deal with it. She got married, man. You know what I'm saying?"

Yeah, and he's lucky a couple deputies just walked in, or he'd be laid out on the floor.

"I really don't want to talk about her fucking marriage," I growl, and he has the audacity to chuckle.

"Wow."

"You know what? Forget I said anything." I shake my head, grind my molars, and stare blindly at the baseball game playing on one of the TVs. I wouldn't have thought it was possible for one person to regret so much in one week, but here I am.

"Maybe that's your problem," Jesse says, ignoring my last words. "Maybe you should stop sweeping shit under the rug because you don't want to deal with it."

"What the fuck are you talking about? I don't sweep shit—"

"Aiden, it's that number again." Liv pushes her way between our stools, her eyes wide with panic as she holds up her phone. "This is the second time it's called since we sat down."

I blink at her cell for a few seconds before her words register, and then I accept the call with a snarl. "Who the fuck is this?"

Her face blanches at my language, but I'm not in the

mood for games right now. Whoever this is can give me a damn name or stop calling.

Except there's nothing but silence on the other end of the line before it goes dead.

"They hung up." I barely have time to make sure the call is actually lost before Liv slugs me in the shoulder.

"What if that was one of my students, you big jerk?"

"Then they'd leave you a message, don't you think?" I don't mean to raise my voice at her, but my stress level is nearing my breaking point, thanks to Jesse. "Shit, I'm sorry." I scrub a hand over my face. "Maybe we should take our food to go."

"Really?" Liv frowns and glances over to the booth where Amelia waits with a worried expression of her own. "All right. If you think that's best."

I don't know what the fuck I'm thinking right now and that's the problem. My head is a mess and has been for days, and if I don't get my shit together, I'm going to be useless to her and this case. Worse, I could screw it up.

"I'll finish lunch with Amelia," Jesse offers. "You two go and sort this out."

"Thanks," Liv mutters, giving Jesse's arm a squeeze, which doesn't sit well. It's not her touching him that bothers me, but the fact that it's an apologetic gesture. She shouldn't be the one apologizing when I'm the one who's made this whole thing such a fucking mess.

I lift a hand to Finn. "Could you box our food up instead?" I gesture to Liv and then dig a wad of cash from my wallet and toss it onto the bar.

Looks like I'll be hitting that woodpile again today, won't I?

CHAPTER 25

OLIVIA

*A*iden never touched his lunch, and I barely picked at mine before I tossed both containers into the trash.

He also refused to come in the house and talk to me, even though I'd practically begged. Instead, he's kept himself busy outside by cutting the lawn, fixing the gutters on the garage, and now he's back at the woodpile, beating the living hell out of every chunk of wood he swings that axe at.

I don't know what transpired between him and Jesse, but whatever it was had him wired like a time bomb that went off the second he answered my phone. The only good thing that came of his momentary explosion was that the calls stopped. For now, anyway.

I know better than to poke the bear, but nothing good can come from him letting all this anger and emotion fester like he is. So, I make my way to the backyard and start piling the wood on top of the stack he's already started.

"What are you doing?" he pants, swiping the back of his hand over his forehead. "Go back in the house."

"No one is going to shoot me while I pile wood, Aiden, jeez." I ignore his command and continue to pick up and organize the mountain of wood he's created.

"Liv, I'm not fucking around. Get your ass back in the house." There's more bite to his words than breathlessness this time, and I spin on him with a glare.

"Will you quit telling me what to do? I'm not a fucking toddler."

He glances away toward the tree line with an irritated laugh. "I'm not in the mood for this today, Liv."

"I haven't been in the mood for a lot of things for a long damn time, Aiden, so stop with your tough-guy bullshit, okay?"

His jaw snaps shut and his nostrils flare as his grip tightens on the axe handle. "It's not safe for you out here."

"With you? Oh, I know. You're the last person I should be with right now."

His stormy gaze swings to mine. "What the hell does that mean?"

"You're a walking time bomb of emotions, which I can understand to a point, because I've asked a lot of you this past week and I've unloaded even more. But you have to stop trying to push everything you're feeling aside, because you think it's what's best for me and this case."

"It is what's best."

"Is it? How do I know it won't get to be too much for you?" I prop my hands on my hips. "How do I know your anger won't get the best of you and cause you to snap and do something crazy?"

"What? I would never." He lowers his chin while I lift mine and stare him down, undeterred.

"Never what? Never scream at me? Never put your hands on me?"

"You know damn well I'd never do either of those things."

"Do I?" I tip my head, praying like heck I'm not making things worse.

"Are you fucking kidding me right now?" He lets the axe drop to the ground and takes a step forward. I simply blink at him, once again, holding my own. "You think I'd hurt you?"

I finally give in and shake my head. "No. I *know* you wouldn't."

"Then what the hell is this all about?" He throws his hands in the air, and I lift mine.

"You tell me."

He scowls. "What?"

"I heard what Jesse said earlier about you sweeping things under the rug to deal with later and that's what you've been doing since I told you I was assaulted."

He opens his mouth, but I hold up a hand.

"You're not dealing with your feelings, but you are letting them eat away at you and somehow convince you that you're responsible for what happened.

"The truth is… you could never hurt me. Even at your worst, you would never raise a hand to me, or god forbid, do worse, because that's not who you are." I move toward him, stopping with only a foot between us. The proximity means I have to look up to see his face and he has to look down to see mine. "I'm not going to let you do this to yourself."

The tension in his expression breaks and he glances away quickly, but not before I see the torment in his eyes.

"You are not to blame, okay? You didn't give me this scar." I touch my temple. "Or this one." I lower my hand to my lip. "And you didn't force yourself on me either." I press my hand to my stomach. "All you've ever done"—I reach for his hand and hold it against my chest, right over my heart—" is love me."

"That's not true." His voice is so raw and vulnerable, but he doesn't try to pull away.

"You didn't love me?"

"You know I did."

"Then what isn't true? Tell me." I turn his face back to mine as he swallows hard. "Don't tell me I'm wrong about what you're doing, because there's no way Jesse and I are both wrong."

"It's not that. It's just... I don't know if I can do this. I don't know if I can keep you safe."

"Of course you can." I curl both of my hands around his jaw and stroke his cheeks with my thumbs. "I wouldn't have asked you if I didn't already know you could."

He closes his eyes. "I can't stop thinking about his hands on you. The shit he put you through..."

I nod. "I know, baby. I did the same for a long time, too."

"I don't know how to make it stop."

"You have to face it head-on, not push it away."

"How are you so fucking strong?" he whispers.

"I wasn't always. That's why I left." My voice cracks and he opens his eyes again. "I wish I'd been strong enough to stay, and that's my biggest regret next to hurting you."

His hand slides from my chest to the side of my neck. "I don't know if I can forgive myself for not being there for you."

"That was my choice, not yours. We can't blame ourselves for other people's choices, Aiden. That's what I'm trying to tell you."

He shakes his head. "You don't understand..."

"I do." I smile through watery eyes. "I hated myself for a long time. Years actually. And it took twice as much therapy for me to realize that I had to let go of the things I had no control over. All we can ever do is be accountable for what we've done, make amends where we can, and learn from

233

those mistakes. If we try to change the things we never had control over in the first place, we'll never be happy."

"I could have told Bren," he says in a pained voice, and I nod.

"I could have, too. But telling him wouldn't have changed what Kyle did."

"You keep saying that…"

"Because it's true. Nothing we did caused what happened, Aiden. Nothing." And I will tell him that a thousand more times if I need to. "I'm not saying you shouldn't feel the way you do. In fact, knowing you care so much…" A tear slips down my cheek and I pull in a shaky breath. "I wasn't sure you would."

"Of course, I care." His hand pushes back into my hair. "But caring too much is a weakness."

"Or it's the ultimate strength," I counter, and he looks down at me like it's the craziest thing he's ever heard. "I need you because you care. And I think right now you need me, too."

His hand fists in my hair and I feel his body shake against mine as he fights to believe me.

"I can't let you run because you don't think you're enough…" I whisper. "When you are everything I've needed all along."

His lashes flutter over emotion of his own, and my heart squeezes so hard that it's hard to breathe. Still, I manage one more plea.

"Lean on me, Aiden, please."

AIDEN

How can something so terrifying also feel so fucking right?

Liv wraps her arms around my neck and holds on so tight that I couldn't pull her off if I wanted to. "Lean on me, Aiden, please."

The feel of her body pressed to mine, her breath on my skin, and her words in my ear...

It's all too much, so I give in, and I press my nose to her temple and do nothing but breathe her in until I lose track of time.

I understand what she's saying, because I've been on the other side before, too. Hell, I've sat beside dozens of women in the emergency room, trying to convince them that the assault they just survived wasn't their fault. And in some instances, I've had to reassure their partners of the same.

My logical brain knows the blame belongs to Kyle Weston, but I still can't help but feel like my choices gave him a way in. If I would have told Bren and Liv and I hadn't tried to keep our relationship hidden, I might've been in Madison that weekend. Or she might've been back home with me instead of that party.

I also know we can *what if* the hell out of a situation until it eats us alive, but it's a lot harder to gag that nasty voice when it's *your* conscience doing the talking.

"Come inside." Her lips press against my bare shoulder at the same time her fingers feather into the hair at the back of my neck. "Help me make dinner and relax for a little bit. Please."

As good as that sounds, there's something I need to do first.

"I'm going to go and talk to Bren." I pull back and sweep my thumb across her cheek. "That's something I have control over."

She smiles before she lifts up on her toes and gives me a sweet kiss. "Okay, but don't take too long. There's something else I want us to do today."

I lift an eyebrow and she swats at my arm.

"Not that."

Obviously.

"But seriously, go. I'll be fine here. I'll keep the doors locked and I have Gertie to keep me company." The damn cat meows from atop the woodpile a few feet away as if to agree.

"I'll call Bolinger and have him come over—"

"I took self-defense classes, Aiden. Lots of them." Her dark eyes blink up at me. "I can handle myself for an hour or two. Now go."

I hesitate, but ultimately give in. Bren should still be at the station, less than three blocks away. I don't like the idea of coming clean there, but I can't put this off any longer.

"All right. Go inside and set the alarm. I won't be long." I give her a quick peck on the cheek before I swipe up my T-shirt from a chunk of wood and pull it over my head.

While she heads inside with Gertie in her arms, I head for my truck. Five minutes later, I walk through the Pine County Sheriff's Office door to find Bren at the front desk talking with none other than Special Agent Bolinger.

Fuck. What are the chances I'd run into him the one time I leave Liv alone?

"Detective." Bolinger glances over, and without missing a beat, asks, "Where's our girl?"

No point in lying when the only two people she's approved to be alone with are standing right in front of him.

"She's at my house, Special Agent. Behind locked doors and a tight security system, I assure you." I don't bother to look at Bren, because I can already feel him glaring at me and wondering what the hell I'm doing here.

"I just need a flash drive from my office," I lie, and add another ten pounds of fucking weight to my shoulders.

"Ah." Bolinger nods, and I tip my head toward the hall.

"Gonna grab it and get going." And pray to god he doesn't immediately call Nolan to have me pulled from this case.

As messed up as my head has been, it'd probably be the best thing for Liv, but I'd never let myself live it down either. At this point, I need to finish out this case for me almost as much as I need to do it for her.

Grabbing a random flash drive from my desk, I return to the front of the building where Bolinger excuses himself from the conversation with Bren and follows me outside.

"Don't look so paranoid, Detective. I'm not going to rat you out."

I chuckle even though his statement doesn't make me feel any better. "I swear this is the one and only time I've left her alone. Figures you'd greet me at the door."

He shoves his hands into his khakis and nods. "How's it going anyway? You two claw each other's eyes out yet?"

"Not quite." But she might've tried earlier if I hadn't let my guard down. I still don't know what I'm doing as far as our past is concerned, but she and Jesse are right—nothing good ever comes from ignoring a problem.

"It may be of interest to you that her uncle and I had a private conversation a couple weeks ago before you came on board. Off the record, of course."

"Of course."

"I'm not sure why he didn't tell Nolan, but I figure he had good reason, so I didn't ask questions."

"And let me guess—you're going to tell me so I can wonder, too."

He dips his chin. "I figure if I'm going to turn a blind eye to your indiscretion, you can do the same to mine and maybe make some use of it."

"Okay…" I'm not sure, but I suddenly feel like I'm making a deal with the devil.

"He said Jelanovich's involvement with the SSP goes way back and he thought himself some sort of vigilante."

"Isn't that the modus operandi of the entire organization?"

"In Chicago, yes, but not overseas."

"All right."

"He was siphoning money the whole time he did the books for the SSP, but it was negligible, so they didn't catch on until he aligned himself with the rebel group and got greedy."

"We already knew that. What we don't know is who the other assholes are. Did he tell you that? Because that's what I want to know."

Bolinger shakes his head. "No. But Zieliński did tell me to be careful."

"Why?"

"Because not everyone is as well intentioned as they appear to be."

CHAPTER 26

OLIVIA

"*I* need you to do two things: trust me and relax."

Aiden gives me a sidelong glance from the passenger seat of his truck. "You're behind the wheel of my baby. Neither of those things is going to happen anytime soon."

"Oh, come on." I laugh, put the vehicle in reverse, and back out of his driveway. "You used to let me drive all the time, and that truck was way bigger than this one."

"I didn't give a shit about that piece of crap. But this one I just paid off. Jesus fuck, woman!" His hand flies to the handle above the door when I turn onto the road too soon and run over the culvert.

"Whoops!" I flash a cheeky grin. "Good thing you've got big tires."

He shoots me an irritated glare and continues to hold on as I navigate toward the back roads we used to practically live on as horny teenagers.

"I'm not sure how this is supposed to help me relax," he

mutters as we bounce along the ruddy dirt road, the trees a kaleidoscope of green on either side of us. It's still light outside, but the sun has already started to drop in the sky, creating an earthy, tranquil sort of ambience. That is, if you allow yourself to appreciate it.

"Let's try this…" I power down the windows, and the cool evening air instantly permeates the cab. "Take a few deep breaths. Close your eyes if you have to."

"This isn't some kind of intervention, is it? Because I'm gonna be pissed if Jesse and Jinx are out here waiting to gang up on me."

"*Noo.*" I laugh. "But that would've been funny."

He gives a begrudged grunt and rests his arm along the open window, drawing my attention to his bulky forearm and the massive hand gripping the edge of the door.

"I like all the new ink, by the way. It looks good." Sexy, if I'm honest.

He makes a fist and rotates the arm on the window to give me a better view of his tattoos. "Thanks. They were my obsession for a while."

"Yeah?" I slow down and turn onto another road, this one narrower and less traveled than the last. It's been at least a dozen years since I've been this deep into the backwoods of our little town, but the place I'm taking us is one I'll never forget.

"You know how they say new ink is like therapy for some people?"

"True for you?"

"One hundred percent."

"Do they mean anything?" He'd only had a handful when we were together before, but there must be at least twice that many now, some big, some small, but all of them various shades of black, gray, and white.

"Not really. I just liked the art." He taps his finger on a

small design tucked between a few larger ones just down from his thumb on the bony part of his wrist. "This one does though."

"Yeah? Tell me about it." I can't make out exactly what it is from here, but it looks like a bird of some sort.

He gives me another sidelong glance, this time with a slow, slightly askew smile. "I'll let you take a look when we stop. Maybe you can tell *me* what it means."

Phew. Is that heat in his voice or am I wishful thinking?

"All right, Mr. Mysterious. I'll bite."

He chuckles, and a handful of minutes later, the final road comes into view. "This ol' place, huh?"

"It was hot and humid today. I figured we could use a swim."

"We could have gone to Amber Lake."

"We could have, but I like the privacy here more."

Sunset Lake is a third of the size of Cole Creek's tourist-laden Amber Lake, and it's part of the National Forest, so there are no cabins or formally developed beaches, and most vacationers don't even know it exists.

"You should have told me. I would've brought my swim trunks."

I press my lips together in a devious smile as I park and unbuckle. "Oh, come on, Enders. That's never stopped you before."

Before he can reply, I hop out of the truck and whip my T-shirt over my head. My flip-flops and my shorts disappear next, and I hurry to the water like I've done so many times before at this very spot with this same man.

"What if I'm not wearing underwear?" Aiden calls when he steps out of the truck after me. "You didn't think of that, did you?"

I toss a saucy glance over my shoulder. "Or maybe I did."

He tips his head toward the sky and groans. "You're gonna be the death of me, woman."

"I sure hope not. You're not even wet yet." Without another word, I dive in and relish in the soothing caress of the cool water against my skin. I've spent lots of time in the pool on campus over the years, but there's nothing quite like fresh lake water to calm the spirit and refresh the soul.

I swim out several yards before I twist around to my back and float lazily back toward the shore. Out of nowhere, big arms wrap around my waist as Aiden swims stealthily beneath me.

"You've gotta be careful," he says into my ear as he pulls me against his chest. "Rumor has it this lake is now home to a mysterious serpent."

"Oh really?" Goose bumps rise on my shoulders as they break the glassy surface of the lake and cool air kisses my skin. "Is it big?"

"Huge." With one arm still wrapped around me, he treads farther out into the lake with the other. "And it only appears at sunset."

"Oh no." The sun dances above the tree line in the distance, painting the sky in shades of pink, purple, and orange. For some reason, the sunset always seems brighter and more vibrant out here, hence the very fitting name of the lake. "Maybe we should get out."

"We'll be fine as long as we stick together. But the second we let go of each other, all bets are off."

"That sounds dangerous."

"It is. You should probably wrap your legs around me just in case."

I giggle and do as he says, turning in his arms so I can curl my legs around his torso and loop my arms around his neck. Beads of water glisten on his face and broad shoulders as dark tendrils of hair rest in spikes against his forehead. And those eyes... those deep-blue eyes that hold so many of my secrets... I swear they have some sort of magical powers because every time I look into them—really look into them—everything in the world feels right.

"I see you were giving me a hard time about the underwear," I tease, as the cotton of his boxer briefs rubs against the inside of my thighs. And with a simple flex of my hips, I'd feel a lot more than boxers.

He gives a soft snort and glances down to my chest where the dark water ebbs and flows against the pale swells of my breasts, barely covered in navy lace. "And I see you already misplaced your new suit."

"It's in the wash," I lie. I almost wore it beneath my clothes but decided my bra and panties were more like old times. And tonight, that's what I want him to remember. I want him to remember what life had been like for both of us before everything changed.

We can't go back and alter the direction that life took us both, but beneath the pain, the heartbreak, the guilt, and the shame, I have to believe we built the foundation of something stronger and more resilient.

I don't know if Aiden wants to find that place again, but something tells me he wouldn't be here now if part of him didn't miss the people we were back then, too.

"I haven't been out here in years," he says, scanning the lake and the trees surrounding it.

"No fishing trips with Jesse or Jinx?"

"Nah, we usually fish at the creek. It's easier with Jett." He takes us a few feet closer to shore so he can stand and adjust his hold on me. With an arm beneath my butt, he lifts me just enough that my lady bits are pressed against his manly bits, which the flutter of his eyelashes and the pulse of his jaw assures me was an accident. An accident he doesn't move to correct. "I think the last time I was here was with you."

"Really?" That knowledge probably shouldn't excite me as much as it does.

A grin lifts one corner of his mouth, just barely showing a flash of perfect white teeth. "Places like this are always more fun with a pretty girl in her underwear."

I laugh and lace my fingers behind his neck. "You really expect me to believe you've never taken the opportunity with anyone else?"

He gives his head a solitary shake. "Nope."

"Aiden Enders, you are so full of shit."

"Hey, I'm not saying I couldn't have; I'm saying I never wanted to."

"Oh." Well, that's something entirely different. "Why not?"

"Why do you think?" He tips his head and something a little naughty flashes in his eyes.

"I'm not sure." I press my lips into a playful smile. "Maybe you should tell me."

A low, husky laugh vibrates his chest. "We had a lot of firsts at this lake."

"Not all of them." Our first kiss and our first time had been at Amber Lake, not here at Sunset Lake.

"I got to second base with you here," he says softly, his eyes lowering to my breasts once again. "And this is where you gave me the honor of being the first guy to see these, too."

A shiver slides down my spine at the memory. I'd been so nervous and self-conscious. All the girls in the locker room had tiny pink nipples. Not only are mine large and dark, but my right boob has always been a half a cup size bigger, too. But Aiden didn't care. In fact, he couldn't get enough of them.

"Remember when I almost made you come just by teasing you?" His free hand slides up my rib cage beneath the water so he can stroke a thumb over my nipple.

Another wave of goose bumps flashes across my skin and I shiver.

"How could I forget?" It was the first time I'd ever felt the buildup and the promise of a real orgasm. It had excited me and embarrassed me at the same time.

"And when I put my mouth on you for the first time, I blew my load in my jeans like I was twelve." He grins, completely unabashed, but I bite my lip.

I'd give anything to feel his mouth on me again. His tongue and his lips and his beard and his heat. And I can promise there would be no *almost* this time... I *would* come. Because no one has ever made my body sing quite like Aiden. Not even my husband.

"I'd let you again," I whisper, and his lashes lower over hazy eyes.

"I don't want to rush this, Livi."

Rush? I've craved this man and his touch *for years*.

"I just need a little more." Covering his hand with my own, I urge him to tug down my bra. "Please." And he does, groaning low in his throat as he takes me in.

"Still so fucking pretty."

"Touch me." I push myself into his hand, the need for him growing stronger by the second. I know he's afraid to hurt me or to ask for too much too soon, but the truth is... the memory of moments like this—*with him*—was what helped me heal.

We were just kids, yet he'd shown me how a real man should treat a woman. He was so patient and tender, so loving and kind, and he always made me feel like what I had to give was exactly what he needed from me, too.

"Is this okay?" he asks, circling my puckered nipple with a fingertip before giving it a gentle tweak, making me gasp and twitch and physically *ache* for him.

"It's perfect," I whisper as I lower my chin to watch his

long, work-roughened fingers play. There was always something so erotic about watching this big, rough-around-the-edges man work magic on my body. It made me feel so feminine and sexy, and it's no different now.

"It's a dove," I gasp, finally seeing the detail in his tattoo. At first glance, it looks like nothing more than a space between the other tattoos, but it's far from nothing. It's soft and delicate and pretty with its white ink and pale-gray shading.

He nods, and his voice is hoarse and a little vulnerable when he speaks. "Olivia means peace, and since doves represent peace…"

He tattooed me—or rather, a symbol of me—on his body? Right where he would see it every day?

"Aiden…" Holy crap. I don't know what to say. I… "Oh my god."

He lifts a shoulder like it's not a big deal, but it's *everything*.

"When did you get it?"

He glances away and swallows, but I turn his face back to mine.

"When?"

"About five years ago," he confesses, a mix of uncertain emotions in his eyes while every restless part of me weeps with long-awaited relief.

Five years. Not ten or even nine. But five years. When both of us should have long been over each other.

"Oh, Aiden…" I crush my mouth to his in a kiss that's full of so many unspoken words. *I'm sorry. I've missed you. Please don't leave me again. I love you.*

"It's always been you," he whispers against my lips. "All this fucking time, it's always been you."

My heart swells with so much happiness that it's hard to

breathe. I was so afraid that he'd hate me, but the truth is he'd wanted me, too. Maybe even waited for me.

Kiss by kiss and breath by breath, the tension in his shoulders eases, and I feel him give in to me and into us, leaving no doubt in my mind that I'm not alone in how I feel. He's been just as scared and yet just as hopeful, too.

He breaks away only to seek out my jaw and then my neck, running his nose along my skin as he places a trail of wet kisses all the way down to my breast.

"Need to taste you," he murmurs before his lips close around my nipple, followed by the caress of his tongue and the gentle tug of his teeth.

"Yesss." My head falls back as he licks and sucks and drives me absolutely crazy, only to pull away, free my other breast, and begin the glorious torture all over again.

"Touch yourself," he husks as he shifts from one nipple to the other, his endgame clear. "You're already so hot against my dick. Slide your hand into your panties and play for me."

Yes, please. I dip my fingers into the lace beneath the water and shiver the second they graze my clit.

"Feels good, doesn't it?" He smirks as my eyelids begin to flutter, the promise of release already blooming. "Are you gonna get off like this, Livi? Like you used to while I'd suck your tits?"

"Uhhh..." A throaty moan vibrates through my chest as every flick of his tongue and every stroke of my fingers winds my impending orgasm tighter.

"Good girl," he praises. "Now pinch that clit for me, baby. Make it feel even better."

My only response is a whimper as I obey and am rewarded with his fingers and his teeth doing the same to my aching nipples. The culmination of sensation from all three points is exactly what I need, and I come harder than I have in forever, my pussy pulsing against his erection beneath the water.

My head drops to his shoulder as he holds me close, his hand running up and down my back as I savor every last flutter and pulse of pleasure.

It isn't until he urges my feet down to dry land that I realize he's walked us out of the water.

"Still so fucking perfect," he murmurs as he kisses my forehead and reaches for his T-shirt on the hood of his truck. "Here, let's get this on before you start to shiver."

With my focus still cloudy, I let him help me into the shirt before it dawns on me that one orgasm between two people doesn't add up.

"Wait, what about you?" I reach for him as he sticks one leg and then the other into his jeans.

He flashes a wicked smile. "Who says we're done?"

"Oh."

"Get in the truck, Livi."

CHAPTER 27

AIDEN

Fucking Craig.

Of all the nights to come back, he had to pick tonight, didn't he?

"Kinda late for company, isn't it?" Liv frowns when I turn into the driveway and my headlights pan across the truck parked in front of the garage. The lights in the house are on, too, and ten bucks says my temporary roommate is already sprawled out on the couch like he owns the place.

"It's Craig," I mutter as I kill the engine and rub the heels of my hands into my eyes. I didn't plan on things getting too out of hand with Liv tonight, but I'd kinda hoped we'd at least be alone. "I'll get rid of him. I—"

"It's okay." Her fingers curl around my forearm. "I mean, he's going to see me in this, but it's not a big deal." She glances down to my T-shirt and a small, secretive smile tips her lips.

"What's that look for?"

"I don't know. I always thought it'd be kinda fun if Bren caught me in one of your shirts."

I might've had that same fantasy a time or two myself. "You got a kink for getting caught or what?"

She purses those pretty lips of hers and gathers up her clothes. "With you? Absolutely."

My laugh turns to a groan as she hops out and starts for the front porch. The shirt leaves the lower curve of her ass cheeks bare, and while the thought of getting busted with her gets me a little hot, too, my friends checking out my girl does not.

"Hold up, babe…" I jog to catch up just as the front door opens and Craig appears with a bottle of beer and a wide grin.

"Well, hey there, kids." He opens an arm to Liv and pecks her on the cheek when she gives him a quick side hug. "Fancy seeing you here, Ms. Bishop."

"Hey, Craig, how are you?" She holds her clothes to her chest and glances back as I follow her up the steps.

"Oh, I could be better, but forget about me. Let's talk about you two." He shifts his gaze from me to her and back again, and I glower.

"Let's not." Wrapping an arm around her waist, I guide her around him and into the house. "Why don't you grab a shower?" I say into her ear from behind. "I'll handle this."

"Okay." Her hand comes up to caress my cheek. "I'll probably go to bed afterward if you don't mind."

It's probably for the best. We crossed a few lines tonight and we need to figure out what that means for this so-called fake relationship of ours before we let it play out in front of everyone else.

"Sounds good." I kiss her cheek and she smiles, holding me close for just a second longer before she sighs.

"G'night."

"Night." I give her hip a gentle squeeze, wishing I could do a hell of a lot more, before she heads for the bedroom at the back of the house.

As soon as the door clicks shut, I turn to my friend and temporary roommate. "Don't fucking say it," I warn him, and he holds up his hands, one of which is still wrapped around his beer.

"I already heard about you two, man, so this ain't no surprise. Yet, it kinda is." One eyebrow lifts as he smirks. "You know?"

No, I don't know. As far as he's concerned, Liv and I have been seeing each other for weeks now. If he's insinuating something else...

"Not sure I do," I say, lifting my chin and leveling with him. If he thinks he's going to give me shit about Liv when his own love life is such a fucking mess, he can think again.

He studies me for a beat before running a hand around the back of his neck. "Bren might've asked me to keep an eye on you two."

He *what*? My heart begins to pound in my chest at the same time red-hot fury boils in my veins. The *sheriff* wasn't supposed to say anything to anyone about me and Liv.

"Don't get pissed, man." Craig puts up another hand. "He didn't give me any details—"

"That's not the fucking point," I seethe. If Bren thinks there's something more going on with me and Liv, he should've come to me about it instead of jeopardizing this case. Yeah, I talked to Jesse, but only because he'd already figured out the truth. "Is that why you're here? Because he asked you to fucking spy on us? If so, get your shit and get the fuck out."

"Dude, relax." He sets down the beer with a nervous laugh. "It's not like that."

I grind my teeth together and glare. It better not be like that or there's going to be hell to pay.

"I saw him at the Cole Stop and told him I was headed over here for the night since Cady's pissed at me. He said you had Olivia here, too, and I thought for sure I'd heard him wrong, because if that were true, one of you fuckers would be behind bars." He shakes his head and grins, but when I don't reciprocate, he clears his throat. "Anyway, he said it wasn't what I thought, but he couldn't tell me more. Then he got a little weird, and said that if I was gonna be here, maybe I could let him know how it was going."

Because I haven't been telling him enough or because he suspects something else is going on? Either way, Bren Bishop can fuck off.

"I don't know what I just saw, but I got enough of my own shit going on. I'm not about to get mixed up in your business." He goes to the fridge and pulls out two beers before sliding one across the kitchen island to me.

I eye it for a second before I snap it up, twist off the top, and take a pull.

"She looks good," Craig says, but there's no creepy undertone to his words, just sincerity. "Even with you."

I make a throaty sound and toss the bottle top in the trash. "I thought you weren't getting mixed up in my business."

He lifts his beer like a white flag. "I'm just saying."

Fucking guy. I down the rest of my beer in two gulps and set the bottle on the counter more aggressively than necessary. He may be one of my best friends, but my circle of trust isn't very big these days.

"I'm gonna hit the shower, but do me a favor, will ya?"

He nods.

"Tell Bren there's a reason Liv's here with me, and it

doesn't have a goddamn thing to do with him being my best friend."

"What the hell does that mean?"

I flash a conniving grin. "Exactly what you think it means."

OLIVIA

THE BEDROOM DOOR opens a half hour later and Aiden quietly slips inside.

"Hey." I set my book on the nightstand and sit up. "Everything okay?"

"Yeah, I just want to grab a shower if that's okay." He thumbs toward the hall. "It'll look weird if I use the other bathroom."

"Of course. This is your room." Which I've been dwelling on since I climbed into bed. If Craig is here, does that mean Aiden and I will be sharing a bed tonight? I think we might've been headed that way anyway after the lake, but now that we have company…

Aiden goes to his dresser for fresh boxers and shorts. "Craig had a fight with Cady, so he might be here for a few days. He also said he ran into your brother at the gas station, and Bren hinted that what's going on with us isn't real."

"What?" My heart stills in my chest. "I thought we were keeping that quiet."

He nods agreeably. "Yeah, I don't know. I'm not fucking happy about it."

I'm not either. Craig has been a good friend to my brother for years, and he and Aiden are obviously still close, but if his behavior as of late is any indication, he may not be as trustworthy as he used to be.

"Anyway, we don't have to worry about him expecting us to sleep together."

And the disappointments keep coming, don't they? "Okay, but if you don't, he'll know you've been sleeping on the pullout in your office."

"Fuck." He pinches the bridge of his nose. "I forgot about that."

"You're welcome to stay in here. I mean, all things considered, I think we'll be fine."

He glances over at me with his eyelashes cast low. "All things considered, I'd be better off pissing off Craig."

My lips twist into a lopsided grin, though I'm just as disappointed as I am amused. "So, you were lying at the lake when you said we weren't done."

"I'm gonna take that shower," he says instead of refuting the accusation, and I let him go.

It's not hard to see that the guilt has crept back in again, probably because he wasn't able to talk to Bren. But the thing is... Aiden and I are adults. We don't need my brother's permission to have a cup of coffee, much less rekindle an old flame.

I understand Aiden wants to do the right thing, but we've lost too much time already. I don't want to lose any more. Starting now.

The second the water turns on in the shower, I creep off the bed and toward the bathroom door, left slightly ajar. I can't see a lot through the narrow opening, but it's just wide enough to see a sliver of skin as Aiden steps into the glass stall and dips his head beneath the spray.

Closing my eyes, I take a deep breath. I've come too far in life to not take chances on the things that I want. More than that, I've lived the last several years wanting this very opportunity. If I don't go after it when it's right in front of me, I'll have no one to blame but myself.

My shorts and panties hit the bedroom floor followed by my tank top before I tiptoe into the steamy bathroom with my heart pounding in my chest.

Aiden's back is to me as he pumps body wash into his hand and rubs it over his shoulders and arms, making rivulets of sudsy water run down his back and the curve of his ass like my hands itch to do. The need to touch and kiss him everywhere is almost overwhelming. I want to taste his tattoos, and I want to relearn every muscle and hard plane of the body I once knew as well as my own.

With his back to the shower door, he doesn't see me approach, but the moment my hand touches the glass and the door creaks open, I'm caught. His eyes go wide for a split second before they darken and slide down the length of my naked body. His gaze turns even hungrier when it falls on my breasts, one of which is pink and abraded from his beard at the lake, and then again at the apex of my legs, where I'm freshly bare from the shower I took less than an hour ago.

He opens his mouth, probably to protest despite the undeniable desire in his eyes, but I push up on my toes and silence him with a kiss.

"Shouldn't be here," he growls, even as he turns beneath the spray, his big hands lifting to grip my hips.

"I'm exactly where I should be." My own hands lift to his chest and then slide down his muscled and tattooed arms. "Why are we fighting this, Aiden? We both want it."

"It's not right." Still, his mouth drifts from mine to the curve of my jaw and then the soft spot behind my ear. "Your brother," he rasps as the tip of his nose glides along my skin and he inhales deeply like my very essence is his air. "Your past... fuck, you're still grieving."

A small sigh escapes my throat as I close my eyes and savor his touch. "You know I'm not. Not like everyone thinks I should be."

"It's still not—"

"Aiden…" My eyes snap open again, locking on his. "I grieved losing you more than I ever will him."

His lashes flutter over stormy eyes and the tendons in his neck strain as he swallows. "I don't want to hurt you, Livi."

"The only way you'll hurt me is by denying us the second chance we deserve," I whisper, and his mouth is on mine a breath later.

His hands lift to my jaw as he kisses me hard and deep, leaving no part of my lips and tongue unclaimed. He tastes like sweet concession and of the forgiveness I've been craving, but the low groan in his chest is still pained. Still so full of guilt.

Gripping his cheeks, I pull him away. "I need you to forgive yourself, too. To let go of the past and what was never your fault in the first place."

His jaw tightens and he tries to look away, but I jerk his face back to mine.

"Start by showing me how a real man touches a woman."

His eyes flash as if challenged, and his nostrils flare as he stares down at me. For a moment, I expect him to try and argue once more, but he pushes me against the glass instead. Hiking one of my legs to his hip, he presses the hard length of his cock against me, and I shiver.

"I'm so fucking scared I'm gonna do something wrong," he murmurs, lowering his forehead down to mine. His hips flex ever so slightly, seemingly of their own accord, and mine follow suit as if my body is reaching for him. Begging for him.

"Nothing between us has ever been wrong." And if he doesn't know that by now, I fear he never will. "Touch me. Please."

His grip on my hip tightens for just a beat before those long fingers slip between our bodies, expertly finding my clit. I gasp the second the rough pad of his finger grazes my already aching bead, knowing exactly how to touch me. Gentle at first and not too direct. Soft, taunting strokes just shy of where I actually need him to build up the anticipation.

"God, I've missed you." My head falls back against the glass as the fire between my legs begins to flame. I will never forget what happened that awful night, but this is what got me through. The memory of how it felt to be adored by a man who loved me. A man who knew when to be patient and gentle... and when not to be, too.

"Do you know how many times I've thought about you in this shower?" His lips shift to my ear again as his free hand guides one of mine to his cock. "How many times I've made myself come with your face and your body in mind?"

"Tell me." I wrap my fingers around him and begin to play.

"I've imagined your mouth," he husks against my neck as his ministrations between my legs become more intentional. "I've thought about you on your knees, sucking me off like I taught you."

I groan and my pussy tightens at the thought.

"You always wanted to be a teacher, but fuck if you weren't a good student, too."

My groan turns into a soft, throaty laugh, and I feel him smile against my skin before his teeth take a gentle bite.

"But my favorite memory is how it felt to slide into you for the first time. I fucking love that you gave me that."

Goose bumps rise on my skin even as the hot water continues to spray around us. I love that it was him, too. He was my first and I would give anything for him to be my last.

"You're mine, Livi. And I hate knowing that someone else touched what's always. Been. Fucking. Mine." He enunciates the last words as he shoves two fingers inside me. The action is rough, but it's exactly what I need, because stars light up behind my eyelids and a shiver rocks my body.

"Always yours," I murmur, my hips picking up pace and working with his hand. I'm already getting close. Just a little more...

"Damn right you are," he growls, framing my jaw with his hand and lifting my face so my lips are just a breath away from his. "And no one will ever touch what's mine ever again."

The second his mouth crushes to mine, I explode. His touch, his words, his kiss... I've craved it all for so long. Since I began to heal and realized this man would be my only true salvation.

"I need you inside," I plead before the flutters of my orgasm have even subsided. "Need you to make me forget."

His snarl of possession vibrates against my lips straight through to my soul, and I open for him in all ways, letting him reclaim every last bit of me.

He lifts me against the glass stall and slides inside in one easy stroke, and I swear nothing has ever felt more right in my life. He's wrapped around me, buried inside of me, and utterly consuming me. Yet, I am more *myself* than I've been in years, maybe ever. I'm older now. *We're* older now. And I understand the magnitude of what we have more than I ever could have back then.

"Fuck, Livi." His nostrils flare as an arm tightens around my waist and he pumps into me over and over again. "Missed you so goddamn much."

"Missed you more." I grasp his face in my hands and kiss him slow and deep. I taste his unspoken promises and spill my own into him, hoping he knows that he is more than my first love and my protector—he is my heart and my soul, and no matter the time we've spent apart, a part of him is woven into every part of me.

"Never gonna lose you again," he murmurs against my lips, and his words blaze through me like wildfire.

"*Aidennn!*" I cry, as my back arches and a second orgasm burns through me. This one is so heady and intense that my vision tunnels and my limbs go numb, but he holds on tight as I clench around him.

"Yes, baby, milk my cock." He grunts, giving me short, deep thrusts to draw out the orgasm. "Fuck, you're gonna make me come, too."

"Do it," I pant. "Come inside me."

A low, feral growl rumbles in his chest and then I feel that telltale pulse inside me. He buries his face in my neck and groans. "*Fuuuck!*"

There's never been anything sexier in my life than witnessing this guarded man come undone. When he lets down his walls and bares himself in the most amatory way. I know he's been with other women, but this feels like mine.

After a long beat, he pulls back and his mouth finds mine for a soft, languid kiss. "I never stopped loving you," he whispers, and all of my uncertainties melt away.

He is mine just as I am his, and I'm not losing him this time.

CHAPTER 28

AIDEN

"Oh my gosh, this is gorgeous!" Liv gasps as we pull up to Jesse and Hayden's house just before dinner-time on Friday night. "He built this himself?"

"Yep. Jinx, Dad, and I helped, too." It's been four years, since the summer after Jett was born to be exact, but my back still aches thinking about the time we put in making a home for that little tornado.

"Wow. I mean, I already knew you were good with your hands, but dang, Detective, I'm impressed." She shoots me a flirty grin, and I laugh. "I'm surprised you haven't built the same for yourself."

I unbuckle my seat belt and point to the line of pine trees along the east side of the yard. "When I do, it'll be over there. Just need to find the time." And someone to share it with.

Liv's brows lift and something quiet passes over her face, but she pastes on another smile. "I'm sure it'll be beautiful. And I love that you'll be close to Jesse, too."

I do, too, but I'd love even more if we both had kids that could grow up together.

Holy shit, where did that come from?

I clear my throat and shove the wayward thought out of my head. "We better get inside before they send Jett out to find us."

"I can't wait to meet him." Liv hops out and takes my hand as we climb the steps to the big front porch that I sat on not all that long ago, trying to convince my brother to pull his head from his ass before he lost Hayden for good. Now, I'm the one all up in my head about a woman.

"Uncle Aiden!" Jett yanks open the door before we hit the top step and launches himself into my arms. "Do you wanna play trucks in my sandbox?"

"I would love to, little man, but I think your mom would rather we eat the dinner she's made for us first."

Liv laughs softly behind us and reaches up to tousle my nephew's mess of blond hair. "You must be Jett."

"Uh-huh." He eyes her curiously over my shoulder, then breaks out into a grin. "You're pretty."

"Hold up there, dude." I chuckle and set him back on the porch so I can reclaim Liv's hand. "Don't you be flirting with my girl."

Liv steps into my side, wrapping her hand around my arm, as Jett streaks back into the house yelling, "Uncle Aiden has a girlfriend!"

"Jett Alexander!" Hayden calls as she rounds the corner into the foyer with a kitchen towel in hand. When she spots us outside the door, she sighs. "I am so sorry about that."

Liv shakes her head and steps inside. "No worries at all. I'm Olivia, and I *am* Aiden's girlfriend." She offers her hand to Hayden, who pulls her in for a hug instead.

"I'm Hayden, and you have no idea how glad I am to hear

that. I was worried he'd work himself to death and never settle down." She winks over Liv's shoulder, and I scoff.

"Hey now. There's nothing wrong with being married to your job."

"Sure." Hayden opens her arms to me next. "Ask your brother how that worked out for him."

A minute later, Hayden has us seated at the bar in the kitchen while she finishes dinner, a beer in front of me and a glass of wine in front of Liv.

"Speaking of my brother, where is he?"

"Finishing up in the shower, I hope. Even though I cleared his schedule so he'd be home in time tonight, he had to squeeze in one more estimate before the weekend." She rolls her eyes, and Liv smiles.

"Are you sure I can't help you?"

"Not a chance. You're our guest tonight, and from what I've heard, you're on vacation. So, please... sit back and relax."

Liv sighs and reaches for my hand beneath the bar. "So, you and Jesse work together?"

"Yep. I'm the office manager at Enders Excavating, which means I get the privilege of keeping Jesse in line at home *and* at the office." She waggles her eyebrows suggestively, and I groan.

"I really didn't need that visual, Hay."

"What? You know damn well Dad and Grandpa made out with Ma and Grandma at the office, too." Jesse strolls into the kitchen with wet hair and a smug grin. "In fact, I think you were the one that caught Ma on her–"

"Don't say it!" I throw up a hand and clench my eyes shut, but the memory of my mother on her knees has already resurfaced, and my stomach sours at the thought. "Jesus fuck, Jesse."

My brother tips his head back and bellows, and Liv's hand shakes in mine as she laughs, too.

"And this is why I've always loved your family so much," she says.

"Right?" Hayden removes a pan of what looks like extra cheesy lasagna from the oven and carefully sets it to the side before she pops a pan of garlic bread in after it. "Never a dull moment with the Enders crew. Anyway, I hope you like lasagna. We were going to grill out, but it's supposed to rain anytime now."

I glance toward the big windows in the dining room, facing my property. Sure enough, a mass of dark-gray clouds makes its way across the sky. "Damn, I guess it is."

Liv follows my gaze and squeezes my hand. "I hope it's a good one. You know how much I love storms."

Jesse clears his throat, and I shoot him a glare. Of course, I would know she loves storms, since she's my girlfriend and not at all because she was my secret lover all those years ago.

"I should probably check on Jett and make sure he's not ordering pay-per-view and racking up my credit card bill." Jesse tips his head toward the back of the house. "Join me?"

I glance to Liv as she leans in for a kiss. "Go. I could use some girl talk anyway." She pecks my lips and I instinctively slide a hand around the back of her neck for more.

Fucking hell, what is this woman doing to me?

"So, that seems to be going well," Jesse says as he plunks down next to Jett on the couch in their family room.

"It's all right." I shrug.

"Looks better than all right to me."

I shoot him a glare that slowly melts into a grin. We may be brothers, but I'm not about to give him any details. I've always been a little selfish about my time with Liv and probably will be even more so now. We have ten years to make up for. "Fine—things are great. But that's all you're getting."

A knowing smile spreads across Jesse's face just as the doorbell rings. A second later, my younger brother's voice calls down the hall. "Honey, I'm home!"

Jesse groans, and Jett's face lights up. "It's Uncle Jinx!"

"Yep, little man. Why don't you go say hi and bring him on back?"

Jinx sprints out of the family room and toward the front of the house, hollering for my kid brother only to be scolded by Hayden.

"You should have another one of those." I wink and take a pull from my beer as Jesse chuckles.

"Someday, man, but probably not anytime soon. I gotta get that girl to marry me first." He tips his head toward the kitchen, though the family room is divided off from the rest of the mostly open-concept layout. "You gonna do that right this time?"

"What do you consider *right*?" I want to see where this goes for sure, and I'm not going to intentionally hide it from Bren or anyone else. But Liv and I have a lot to consider if we're going to be together long term. She has her career in Milwaukee and I have mine here. Not saying I wouldn't give mine up, especially if the FBI offered me something more permanent, but I'm not getting my hopes up. Hell, this case isn't even over yet.

"Don't let her get away this time," Jesse says easily. "It's as simple as that. Whatever you have to do, do not let that girl slip through your fingers a second time."

"I don't plan to." But first I have to make sure I keep her alive.

"I'm still pissed at Craig for fucking up things with Rachel. I'd hate to be pissed at you, too."

I snort as Jett and Jinx stroll into the room. Jett is carrying a juice box and Jinx has a beer.

"Speaking of Craig, I've got a bone to pick with him." My youngest brother scowls as he claims a chair.

"Yeah? What about?" Jesse asks.

"I was doing a landscaping job at the Pruitt place yesterday, and the grass at Rachel's place was midcalf. Mason was outside messing with the lawn mower but couldn't get the damn thing going. I know Craig's not living there anymore, but the least he can do is make sure his kids aren't living like that. Poor kid was embarrassed as hell when I offered to help with the mower."

Jesse lets out a long sigh. "I'll see if I can weave it into conversation on Monday."

Jinx shakes his head. "Don't bother. I went back last night and cut the lawn myself."

Damn. "I'm sure Rachel appreciates that," I say. And next time I see Craig, I'll mention it, too. If nothing else, he could help his kid fix the friggin' mower."

"She was humiliated." Jinx clenches his jaw, and his knuckles turn white around his beer bottle. "So, next time I do it, I'll make sure she's not home."

"Next time?" Jesse cocks an eyebrow.

"She's on my weekly rotation now, whether she likes it or not."

I snort. "Dude, you can't just show up and cut her grass when no one is there. That's trespassing."

"What are you going to do, arrest me for being a nice fucking guy? Go ahead, I dare you."

Jesse chuckles. "Rachel may be a kindergarten teacher, but she's a spitfire, man. You don't want to get on her bad side."

No shit. She showed up on my doorstep a couple months back to chew Craig out for missing a visit with the kids. I thought the guy was going to piss his pants by the time she was done.

"How the hell can you two stand by that guy?" Jinx looks between me and Jesse. "He's screwing up his family, and for what? A trip down memory lane?"

I lift a hand. "I don't know, man."

We share a moment of silent confusion before Jinx speaks up again.

"Oh, and don't think I didn't notice Olivia Bishop sitting in the kitchen with Hayden, either. You want to tell me what that's about?"

"Not really."

He narrows his eyes. "Something going on between you two?"

Jesse laughs. "You really need to pay more attention, dude."

"Uncle Aiden has a girlfriend," Jett says on cue, and Jinx's jaw drops.

"You serious? You and Olivia?"

I tip back a swig of beer and nod. "Yeah, you could say that."

"Bren kick your ass yet?"

This time, I'm the one who laughs. "Not yet, but I'm sure it's coming."

OLIVIA

"So, you're the one."

"The one?" I frown as Hayden adds the last of our dinner plates to the dishwasher. We finished eating a half hour ago, and since then, the Enders men retreated to the back deck for an after-dinner drink.

"The one Aiden's been pining after all these years." Her lips tip with a soft smile. "When Jesse and I first got together, I asked him why Aiden didn't have a girlfriend. He said he was pretty sure there was someone from his past he hadn't gotten over yet. That was five years ago."

I blink as her words sink in. "Really? Jesse said that?"

"Yep. He never said who, but it's obvious he was talking about you." She closes the dishwasher door and hits the power button.

"What makes you think that? I'm sure Aiden's dated lots of other women since we were together." Not that I want to think about that, but I'm not naive.

"I've seen him with exactly one other girl the entire time I've known him. Granted, I only just recently moved to Cole Creek, but I spent lots of summers here. He's had lots of opportunities, but he rarely took them."

"Wow. I'm not sure if that makes me happy or sad." It says a lot that he held on, but it makes my heart hurt that he might've done so while I'd been married to someone else. For all he knew, I was happily married, not living the lie I'd tried to convince myself was all I deserved.

"These Enders boys love hard and fierce. It doesn't surprise me that Aiden held out hope that you two would find each other again someday."

A lump forms in my throat, and the best response I can offer her is a nod.

"Aww, don't do that." Hayden pulls me in for a hug when she spots the tears welling in my eyes. "A wise woman once told me that the journey of love is rarely a straight line. And the couples who find each other again after taking different forks in the road are usually the strongest because they know better than to take each other for granted."

I take a shaky breath. "That sounds like something Janice Enders would say."

Hayden laughs softly. "Yep. And lord knows it was exactly what I needed to hear, considering how crazy and twisted my journey with Jesse has been."

As we pull apart, I wipe the tears from my cheeks. "We've put our guys through the wringer, haven't we?"

"Yes, but it's part of the growing process. And what's important is that we've found our way back to them."

"I hope you're right." I don't expect everything with Aiden to be sunshine and roses, especially when the men who want their money or my head are still lingering in the shadows. But I do hope we're headed in the right direction.

In the distance, a phone rings and Hayden and I both glance around.

"You or me?" she asks as my screen lights up on the island.

"Me." And I'm not sure why, but something about receiving a call instead of a text at this time of night makes me nervous. As soon as I reach the phone, I see why. *No Caller ID*. "Crap."

"What's wrong?" Hayden frowns, but I'm already headed to the front door.

"I'll be right back." I sprint to the front porch and put the call on speaker as soon as I step outside so whoever it is doesn't hang up. "Hello?"

Aiden and his brothers stop their conversation and turn to me with questioning expressions, but it takes Aiden only a second to figure out what's going on. He's on his feet and headed toward me before a familiar voice sounds.

"Olivia! It's Lena!"

Everything in me sags in relief. "Len. Thank god. Where the heck are you calling from?"

"Home. But I'm using a prepaid phone because I accidentally drowned mine in the toilet last night. My new one won't be here until tomorrow."

Aiden pinches the bridge of his nose as his shoulders shake with silent laughter.

"That explains why you didn't text me back earlier."

"Yep. Wendell almost sent out a search party when I didn't reply to him either. That man cannot get home soon enough." She sighs, and when I gesture to Aiden's truck, indicating that I'm fine to talk alone, he nods and returns to his brothers.

"So, is he on his way back yet?" I ask as I climb into the vehicle.

"Caught his first flight earlier this afternoon. He should be in the States by morning, but he has some business in Virginia to take care of before he can come home. I pick him up from the airport here on Monday."

"That's so exciting. Please tell me you went out and bought some fancy new lingerie to wear."

She laughs. "Girl, you have no idea. I am going to blow his damn mind."

I have no doubt she'll do exactly that and then some.

"How's Aiden? Has there been any drama?"

"He's good. And no drama. Well, not really."

"What do you mean 'not really'? Did something happen?"

I tell her about the calls and the one where Aiden blew up. "I almost didn't answer tonight."

"Oh shit. I didn't mean to freak you out. I'll have my other number back tomorrow, I promise."

"It's fine. Besides, Aiden is here."

"Are you any closer to figuring out who's behind this?"

"No. But I think whoever it is has figured out I'm no longer in Milwaukee. Aiden is expecting we'll have company any time now."

"Oh god, that's scary."

I shove a hand through my hair and gaze out over the

269

lawn toward Aiden's property. "It is, but I feel safe here. It's so strange after avoiding this place for so long."

"Because you're with him?" Her voice is soft and knowing, and I can't help but smile.

"Yes. It's been amazing, Len. I mean, we still have a ton to work through, but being with him again, especially in Cole Creek... I wish I would have come home sooner." Mobster or not, I hate that Jake had to die in order for Aiden and me to have this opportunity, but I'm nonetheless grateful for it.

"I wish you had, too. You tried to be strong for so long, but as your best friend, it was obvious your heart wanted more."

She's right. My heart wanted Aiden.

"I'm proud of you for doing this, Olivia. I stand by the fact that you are the toughest cookie I know, and with Aiden on your team, these guys don't stand a chance."

I pull in a deep breath as the last of the sun slips behind the trees in the distance. "I hope you're right."

Because I'm ready for my second chance with the man I love, and I will stop at nothing to get it.

CHAPTER 29

THE KILLER

"*H*e's a cop. You can't tell me that's a coincidence."

"He's also her ex," the other guy says. "Maybe it's not a setup."

Fucking idiots, the both of them.

I swirl the bourbon around in my glass and lean back in the leather chair. "It doesn't matter who he is. He needs to be eliminated." Because I'm sick of waiting around. It's been weeks… shit, it's been years since we caught on to Jake's bullshit. I want my goddamn money.

"I say we walk," the gullible one suggests, and I snort.

"We didn't come this fucking far to walk."

"It's a million dollars," the first one says like it's pocket change. And he's right—we don't need the money—but that's not the point.

"We started this, and we're going to finish it." I don't give a damn what it takes.

"If they are trying to play us, then they're doing it because they're desperate to draw us out. They can't get to us on their own."

"The feds don't know who we are," the stupid one says, and I pinch the bridge of my nose and laugh. Sometimes I wonder why the hell we brought him on, never mind how the dumb fuck managed to earn a badge.

"He showed up here, you fucking moron." He might not have figured it all out, but he's putting the pieces together, and I'm not taking any chances. "I want him gone."

"I don't know..." He sits forward and scrubs his hands over his face. "The plan was to scare Olivia into giving us the money, not take anyone else out."

"Yeah, well, it wouldn't be the first time we changed plans, now would it?" I didn't think I'd have to put a bullet in Jake's head either, but when he wouldn't cough up what he took from us, I'd had no choice.

"He's right," the other one says. "The boss won't be fond of us taking out a cop when he's put in so much work to get on their good side."

"Their good side..." Guttural laughter rolls through my body. "There's no fucking good side with the feds. It's always gonna be us against them. And you're kidding yourself if you think the boss gives a shit about us now. The only reason he hasn't ordered a hit on all three of us is because he wants his money, too, and he's hoping we find it for him."

"It's a drop in the friggin' bucket," the mopey one mutters, and I pull my 9mm from my back so fast he doesn't see it coming until it's pointed between his eyes.

"Piss and moan one more fucking time, and I'll end you right here."

The color in his face drains but he holds his own, staring at me without wavering. "Maybe you should because this isn't what I signed up for. And I'll be damned if I'm going to spend the rest of my life in a prison cell because of your fucking ego."

The pop of the gun sounds at the same time his eyes go wide and his blood paints the basement wall behind him.

"What the fuck!" The other guy jumps from his seat, the heavy wooden chair crashing against the concrete floor. "Are you crazy?"

I shrug as the body on the other side of the table slumps forward, his bloodstained forehead hitting the wood before he falls to the floor in a lifeless heap.

"He was a liability, thinking with his lovesick little heart instead of his head." It was obvious from the second we took out Jake that he'd had his sights set on Olivia instead of the money. Can't say I blame the guy. I plan to have a little fun with her myself before this is over, too.

"What the fuck are we gonna do now?" He begins to pace, his hands flexing at his sides.

"We're gonna get our money."

He spins to face me, nostrils flaring. "What good is the money gonna be when we're locked up? When our families don't get a penny of it because the feds seized it all?"

I laugh and throw back the last of my bourbon. "We'd have to get caught for that to happen."

"How the fuck do we come out of this clean? There's a cop on the floor. A dead fucking cop."

"I didn't say we'd come out clean. I said we wouldn't get caught."

"How?" His hands fly to the top of his head. "How is that possible now?"

"We quit fucking around and do what we should have done all along. That bitch knows where the money is and she's gonna tell us, I don't care what I have to do to get it out of her."

"You're out of your damn mind."

273

"Am I? Or are you just pissed that I'm gonna be the one to get this job done once and for all?"

He frowns as I push to my feet, lift my gun, and pull the trigger a second time.

He stumbles back, trips over the fallen chair behind him, and cracks his head against the concrete wall on his way down.

A smirk curls at my lips as I tuck the gun back into my waistband.

"You don't get caught when there's no one left to snitch."

CHAPTER 30

OLIVIA

"Maybe they've moved on," I say to Aiden as we stroll into the farmers' market Saturday morning. At least a dozen tables are already set up near the entrance of the town's festival grounds, some full of produce and others piled with baked goods that are already making my mouth water.

"I don't think we'll get that lucky," Aiden replies. "If anything, I probably pissed 'em off the other day when they called."

"Ugh, I hope not." The last thing we need is to make things worse.

"Actually, I hope I did. That's the kind of fuel we need to get this done and over with."

Dread niggles in my stomach as I wave to Lorelei Kaminski, adding tomatoes and onions to the baskets on her table. "And what happens then? When this is over?"

Aiden's steps are slow as he turns to face me. "That's

something we'll have to think about, isn't it?" He strokes his thumb across my cheekbone.

"As much as I want the threats to go away, I'm enjoying this part." I curl into his touch, and he smiles.

"I am, too."

"You are now," I remind him. "But a few days ago, not so much."

"I just don't want to mess this up, that's all." He leans in and steals a kiss. "I've waited a long time to get you back in my life."

"I don't plan on going anywhere," I whisper. "It's rather comfy in your bed."

A low growl vibrates in his chest. "You keep saying things like that and we'll never leave that damn bed."

I laugh and loop my arms around his neck for a more intentional smooch. One that leaves me wishing I hadn't practically begged him for this outing today, because going back home suddenly sounds a lot more fun.

"Your old man is castrating me with his eyes," Aiden murmurs. "I'm gonna go and give Mrs. Janikowski a hand carrying her stuff before he decides to make that fantasy a reality."

I giggle and swipe the lip gloss from his lips. "Okay. But you're sticking around, right? Just in case?"

He nods. "The fire department is getting everything set up for the dance tonight, so the farthest I'll go is the next street over. I have it on good authority that your dad is packing, so you should be fine."

"I'm sure I will be." I sigh when he squeezes my hand and starts toward Mrs. Janikowski's car.

I've barely been home a week and there are still people running around who want me dead, but I'm more comfortable and content with life than I have been in forever. And all because of that man and his stolen kisses.

"You and Aiden look cozy," my mom says when I finally meander over to her table, already set up with literally every kind of vegetable imaginable and even some raspberries from my grandma's secret patch.

"Well, he's my boyfriend, so that's how we're supposed to look." I grin playfully, and my dad scoffs from the back of his truck, where he's organizing crates of extra produce.

"We forgot the extra beans, Joanna. I'm gonna run home and grab 'em. Olivia, do you think you can help your mom, or is Aiden gonna come back and suck some more of your face off?"

"Daddy!" I laugh, but his expression remains stoic. Apparently, he's still skeptical about my arrangement with Aiden... and I can't say I blame him. "Yes, I can help Mom. Go and get your beans."

He grumbles something under his breath before he hops into his truck and heads out of town toward my childhood home.

"He's not used to seeing you in this light, sweet pea. Give him some time to get used to it."

"I'm thirty-one, and I was married for nine years," I remind her. "He saw me and Jake together every single Christmas."

"That was different." Mom pastes a placating smile, and I frown. My parents don't know the truth about my marriage... do they?

"I'm not sure I understand."

She sighs as she adds the last bundle of bib lettuce to the table and then gestures to the lawn chairs behind it. "Let's sit and talk."

I nod nervously, because this was not the conversation I expected to have with her today.

"You know the only thing I've ever wanted is for you to be happy, right?" Mom smiles softly, her face shaded by the wide brim of her gardening hat. It's a perfect day with an easy breeze that casts strands of salt-and-pepper hair across her cheek, just as it flits with the hem of my sundress.

"Actually, I'm not sure I did know that," I admit, though it pains me to do it. My parents are wonderful people and they've been supportive of almost everything I've ever wanted. But they failed to realize that, as I grew and changed, so did my dreams.

I always knew I wanted to get my PhD, just like Bren always knew he wanted to be the Pine County sheriff. As a kid, I'd made it very clear that I wanted to get as far away from Cole Creek as possible, because when you're ten years old, the grass is always greener elsewhere.

My small-town heart had big-city dreams for a long time, but as I grew up, those fantasies lost their luster. I no longer cared about living in a fancy high-rise and drinking expensive wine with my smarty-pants friends, which is laughable anyway, because professors do *not* make that kind of money, but I digress.

By the time I was sixteen and coincidentally crushing on my brother's best friend, I'd realized the importance of family. Of wanting to stay close to my parents and to Bren, because they're the only family I have other than Uncle Joe and Aunt Candy.

I smooth the cotton down over my thighs and choose my next words carefully. "I know I was adamant about what I wanted to do with my life, but at some point, those dreams changed. Not entirely, but enough, and it didn't seem like you, Dad, or Bren wanted to see that."

She surveys me for a moment before glancing out over the farmers' market and its patrons, moving casually from table to table. "It's not that we didn't want to see it, Olivia. We just wanted to make sure you weren't changing your mind because your heart was trying to tell you something different."

My breath catches in my throat. "There's nothing wrong with following your heart and your head."

Her gentle smile kicks up a notch as she finds Aiden unloading Mrs. Janikowski's jelly, jam, and preserves onto her table across the way. "I know you loved him. I just didn't know he felt the same way about you until he brought you back home."

My silly heart does a somersault in my chest. "Bren doesn't know yet."

Mom nods. "No, but he isn't blind, sweetie. Even if he were, it would be hard to deny what's so obvious now."

I bite my lip as Aiden's gaze drifts my way and he smiles.

"That boy is smitten with you, Olivia Rae. And I'm sorry I didn't realize it sooner, because then maybe I wouldn't have pushed you so hard to take another path."

"I didn't…" I pause and swallow hard. "I didn't do what I did because of you and Dad. Bren either."

She turns to me with a sad knowing frown, still she asks, "And what exactly did you do?"

"Aiden and I were involved almost the entire time I was in college. But I broke things off." I curl my fingers around the edge of my dress and grip the fabric to keep my hands from shaking. "I didn't do it because I was worried that you would think he wasn't good enough for me—I did it because I didn't think *I* was enough for *him*."

"Sweetie…" Mom reaches over and squeezes my arm. "Why would you ever think that? It's obvious in the way he looks at you that isn't true."

I can't tell her about the rape because some secrets are best left unshared, and telling Aiden the truth was all that mattered, anyway. But at some point, I'm going to have to tell them all my other truth. The one that will forever weigh heavy on my heart, and the one I hope Aiden's love is strong enough to overcome.

"There are a few things that Aiden and I are still working out, but I've realized the error in my thinking, and he's been gracious enough to give me a second chance. Eventually, when the men who killed Jake are behind bars, I hope we can hash everything out and somehow find a way to put the past behind us."

Mom's fingers brush gently over my arm. "I know you cared about Jake, too. And knowing how easily your uncle lives two different lives, I suspect Jake may have been doing the same."

"I hope that's the case, but I'm not sure if I'll ever know the truth."

"I have to believe he was a decent man otherwise it's hard for me to imagine you living with him all those years," she admits, and I know the feeling all too well. It hurts my heart to think he could have played me when I'd opened myself up to him like I did. "We had a conversation once… that time he stayed with me and your dad when he was passing through for work. He told me that you were his sunshine in an otherwise cloudy world and he was so grateful to have met you."

He'd said that? Emotion builds in my chest before I realize the rest of what she's said. "Wait, what? Jake stayed with you?"

"Yes, silly. Last summer, remember? When he traveled to the Upper Peninsula for that Polish artifact for the museum?"

No, I don't remember. In fact, I don't remember Jake ever traveling for the museum, let alone visiting Cole Creek. As far as I knew, he'd never been north of Green Bay.

"When you say he stayed with you…"

She nods. "He spent the night. In your old room. You honestly didn't know about this?"

I shake my head as the already spinning wheels begin to fly.

Why hadn't Jake told me about visiting my hometown? Was it because he knew I'd been nervous to return myself?

He and my parents had always been civil, but they weren't close. I can't imagine him reaching out and asking to stay with them, let alone asking them to dinner when he passed through town.

And he'd stayed in my old room? Surely, he would have given me a hard time about teenage obsession with Ryan Gosling and the color green.

Unless, of course, he hadn't wanted me to know he'd seen any of it.

My phone beeps with a text before the thought can fully formulate in my mind, and I distractedly open the message.

My dear Olivia. You think hiding out with your cop boyfriend is going to keep you safe?

"Oh god." I press my hand to my stomach as it instantly knots.

"What's wrong?" My mom's brow furrows with concern.

"I need Aiden." I look over to Mrs. J's table, but he's not there. "Do you see him?"

"Not anymore. He was just talking to his mother. He couldn't have gone far."

Who is this? I text back with shaky fingers, and the reply comes immediately.

Ah, but telling you wouldn't make this game as fun, now would it?

I don't have what you want. I never have. Please leave me alone. And where the hell is Aiden?

Unfortunately, I can't do that. You either give me my money, or I'll be forced to take what's owed to me in other ways.

My blood runs cold and I rush to my feet so fast that the world spins around me.

"Whoa, babe, you all right?" Aiden's voice sounds from behind me just as one of his arms wraps around my waist to steady me.

"No!" I turn in his arms and shove my phone at him. "They're texting me."

His concerned expression instantly turns to ice as he reads the messages and begins to type.

"What are you saying?"

He angles the phone so I can see the screen. **Not if I have anything to say about it.**

Detective Enders. Or should I say Special Agent Enders?

"Fuck." Aiden scrubs a hand over his jaw. "I had a feeling this was what Bolinger was talking about."

"Bolinger?"

Aiden's jaw tics as he swallows. "He followed me out of the station the other day and told me he'd had a conversation with your uncle. Off the record."

"Uncle Joe? When?"

"Not sure, but Joe told him to be careful."

"What? Why?"

"Apparently not everyone involved has your best interest at heart."

"What? And what does that even mean?" More importantly, why hadn't Joe told *me* that? "Does Special Agent Nolan know about this?"

Aiden shakes his head. "I don't think so. Which makes me wonder why Joe chose to warn Bolinger instead."

Nausea rolls in my stomach as dozens of possibilities come to mind, one of which is especially disturbing. "Do you think..." I can't bring myself to say it.

"Someone on the inside knows more than they should, but I don't think it's Nolan."

I sure hope not, because I'd let him into my home. I shared very personal information with him. For god's sake, I fed him crepes!

"We can't rule it out, but I don't think Joe would have allowed him to work so closely with you if he wasn't someone who could be trusted."

"What if Bolinger is lying?" The question comes out before I really think about it, and bile rises in my throat. "Maybe he's involved, and that's why he's here."

Aiden's knuckles turn white around my phone. "That's a possibility."

"I don't like this." I don't like it one bit. From learning that Jake had been in Cole Creek to Aiden's cover being blown, my nerves are a frazzled mess.

I'd been okay. I'd rolled with the punches, and I'd keep my head above water, but it suddenly feels like I'm drowning.

AIDEN

CAL RETURNS A FEW MINUTES LATER, and despite her protests, I have him take her back to my place to calm her nerves. She's held it together fairly well through all of this, but the texts hit a nerve, and it's not hard to figure out why. Whether they know it or not, these assholes have landed in familiar territory with their threats, and there's no way in hell she will relive any part of that under my watch.

After I call Amelia and ask her to relieve Cal so he can return to help Joanna, I head to Bren's house to give him an update and finally have the man-to-man conversation that's long overdue.

I find him in his garage lubricating his bow, which I suppose is better than one of his guns, though I'm sure he has at least one stashed within reach.

"Hey, man." He glances up from the worktable with a grin that quickly turns to a scowl. "Starting to become a thing, you leaving my sister unattended."

"Relax. She's at my place with your dad, and Amelia will be there shortly so he can get back to your mom at the farmers' market."

He continues to glower as I approach, quickly spotting Liv's phone in my hand. "What's going on?"

"Liv got a few texts today, I'm assuming from the same person who tried calling earlier in the week."

He wipes his hands on a rag and exhales a heavy breath. "Okay…"

"They know I'm working with the feds."

"Fucking hell."

"Yeah." I run a hand around the back of my neck and debate whether I should tell him about Bolinger. I don't want to breach the agent's trust, but frankly, I trust Bren more than the FBI right now. "I had a chat with Special Agent Bolinger the other day…" I give him the rundown and show him the texts on Liv's phone.

"Who the hell is behind this?" Bren snaps when he hands the phone back to me. "Do you still think it's the guy from the museum?"

I shrug. "He's the only one that makes any sense, but he's obviously not working alone. The museum's vice chair owns the pub Liv and Jake used to frequent. That guy's brother-in-law is a professor at U of M. He was at the pub that night, and not the least bit happy to see Liv with someone who wasn't him. Then there's O'Reilly, the cocky fucking fed who somehow didn't see the creep in Liv's backyard. I don't know what it is about that guy, but he rubs me the wrong way."

"What about the neighbor? The other immigrant."

"He's the one guy I didn't meet, but his wife called Liv the other day when we were at the lake. She asked a lot of questions, but nothing I wouldn't expect two friends to talk about."

He eyes me for a moment before he knuckles his nose. "So, when did you plan on telling me the truth about you two?"

I survey him back and take a slow breath. He doesn't look like he's ready to kill me, but that doesn't mean much. I've seen him flip faster than a quarter plenty of times over the years. "Which truth are you referring to?" I ask carefully.

"Aren't they basically the same? You were messing around with her years ago and now you're doing it again. Same thing in my book, man."

Fuck. "I wasn't messing around then and I'm not now. I care about her."

He sticks his tongue in his cheek and glances out over his lawn. "Why didn't you tell me?"

"As kids? Because I liked having her to myself, and because she was worried about what you and your folks would think. But now... I don't want to fuck this up, man. Hell, I didn't even want it to happen until the case was over and she'd had some time to heal, but she needed something different, and I've never been good at telling her no."

He scoffs. "Yeah, well, you've never been good at taking no for an answer yourself."

"This has nothing to do with you, Bren. It never has. I know you wanted better for her, but what about what she wanted? What about what made her happy?"

He swings a scowl my way. "She *was* happy. Until her husband turned out to be a fuckup."

"No, she wasn't." Heat begins to burn up my neck. I won't spill her secrets, but I'm done hiding the truth when it comes to me and her. "She didn't stop coming home because she was too busy—she stopped because the life she was living was a lie. She knew I'd take one look at her and see the truth, and I think if you would have looked harder, you would have seen it, too."

He lifts his chin as quiet acquiesce slips over his gaze.

"I'm not saying she did everything she did because she was worried about living up to your expectations, but it damn sure played a part."

"What's that supposed to mean?"

"It means you and I both fucked up, and while I work on making things right with her, maybe you should do the same."

"Oh, and what, you're suddenly the authority on what she needs because of this case?"

I look him dead in the eye and shake my head. "I know what she needs because I love her. I have since I was eighteen, and this time around, not even you are gonna get in the way of that."

CHAPTER 31

OLIVIA

"Are the boots too much?" I bite my lip in front of the full-length mirror in Amelia's walk-in closet. Somehow, she managed to sweet-talk Aiden into letting me get ready for the street dance with her since he's so obviously been monopolizing my time and depriving me of much-needed girl talk.

"Girl, the boots are perfect with that dress!" She sidles up beside me in a navy dress that's cut a little lower in the front than my white one, but our hems are both short and sassy. "I also happen to know that my big brother has a thing for girls in cowboy boots. Just don't tell him they're mine, or he might get weirded out."

My cheeks heat and I try to laugh it off, but it's too late.

"Aww, look at you, blushing at the thought of getting my brother all hot and bothered. It'd make me nauseous if I weren't so freaking grateful that you'll keep his focus off me tonight. I swear, I can't do anything in this town without one of my brothers getting up in my business."

"I hate to break it to you, but that never changes. I'm thirty-one, and I swear Bren still treats me like I'm fifteen."

She wrinkles up her nose. "That's not what I want to hear."

"No, but eventually you'll stop caring what your brothers think, so there's that." I slip in a hoop earring as she presses her lips into a knowing smile.

"Is that what happened with you and Aiden?"

"Kinda?" I can't tell her about the case, so I choose my words carefully. "Let's just say that I've turned the phrase live and learn on its head. I learned the hard way, and now I'm ready to live." Providing, of course, someone doesn't *unalive* me first.

"Well, I'm glad to hear that, because if I know anyone else who deserves to live, it's Aiden. But don't tell him I said that or he'll get a bigger head than he already has. And that is *not* an invitation to tell me what he's packing." She shudders, and I bite back a laugh.

"Are you sure the boots don't look silly?" I give myself a once-over in the mirror and make a mental note to thank Lena for sneaking this dress into my bag.

"Not at all." Amelia loops her arm through mine and smiles at our reflection. "Just do me a favor and make sure you don't get anything funky on them later, because I can guarantee that's where my brother's mind is going to go the second he sees you tonight."

AN HOUR LATER, we arrive at the town festival grounds as the first band of the night takes to the stage. They start the night out with a George Strait classic that sends a handful of two-stepping couples out onto the asphalt to warm things up.

"Oh, and be warned that my dad doesn't dance anymore

288

because of his knees, so my mom will pull anyone she can get her hands on onto the dance floor," Amelia says as we head toward the bar, where a long line of patrons has already formed. "And knowing Aiden, he will sacrifice you to her just to avoid having to do it himself."

I chuckle as the man in question comes into view, standing off to the side of the dance area with Jinx and another Pine County deputy. He glances over as if feeling someone watching him, and his gaze immediately drifts down my body before slowly sliding back up again. When our eyes meet, he flashes a wicked grin and mouths a silent, "Wow."

"See?" Amelia bumps her shoulder into mine. "What'd I tell ya?"

"I apologize in advance for potentially exposing your boots to your brother's wily ways."

She laughs softly before she spots someone in the line ahead of us and waves. "Hey, why don't you go and give your man a proper greeting while I grab us something to drink? I'm almost positive I can cut in by Mia without anyone noticing."

"I think I'll take you up on that. Could you get me a hard seltzer?"

"Absolutely. See you in a few."

While she hurries ahead to her friend, I cut over to Aiden only to be intercepted by Jinx first.

"Hot damn, Dr. Bishop. You're looking mighty pretty tonight." He leans down and pecks my cheek, blatantly ignoring Aiden's warning to back off. "Any chance I can get your first dance tonight since this asshole will probably get your last?" He angles his head toward his brother and makes an annoyed face that earns him a hard fist to the shoulder.

"Do you need your ears checked, bro?" Aiden snags my hand and tugs me to his side. "Get your own girl."

289

"Dude, you have no idea how hard I'm trying." His eyes flick to a group of women eyeing up the shirtless firefighter climbing into the dunk tank. I can't tell who they are from this far away, but I'm pretty sure the one with auburn hair is Rachel Perry, Craig's soon-to-be ex-wife. "Anyway, we all know you don't like to dance, so think of it as me doing you a favor."

"I did you a favor by not punching you when you kissed her." He snakes an arm around my waist, and I curl into him with a light laugh. He smells amazing, like something spicy and citrusy, and he's wearing a black T-shirt that hugs his biceps and shoulders in all the right places. I would be perfectly content to snuggle close like this all night if he'd let me, which he probably would if it meant keeping his brother away.

"So, is this a thing?" The young deputy asks, shifting a grin from me to Aiden and back again. "You're the sheriff's sister, right?"

I nod and begrudgingly peel myself from Aiden to offer my hand. "Olivia Bishop."

"*Doctor* Olivia Bishop," Aiden corrects, and I roll my eyes.

"Ignore him."

The deputy smiles, his dark eyes sparkling beneath the lights strung over the dance floor. "Ty Crawford. Nice to meet you."

"And to answer your question, yes, this is a thing," Aiden says unnecessarily. "And her dance card is full."

Jinx snorts and mutters something under his breath that sounds an awful lot like, "We'll see about that," before he lifts a hand in greeting to his parents as they approach. "Be glad you missed the Polish Heritage Festival. Ma would've had you dressed up with the rest of us."

"Oh, believe me, my own mother would have insisted,

too." And as much as I'd detested the tradition as a kid, I'd probably enjoy it now.

"Hey everyone!" Janice says with a wide grin before she gives me a quick hug. "Have you seen Jesse and Hayden yet? I hope their babysitter didn't back out."

"They're probably knocking one out in the parking lot," Jinx mutters, and Janice slugs him in the same shoulder Aiden punched a minute ago.

"Justin Andrew, was that necessary?"

"Was hitting me necessary?" he counters, and Janice and Aiden simultaneously answer with a resounding, "Yes!"

The lighthearted banter continues for another hour, and Janice manages to drag everyone except Aiden onto the dance floor.

"What are the chances you'll twirl *me* around?" I tug on his arm when an upbeat song comes to an end and the familiar chords of one of my favorite country ballads begins.

"I'll always make an exception for you." He sets his beer on a nearby table and leads me to the asphalt square where at least a dozen other couples come together, as well.

"You're sure good for a lady's ego," I tease as I loop my arms around his neck and he pulls my body tightly against his, leaving no room between us. "Mmm, and you're good for my libido, too."

He chuckles and leans down, placing a line of kisses along my jaw. "Then you'll be happy to hear that Craig and Cady made up. We'll have the house to ourselves tonight."

"Ah." My fingers feather into the hair at the back of his head, and he shivers. "Does that mean we'll be ending the night early?"

"If you keep touching me like that, yes. Unless you want to show everyone in town just how real this is."

A soft giggle rises in my throat. "Bren would kill us."

"Your brother is no longer an issue."

I pull back in surprise. "He's not? Did you talk to him today?"

"He brought it up before I could."

"And?"

"And nothing. He may not be happy about it, but it's out of his hands. We're not kids anymore."

I'm not sure what I expected, but the relief in knowing there was no bloodshed is immense. "Thank you."

"For what?"

"For doing that."

He shakes his head. "I should've done it a long time ago. Maybe then—"

"Don't say it."

His pale eyes shine down on mine, and I see the fight in them. The desire to give in and forgive himself. But something inside of him won't let go.

"I love you," I whisper, and a tender smile graces his lips.

"Say it again."

"I love you, and though I hate the circumstances that brought us together again, I'm grateful for them, too." My hand curls around his bearded jaw as he swallows. "My heart has ached for you since the moment I walked away."

"Livi…" He drops his forehead to mine and closes his eyes.

"I have to believe I went through all of this for a reason, and that reason is so I could find my way back to you. If we weren't meant to put the past behind us and be together again, none of this would have happened."

"I'm not saying we can't be together…"

"I need all of you, Aiden, and you can't be one hundred percent in this if you're still blaming yourself."

He's quiet for a moment before he sighs. "You drive a hard bargain, Dr. Bishop."

"I've put myself through enough hell for one lifetime. I'm over settling for less than what I truly want."

His eyes open again, and one corner of his mouth lifts. "You're finding your spunk again. I like it."

"Yeah? Well, I have a lot of time to make up for, so be warned."

He chuckles as the song ends and another begins. We linger under the lights, in no hurry to let each other go, when someone clears their throat nearby.

"Sorry to break this up, but I am long overdue for a dance with my favorite niece."

I glance around Aiden and find Uncle Joe waiting patiently. We saw each other just a few weeks ago in Milwaukee, but it still feels like forever.

"Joe!" I let go of one man to embrace the other, so grateful for the help both have given me. "Oh my gosh, how have you been? I've been meaning to come and visit, but we haven't had time."

Joe lifts his chin to Aiden. "I see that."

Aiden lifts his hands innocently. "Hey, I'm just doing my job."

"Uh-huh. Get out of here and let me dance with my niece." Joe shoos him away, and I smile.

"It's so good to see you again. On home territory this time. How are you and Aunt Candy?"

"We're good, kiddo. How are you holding up?"

"Better than I was, thanks to Aiden."

He glances toward the Enders family. "I'm glad things are working out for you."

"Me, too. But I'd be happier if the guys who killed Jake would surface already."

Joe nods, something brewing in his dark eyes. "That's actually why I wanted a moment alone. I'll talk to Aiden, too, but I wanted to give you a heads-up first."

My feet slow until we're barely dancing at all. "What is it? Did something happen?"

"There was an incident last night at the Polish Exhibition House."

"Eli?"

Joe shrugs. "I'm not sure. But one guy is dead, and another is in the hospital in critical condition. He hasn't woken up yet to talk."

"You do know, Joe. I know you do. Why can't you tell me?"

"I actually don't, kiddo. There were a bunch of guys who got pissed at the boss and started side shenanigans. The dead guy isn't even SSP. The rebels recruited him on their own."

"If he wasn't SSP, you can tell me his name. Right?" My heart pounds so fast that my ears begin to ring. Two more people had been shot. Will I be next?

Uncle Joe hesitates, but finally gives in. "Derek O'Reilly."

And just like that, my world goes black.

AIDEN

"Why the fuck didn't you tell me?" I pace back and forth across my front porch, hands balled into fists as rage rolls through my veins. "O'Reilly was at her house every damn day. He'd been *inside* her house, Joe."

The older man hangs his head as he sits in one of my chairs with not only me waiting on answers, but Bren and Cal, too.

"I didn't find out about O'Reilly until recently, and then you came on board. Like I said, he isn't SSP, and I figured she was safe with you there."

"Would have made things a fuck of a lot easier if I would have known." For one, I would have never let the guy within a mile of Liv. And that whole cat incident? He didn't see it happen because he's the one who did it. He knew where to walk to avoid the cameras, and he'd been close enough to get back in his car and look like he'd been there the whole goddamn time.

"You knowing would have made a mess of things. Hell, the feds didn't even know, and if they had, it would have turned everything upside down and drawn this out even longer. I couldn't do that to Olivia."

Cal scoffs. "All I've got to say is that you're lucky Aiden was there, because if you would have left her to fend for herself, you'd be the one on life support right now."

Joe's face turns pale as he glances from Cal to Bren. "I would have never let that happen. Even if it meant going against the SSP."

Bren lifts a hand. "Look, I understand the mob is like family, but we're blood."

"And that's why I've done everything I can to help. You think this is easy for me?" Joe shakes his head and then scrubs his hands over his face. "It's not all bad, you know. Even Jake… he got himself messed up in some shit, but he was a decent guy."

My lip curls. "If he was such a decent guy, we wouldn't be having this conversation right now. Liv's life wouldn't be in danger, and she wouldn't be so fucking stressed that she passed out."

The front door creaks open and her mom steps out onto the porch, her arms wrapped around herself. "She's feeling better now that she's had something to eat."

A collective sigh of relief moves across the porch like a wave.

"But I'm not happy about this, Joe," her mom continues

on. "You promised you would never bring your lifestyle to my doorstep."

He gets to his feet and goes to his sister, wrapping her up in a hug even though she resists. "Jojo, this wasn't me, I swear. All I've done is try to keep our family safe."

The desperation in the guy's voice... the sincerity... it annoys me as much as it eases my mind. I wish he'd told me about O'Reilly, but I know the position he's in made it difficult. He did what he could do without jeopardizing his loyalty to the SSP, which would have landed him in the morgue, not just the hospital. More than that, he made the decision he did because he trusted me to do what he couldn't. I have to respect that.

"Look, it's been a long night. Let's give Liv some time to rest, and we can figure out where to go from here in the morning." I squeeze the back of my neck, trying to ease the tension.

"All right." Cal pushes off the railing and gives Joe a stern glance as he passes by to collect Joanna. "Don't think I was kidding about what I said before. If something happens to my daughter—"

"Dad." Bren claps his old man on the shoulder and urges him toward the steps. "I think we've said enough for one night."

One by one, they all head to their cars until the only vehicle left in the driveway is mine.

Blowing out a breath, I retreat to the house and activate the security system before shutting off the lights and making my way to the bedroom.

The bedside lamp is on, casting Liv's face in a pretty golden glow as she sleeps quietly, looking far more at ease than she had earlier, when I'd picked her up off the asphalt.

Anxious to hold her, I get undressed, shut off the lamp, and climb in behind her.

296

"Hi," she whispers sleepily. "I've missed you."

I press a kiss to her shoulder and hook an arm around her waist. "It's only been an hour, babe."

"Too long."

I bury my face in her hair and laugh quietly. "Well, I'm here now. Go back to sleep, Sleeping Beauty."

"Okay." She sighs. "I love you."

I smile, because even with all the noise in my head and all the unknowns of this case, something about those three little words on her lips promises it's going to be all right.

"I love you, too," I whisper back, and then I close my eyes and follow her to dreamland.

CHAPTER 32

OLIVIA

*A*iden's soft snores and warm breath puff against my neck as he sleeps soundly behind me. So soundly, in fact, that not even Gertie's incessant scratching at the back door, complete with throwing her food dish around like the diva she is, has caused him to so much as stir.

It's just as well, because I'm thirsty anyway.

Slipping carefully from the bed, I creep out of the bedroom and close the door quietly behind me. No sense in both of us being up with the cat.

I push the buttons on the alarm and disengage the system before I unlock the door and flip the light on for the backyard.

"Come on, Gert. Get your fluffy butt in here," I rasp into the night. But the black-and-white terror is nowhere to be seen. Her dish, however, is a good ten feet into the grass, which is consistent with the clanking and banging I'd heard.

Sighing, I pad out into the yard in my bare feet, panties, and tank top, praying that no one other than Aiden has access to his surveillance footage, or worse, that I somehow get locked out for hours while he snores.

A flash of movement to my right has me damn near jumping out of my skin before Gertie starts traipsing over from the woodpile.

"You are so sassy," I tell her. "Come in the house and eat before we get stuck out here."

Suddenly, she stops dead in her tracks and begins to back away. I give an annoyed huff, because it's not like she doesn't know me. She's been in the house hanging out with me every single day.

"Gertie, you're such a pain in my—"

Out of nowhere, a hand slaps across my mouth, pulling me back against a hard chest. "Ass?" a low, gravelly voice sounds in my ear. "You mean like you are to me?"

Complete panic surges through my body as the cool metal from a gun presses into my temple, but when I try to scream, nothing comes out.

"Just relax, Dr. Bishop, and this won't be as painful."

That voice... oh my god, that voice!

"In fact, maybe you'd be more comfortable if we went inside. I might even let him watch."

He begins pushing me toward the back door, giving me no time to get my feet beneath me, and I stumble, almost face-planting in the grass before he yanks me up with a fistful of hair.

"Don't play fucking games with me, Olivia," he seethes in my ear, and bile rises on my throat. "I've waited far too long for this as it is, and I am in no mood to prolong it."

"H-how could you?" I cry, my voice shaky and hoarse. "You w-were my friend."

"I was never your friend. But Jake... Jake had been my friend until he fucked me over." Troy jerks hard on my hair again, and I bite my tongue against the pain. "You... you were nothing more than a fantasy. A fantasy I couldn't fucking have because he would have killed me as soon as I touched you."

Hot tears burn in my eyes as we reach the back door. I know I should shut my mouth and cooperate, because if I don't, he might hurt Aiden, too.

But I've come too far not to fight like hell. And even if it blows up in my face, I know it's what Aiden would want me to do.

"Jake may be gone, but Aiden isn't. If you touch me, he'll kill you, too."

"I'm touching you right now, Olivia, and where is he? Where is your big, bad boyfriend?" His laugh is venomous in my ear, and I shiver straight down to my core. "You've never been more than a piece of ass to him. Haven't you figured that out by now?"

"Haven't you figured out that you're not going to get what you want? I don't have your money."

"Oh, I know. I'd really hoped you did so it wouldn't come to this, but now that it has, I'm a little excited. If I can't have the money, at least I can have the girl."

He pushes his crotch into my ass and the feel of his erection makes me physically ill. Vomit fills my mouth and I gag.

"What the fuck?" he pushes me forward when I heave and my hands slam into the back door as vomit spews from my mouth. "You disgusting fucking slut."

His hand winds in my hair again, tugging me away from the door just as it opens and Aiden appears, gun drawn.

"Let her go, McAllister."

"Oh, look who decided to join the fun." Troy jams his weapon against my skull again. "The thing about this game is that we play by my rules, Detective. Or Special Agent. Whatever the fuck you are."

"I don't think so." Aiden steps out onto the sidewalk, and Troy takes a clumsy step back as well.

"I'd suggest you stop, or I'll shoot her in the fucking head like I did Jake and O'Reilly."

"Don't forget about Krol," Aiden mutters. "Then again, from what I hear, you missed."

"I don't miss, asshole. I get what I go after every fucking time, and right now, it's her."

Aiden shakes his head confidently. "Not on my watch."

Troy laughs and the action has him loosening his hold just enough for me to drop my head and shoulders, and for the sound of a single gunshot to echo through the quiet night.

Troy's hold on me disappears a second before his body hits the grass with a lifeless thud.

I feel myself going down after him, but Aiden catches me before I hit the ground.

The last thing I feel before everything becomes blurry is the warmth of his tears pressed against my cheek as the most precious words I've ever heard fall from his lips...

"It's over, baby. It's finally over."

AIDEN

AFTER I GAVE Special Agent Bolinger and Bren my statement and they both put me on administrative leave, I head over to the Bishop's house to check on Liv. Deputy Crawford brought her over when my backyard turned into a crime scene, because the last place I wanted her to be was near the body of the man who'd made her life a living hell for weeks.

He hadn't worked alone, but he'd been the one who'd pulled every trigger and he'd left Krol in rough enough shape that the guy would never wipe his own ass again, let alone be a threat.

Cal opens the door before I even knock and gives me a hug instead of his usual backslap. "How you doing, son?"

I nod. "I'm all right. How's Liv?"

"Okay, I think. She's upstairs. Joanna gave her something to sleep, but knowing her, she didn't take it."

"Mind if I check on her?"

"Not at all. Wouldn't hurt you to get some sleep, too."

"Thanks, Cal. I appreciate you looking after her."

"Yeah, well, the same goes for you. I'd say you did more than look after her." Something awfully close to gratitude and affection shimmers in his eyes, and the realization clogs my throat. I've always known I could give Liv what she needed, but somehow, I'd needed him to know that, too.

With another humble nod, I head upstairs and quietly sneak into Liv's room only to find her sitting on the floor at the side of her bed. There's some kind of antique-looking box next to her and a few pieces of paper in her hand.

"Hey," I say as I sit down beside her and take in her wet, tearstained cheeks. "You okay?"

She shakes her head. "Not really."

"That's understandable. You were really fucking brave tonight. It's okay to not be okay."

She sniffles and clears her throat. "I forgot to tell you something earlier. At the farmers' market."

"What's that?"

"My mom mentioned that Jake had stopped here once while he was traveling through for work. He spent the night."

"Okay..." I wait for her to continue.

"He never told me he visited. In fact, as far as I knew, he'd never been to Cole Creek." She hands me the papers. "He was here so he could leave this."

"What is it?"

"The reason he did it all."

My dearest Olivia,

If you're reading this letter, my assumption is that you've gone home because I am no longer there to hold you back.

I can only imagine the way I was removed from your life, and right now, you probably think I deserved it. Maybe I did. But sometimes we have to make choices to protect the people we love, no matter the cost. You, my wife, will understand that better than most.

My guess is that my life ended at the hands of the men I've involved myself with. Men I, in no way, trusted, but had to align myself with in order to achieve my goal. Olivia, I must be honest with you, and tell you now that I've likely done everything I've been accused of. It was the only way I could keep a promise I made years ago, before we ever met.

You see, Olivia, my beloved Krystyna didn't just pass—she was killed because I made a foolish mistake. I promised to keep her safe, but I let my guard down and then she was gone. The men I was involved with then were far worse than the ones I've been involved with

303

now, and they spared no mercy. You know her death was brutal, and you know the guilt I've carried because of it. I was supposed to protect her—a vow I'd made to her family—and I acted selfishly instead. I wanted her for myself, and my greed cost me everything.

If I'm gone, my guess is they want their money. The truth is, I never kept a penny. I sent all of it back home to Krystyna's family. You know she was the primary caretaker for her parents, and without her, they've suffered. And I blame myself for that. So, I took money from the organization that ultimately took her, and I made things right.

I realize my actions may have put you in danger now, but I have it on good authority that you'll be safe, and I have to trust that you have good people in your corner, even if they walk a little left of center from time to time.

I love you, Olivia. I didn't think I'd ever care for another woman like I did Krystyna, but you own a piece of my heart, too. You accepted me at my worst, and you helped shoulder my pain, all the while carrying your own. You are the strongest person I know, and I can't thank you enough for lending me that strength all these years.

But now I need you to be even stronger. I

don't want your forgiveness or your grief, because I don't deserve either. You, however, deserve so much more than you've allowed your-self. I don't regret our time together or the chance you gave me, but I do regret that, in partnering with you, I kept you from the kind of love you truly deserve.

I'm begging you, sweetheart, to forgive your-self. And we both know the only way you'll ever truly be able to do that is by telling Aiden the truth. Even the parts that still hurt, because he is the only one who can help you heal once and for all.

Thank you for giving me a second chance at life and for trusting me with your secrets. I hope you can understand why I had to keep mine.

Zawsze będę cię kochać,
Jakub

Holy shit.

Liv glances up at me, her eyes red and her cheeks stained with endless tears. "He knew it was coming."

My jaw tics as I nod. "Sounds that way." Sounds like he might not have been the asshole I'd pegged him to be either, just like Joe had said.

Olivia covers her face in her hands, the tears coming harder and harder until she can barely breathe. It's all I can do to hold her and offer her comfort, because it's fucking gutting me, too. To know that she not only married another man, but that she gave him a big part of herself, too. They may not have had the kind of love we do, but he was important to her, and in the mess he'd left for her, she'd never had the chance to grieve. Until now.

"I'm sorry," I whisper into her hair. There's so much more I could say. So many questions I could ask. But nothing is going to help her more than simply being here for her like I should have been all those years ago. Like he'd been for her when I couldn't.

"I feel like I betrayed him," she cries softly, and her words feel like a knife to the chest. "I assumed the worst when I found out he was involved with the mob. I thought he lied to me about everything, and that wasn't true at all."

Maybe not, but he still put her life in danger. His reasoning may have been well intentioned, at least where his ex's family was concerned, but he could have handled matters with Liv a hell of a lot better.

"He still put you in harm's way, Liv. Noble intentions or not, you could have been hurt. Hell, you *were* hurt. And let's not forget that you've lived in fear for the past two months, too."

"I-I know. But we both made ch-choices we thought were best at the time."

I should bite my damn tongue, but this is the woman I love we're talking about. "He chose someone else's well-being over yours, Liv. That's never going to be okay in my book."

She's quiet for a moment before she says softly, "Sometimes we have to make hard choices. Choices that will haunt us forever."

I frown down at her. "What are you talking about?"

She pulls in a shuddery breath before she gets to her feet, goes to her overnight bag, and takes out a leather-bound book I saw in her room in Milwaukee and on the nightstand in my room every day since she started staying with me. I assumed it was a journal, so I left it alone.

Reclaiming her spot beside me, she opens to the beginning of the book, and the first thing I notice is the date at the top of the page. Ten years and a few months ago.

"I started this in the hospital the night I was raped," she explains, her voice clear but still thick with pain. "The sexual assault advocate brought it for me so I could write down everything I was feeling. Memories, too, in case I decided to go to the police."

My hands ball into fists as I listen. Part of me wants to snatch the journal from her hands and read every last word, and another part wants to take the fucking thing outside and set it on fire.

"I ended up using it for something else." She turns the page and a glossy, black-and-white image slides free. I immediately recognize it as a sonogram picture like the one Jesse had put on his fridge while Hayden had been pregnant with Jett.

And my blood runs ice cold.

"I had a lot of pain after the assault, and there'd been blood, too. I thought it was just my period, but the emergency room doctor wanted to be sure the attack hadn't hurt me in other ways. And that's when…" She chokes on her words and the tears she's held in break free. "That's when I found out I was pregnant, Aiden. *We* were pregnant."

"What?" I had to have heard her wrong. She didn't just say…

"The doctors said the assault and the trauma likely initiated the bleeding, but it would have happened sooner or later on its own."

I jolt to my feet, hands tugging wildly at my hair, because holy fuck, *she'd been pregnant*. With my baby.

"It was an ectopic pregnancy," she rasps, her voice filled

with so much shame. "I was twelve weeks along, and my tube had ruptured. There was nothing they could do."

Jesus Christ. As if surviving a vicious rape hadn't been enough, she's gone through a miscarriage on her own, too. What the hell else could the world possibly throw at her?

"I can't have children," she whispers. "The ultrasound also revealed that I only have one ovary, so the surgery… it took away my only chance."

The deepest, soul-crushing pain I have ever known washes over me, and my knees hit the floor in front of her.

I could have lost her forever. That pregnancy could have taken her from me, and maybe it makes me selfish or even cruel, but if losing our baby meant I'd get this second chance with her, I would choose her over and over again.

"I'm so fucking sorry, Livi," I say into her hair as I gather her close. "I'm so sorry you had to go through that by yourself."

We hold each other for what feels like hours before she pulls back, bloodshot eyes searching mine. "Does it change how you feel about me?"

"What?" I rear back in confusion. "Why would it change anything?"

"I can't give you a family," she whispers like it might somehow make her less in my eyes, and I almost laugh, not because it's funny, but because I clearly have more work to do than I thought.

"I would choose you in any storm, Livi. No matter how battered or bruised."

She closes her eyes and I swear I can feel the fear leave her body as she sags against me.

"There's nothing strong enough to keep us apart, and if we've learned anything from this, it's that."

CHAPTER 33

AIDEN

"*T*ime to put the work away, handsome. Your mother made me promise we wouldn't be late, and I can't let her down on my very first Sunday dinner with the family."

"Eh, she'll get over it. I've been showing up late for years." I set my laptop aside and smile. Liv, in turn, rolls her eyes.

"That's what I'm saying. I promised her I would help you change your ways, and you're not making it easy."

"Making promises on my behalf was your first mistake, babe. You know you're the only one I bend for."

"That's kinda why I thought I could convince you." She bites her lip in that adorable way she does and then shrugs. "I even made peach cake."

"Wait, wait, wait…" I get to my feet and move around my desk, my stomach already growling. "You made peach cake? And didn't tell me?"

"I couldn't risk you eating it."

I hold up two fingers and grin. "Second mistake."

"Huh?" Liv steps aside as I exit my office on a direct path for the kitchen. "Where are you... Aiden Enders, do not touch that cake!"

The slap of her sandals follows me down the hall, but it's too late. The second I spot the cake pan on the counter, it's on.

I lift it above her head, laughing a little harder every time she tries to jump to reach it.

"Aiden, come on. I promised your mom I'd bring dessert."

"We'll stop at the store and grab ice cream. But this cake? It's mine." And pretty soon, she will be, too.

She stomps her foot and crosses her arms over her chest. She's wearing that pink sundress I love so much, and her hair is twisted up into a messy bun, which is probably for the best.

"Take off your dress."

"Excuse me?" Her mouth drops open and her dark eyes narrow.

"Take. Off. Your. Dress. And maybe, just maybe, I'll save some of the cake."

"Blackmail is illegal, you know." She makes a snobby face, and I chuckle.

"Not in this house it isn't. Now do as I say."

"Or what? You'll eat the whole cake yourself? Fine, go ahead. Be a pig. I hope you get sick."

"Not a chance." I set the pan down only to grab her around the waist and pull her against me. I've been hard since she walked into my office and there's no way she can miss it.

"We do not have time for this," she protests, but her voice is already softer. Her pupils are dilated, too.

"Just one little piece. That's all I want."

The slightest smile tips her lips. "Of me or the cake?"

"Can't I have both?"

In a matter of seconds, we're both naked and clawing at each other like we didn't just make love this morning.

"We are going to be in so much trouble," Liv pants as she flicks her tongue over one of my nipples and wraps her hand around my cock.

"It'll be worth it." With one arm around her waist, I lift her onto the counter, and she gives a yelp.

"It's cold up here!"

"Not for long." Flashing a feral grin, I flip the lid off the cake and reach in for a handful.

"Aiden, don't you dare!" Liv's eyes go wide as she watches me smear the cake across her chest and then straight down to the center of her legs.

"Like I said, I want you *and* the cake." So, I have them both, right there on the kitchen counter.

Licking and teasing, I make my way along the path from one nipple to the other until Liv's hands are wild in my hair and every part of her trembles.

"This is so wrong," she cries, even as she tugs my head to where she wants me, all the while watching me devour her sweet flesh. "God, I love it."

I smile into the valley between her tits before I begin my descent. "You know what I love even more than peach cake?"

"Torturing me?"

"Your pussy. Can't imagine any sweeter treat than having both at the same time."

"*Unngh.*" She groans as she pushes my head down faster to meet her rising hips. The moment my tongue finds her clit, her head falls back and the lowest, sexiest moan I've ever heard reverberates through the house.

"So good," I growl as I lick her clean, careful not to get

cake in places it doesn't belong. "Fuck, I could eat you for every meal."

"Keep that up and I might let you." Her hips continue to pulse against my face as I tease and play, until she lets out a soft plea for more.

"You want me inside? Is that what you need?" I don't bother waiting for an answer. I stand, lift her from the counter, and follow her down onto the rug. I'm buried inside of her a second later, our bodies slapping together with desperate thrusts as we fuck.

"Yes, oh god, yes!" Liv's nails score down my back as her back arches and her pussy grips my cock for all its worth. She cries out with abandon, and my vision fades.

"I'm gonna come," I grunt, trying so fucking hard not to let go until she's finished.

"Not inside me," she says frantically, and I pull out before it's too late. "I want you in my mouth."

Sweet baby friggin' Jesus.

She's on her knees in front of me a second later, her mouth full of my dick. Two pumps is all it takes, and I unload down her throat before I even realize there's cake on her face.

"Did you just…?"

She flashes a crooked grin, licks her lips, and swipes a little piece of peach into her mouth. "You made it sound so good."

Fucking hell, this woman.

OLIVIA

"So, what's the plan now that you're in the clear?" Jinx asks me later that afternoon on his parents' back deck. "Are you gonna come to your senses and leave this guy? Maybe look for a younger man."

Aiden snorts. "She's not leaving me, bro, and if she did, it sure as hell wouldn't be for you."

I wrinkle my nose at Jinx. "I'm sorry, but he's right. I just got him back, and I'm not ready to trade him in quite yet."

"Quite yet?" Aiden scoffs. "How about never?"

Hayden giggles. "I have a feeling you two are going to end up married before we are."

"You're probably right about that." Aiden winks at me. "But we'll see how it goes."

Uh-huh. It's only been a month since Troy showed up in Cole Creek, but my schedule for the fall and Aiden's work have forced us to make several important decisions on rather short notice.

"I've decided to move back to Cole Creek," I announce, and Janice gives a whoop of approval from inside the house.

"I'm not eavesdropping!" she adds. "Just cleaning up, I swear!"

Jesse rolls his eyes. "Yeah right, Ma. You know what happens when you lie, right?"

Jett's eyes go big. "Your nose is gonna grow, Grammy!"

"You tell her, little man."

I laugh and continue on. "After good feedback from my students, the dean agreed to let me teach virtually on a regular basis. I will have to go down to Milwaukee for meetings and whatnot, but most of my work will be done online."

"I loved that so much," Hayden says. "It worked out so well when Jett was little."

Aiden and I share a quiet smile. We haven't told anyone about my infertility, because it turns out it's not as important to him as I thought it would be. Yes, we'd each hoped to have a family someday, but finding each other again is proving to be plenty for both of us right now.

"How about you?" Amelia prods at Aiden's chair with her sandal. "What badge are you going to carry, hotshot?"

Aiden takes a pull from his beer and then exhales. "Well, it turns out I can have both. I'm going to stay up here and continue working for the county as my primary, but if the feds need me for something, I'll be there for them, too. Turns out I like working with small-town assholes better than big-city ones."

"And it turns out I missed my family more than I'd realized," I add. "Even Bren."

Aiden groans. "Not me. I definitely didn't miss him."

"You've seen him every day!" I swat his arm, and he nods.

"That's what I'm saying!"

"How do you think we feel about you, man?" Jinx asks, and Jesse snorts.

"You better be careful over there." Aiden points his beer at his eldest sibling. "Especially since you're gonna be seeing a lot more of me soon enough."

"Oh yeah? Why is that?"

I waggle my eyebrows at Hayden. "Because we're going to be neighbors!"

She shrieks, and Amelia falls back in her chair laughing as Jesse bites off a curse we all know he doesn't truly mean.

"And when is that supposed to happen? I don't have you on the calendar for any dirt work, and I'll be damned if I'm digging for you in the winter."

"Actually…" Hayden raises her hand. "They are on your schedule. I added them last week. I just didn't get around to telling you yet."

He tries to glare at her, but he can't keep the grin from his face.

"Well, then I guess congratulations are in order." He gets to his feet and raises his beer, and one by one, the rest of us follow. "To Aiden and Olivia... May the home you build together be as strong as the one we were raised in."

Jinx smiles, and Amelia sniffs back a tear. Aiden... well, he wraps his arm around my shoulders and kisses the top of my head.

"Welcome to the family, babe. I hope you grow to love this crazy bunch as much as I do."

CHAPTER 34

ONE MONTH LATER...

AIDEN

"*A*re we really doing this?" A giddy smile spreads across Liv's face as we stand on the front steps of the Pine County Courthouse with our marriage license in hand. The only things missing are the signatures that will make it official.

I reach up and tuck a lock of dark hair behind her ear, as the late September wind kicks up and teases the long strands against her face. "We sure are. Unless you're getting cold feet?"

"Not a chance, handsome." She presses up on her toes and sweeps her lips across mine just as someone clears their throat behind us.

"Pretty sure you're supposed to wait until the judge pronounces you man and wife, bro." Jesse claps me on the back, and Hayden rolls her eyes.

"Ignore him. He clearly doesn't know what he's talking

about, considering he gave me a child before he ever even thought about giving me a ring."

"Hey now," my brother protests. "You were the one who came to town and seduced me. There was no time for a ring."

Liv giggles. "Does the order of things really matter when things work out how they're supposed to in the end?"

I pull her in for another kiss. "I love the way you think, woman."

She slaps my ass. "Good. Now, let's get inside so you can give me your last name."

"Yes, ma'am."

Ten minutes later, the clerk calls us back to Judge Marshall's chambers. Only, the man sitting at the judge's desk is not the burly old man I've sat in court with countless times over the past decade.

"Good afternoon, folks," my best friend says, as he rocks back in the judge's chair like he owns the damn place. "I heard a rumor you two might be dropping in today—on the sly like you apparently do everything."

"Bren, you are out of your mind if you think you're going to stop me from getting married today," Liv says through gritted teeth, and her brother tips his head back and gives a bellow of laughter.

"Oh, baby sister, you have no idea." His gaze, still amused but also a bit spiteful, locks on mine. "Did you really think I'd let you just up and marry my only sibling, Enders?"

Liv stomps forward, her simple white dress swinging around her thighs as her hands ball into fists at her sides. "Brendan Callum Bishop, we are *not* doing this today."

He rises from the chair and comes around the desk. Curiously, he's dressed almost as nicely as I am in slacks and a button-down instead of his usual Pine County Sheriff's Office attire.

"You really love this guy?" he asks her, lifting his chin toward me, but never taking his eyes off her.

"You know I do."

He surveys her for a long moment, his jaw pulsing beneath his ginger beard. "All right. That's all I needed to hear."

The clerk clears her throat and hands Bren a book. "Here you go, Sheriff."

And that's when it clicks. Holy shit.

"Man, are you serious?" My voice is low from the sudden pressure in my chest.

"If I can't be your best man, I figured maybe you'd let me be the minister instead."

Liv gasps, and Jesse chuckles behind us. "Shit, I forgot about that."

"Forgot about what?" Liv demands.

"He's ordained," I explain, and Bren beams like a damn kid.

"Figured it might come in handy someday, and low and behold, here we are."

Liv glances from me to him and back again with tears in her eyes. "Are you serious? He can legally marry us?"

"Yep." And to be honest, I wish I'd thought of it myself. "What do you say, Dr. Bishop? You okay with this guy pronouncing us Mr. and Dr. Enders?"

She waves her hands in front of her face, but I'm not sure if she's trying to keep from crying or laughing. "Who would have thought this is how we'd end up?"

Taking her hands into mine, I stroke my thumbs across her knuckles and the engagement ring we picked out together a week ago. It was a spur-of-the-moment decision, but then again, it really wasn't.

"I knew," I tell my soon-to-be wife as our eyes meet, and from the way she looks at me, she knew, too.

Life may have led us down different paths, but Liv and I were always destined for more than memories…

We were destined for forever.

EPILOGUE

TWO YEARS LATER...

OLIVIA

"*A*re you serious?" Aiden's blue eyes go as wide as mine as we stare down at the bathroom counter in complete shock.

For twelve and a half years, I'd convinced myself that it didn't matter if this day never came. That I would find other ways to fill the void of never being a mother, much less never being the mother to Aiden's children.

But here we are, more in love than we've ever been and about to celebrate our second wedding anniversary with the one thing we thought might never happen.

I pick up my phone and scroll to the first of Jasmine's texts from just a half hour ago. "She said her water broke two hours ago, and when she got to the hospital, she was already two centimeters dilated. This is happening, babe. Maybe even today."

"Holy fuck." Aiden's face goes unexpectedly pale for a guy who takes down bad guys for a living. "I don't have the car seat in the car yet. Shit, do you think we have enough diapers? Maybe we should stop on our way down and grab more."

I laugh and reach up to cup his face in my hands. "Babe, we have plenty of diapers. But we may not have a lot of time." Jas is a first-time mom, but she is two weeks early, so who knows how fast or slow this might go.

"Oh shit. It's a four-hour drive. Are we even packed?" He glances to our bedroom in a panic, and I laugh again.

He's been the calm one through all of this. The voice of reason when my nerves got the best of me, and I worried that Jasmine would change her mind about the adoption. I should have expected that he'd be the one to freak out when the big day actually arrived.

"I'll throw some clothes and toiletries in a bag for us if you can put the car seat and the bag for the baby in the car. I filled the car with gas last night, so we shouldn't have to worry about that. And we can call our parents once we're on the road."

He nods as resolute focus quickly replaces the panic. "Right. Okay. Car seat and bag. I can do that."

"Good." I push up onto my toes and press a kiss to his lips. "I love you."

"I love you more." He snakes his arms around my waist as a nervous laugh rolls through his body. "Holy shit, we're gonna be parents."

"I know. Who'd have thought?"

"Me," he confesses as he pulls back and smooths the hair from my face. "Always knew you'd be one helluva mom."

Fast emotion burns in my throat, and I wave a hand in front of my suddenly watery eyes. "We do not have time for tears right now!"

"Shit. Right." He jumps back and points to the nursery across the hall. "Car seat and baby bag. I'm on it."

Four and a half hours later, a kind nurse who reminds me of Lena tapes wristbands to our wrists before she takes us back to Jasmine's birthing suite.

The pretty blonde opens her eyes and smiles when she sees us, and that simple gesture makes me tear up. I still can't believe this is happening. That the stars aligned the way they did, and Jas chose us to raise her baby.

"Hi, Dr. Enders," she says sweetly before she grimaces with a contraction. "Oh, jeez, they're getting stronger now. Thank god for epidurals."

The nurse by her monitors nods. "They're coming fast, too. I should recheck your progress."

"I was six centimeters last time," Jas explains, and Aiden goes pale.

"There are only ten, right?"

"Yep, we're getting close." The nurse snaps on a glove and Jas lets her legs fall apart so she can check.

"Ah, maybe I should step out." My poor husband turns for the door, but I grab his arm and tug him back to me. We talked about this countless times over the past few weeks, and Jasmine even insisted he be in the room when she delivered, because she wanted him to have the full *new-dad* experience.

"You're nine, girl. Ten is going to come in no time, so we'd better get the doctor here." The nurse grins as she tosses the gloves in the trash and starts for the door. "I'll be right back, folks. If she starts to push, you know what to do, right?"

Aiden's eyes go wide, and I laugh. "She's kidding. I think."

Jas waves it off like an old pro instead of a first-timer. "We got this. Again, all things are possible when you're mostly numb from the waist down."

Aiden and I make our way to the other side of the bed

when it occurs to me that Jas is alone. "I thought your mom was supposed to be here."

She wets her lips and breathes through another contraction before she answers. "She brought me in but decided not to stay. She didn't want to be in the way."

"Oh. There's plenty of room. We don't mind—"

"She was afraid she'd get attached," Jas interrupts. "You know, if she saw the baby and whatnot."

Aiden's hand tightens around mine before he clears his throat. "We talked about that, Jas. If your family wants to be a part of this baby's life, we're open to that."

Jasmine's dark eyes fill with tears. "I know. And eventually, we will be. But I don't know if it's a good idea right now."

This poor girl. My heart has hurt for her from the day she came into my office during office hours and broke down in tears. She'd found out she was pregnant one week and the very next her boyfriend had been killed in a car accident. She'd been scared but so freaking brave, and I'd seen so much of myself in her.

A month later, she came back and told me she'd decided to put the baby up for adoption, because she wasn't ready to be a mom on her own. She'd talked to her family, and though they'd been apprehensive at first, they came around.

Jas had asked if I knew anything about how the adoption process worked, and I think I knew in that moment how this all would end. Aiden and I had been researching our options for a few months, so I shared what I knew. It took Jas two days to come back and ask if I'd be her baby's mother.

The rest happened just as fast. Aiden and Jas met and immediately hit it off. It helped that the baby's biological father had been in the police academy, so they'd bonded over that. And with Jas's plans to teach English as a second language overseas, we really couldn't have been a better match. We could give her baby the life that she would have liked to if things had been different for her.

"I love you guys," Jas rasps as she wipes her tears. "And I don't want you to worry that I'm going to change my mind, so I think it's best if I give you time and space to love this baby and start your family. When the time is right for me to become more involved, we'll know it."

I pull in a shaky breath and let go of Aiden's hand to take hers. "We love you, too. And we'll do this in whatever way you need."

She smiles as a single tear slips down her cheek. "You know, I told Jamie about you. About how much I looked up to you and wanted to be like you someday."

"Oh, Jas…"

"He'd want this, too, I know he would." She squeezes my hand just as the doctor strolls into the room with a wide grin.

"I hear we're having a baby today, folks." She glances at the monitor just as another contraction comes and Jas's hold on me tightens.

"Oh, this is a big one," she grunts. "Something is definitely happening."

The doctor chuckles as she pulls up a stool and a handful of nurses pile into the room. "Let's bring this little one into the world, shall we?"

AIDEN

"Is it weird that I think he looks like you?"

I glance down at our son, swaddled in a hospital blanket with a blue-and-pink-striped hat covering his mess of light-brown hair. There's a tiny divot in his chin, and his eyelashes are so long they touch his cheeks.

"He's way better looking than me, babe. And if he ends up with Jas's dark eyes, chances are he'll look more like you."

Liv snuggles in close to me and rests her head on my shoulder. "What do you think, Jameson? Are you going to look like either of us, or are we just crazy?"

"Crazy in love, for sure." He's only been here for a couple of hours, but I already love this boy with everything in me. I remember Jesse saying something similar after Jett was born, and I thought he was being dramatic. Turns out I'm just as guilty. But there's no shame in this kind.

"No doubt about that." Liv reaches out and strokes a finger down Jameson's cheek, and his little pink lips purse in his sleep. "He really is perfect, isn't he?"

"Just like his mama." I lean over and take her mouth in a kiss. "I love you, Livi."

"I love you more."

"Not a bad anniversary present, huh?"

Liv smiles against my lips. "Not bad at all."

~THE END~

If you enjoyed this story and want to keep up to date on the next Cole Creek book, please **join my mailing list**!

Jinx's book, *Measure of a Man*, is up next, and if you were paying attention, you've probably figured out that he's about to fall hard and fast for Cole Creek's newest single mom. I wonder what Craig will think about that. **wink**

I'd love to stay connected on social media, too!
Join **Molly's Misfits (my reader group)** on Facebook!

MORE BOOKS BY MOLLY

ACKNOWLEDGMENTS

First and foremost, I have to thank Sandra all the late night chats and about this book and this series. From plot to character names to cover pics, you have been my go-to girl for all things Cole Creek, and I cannot thank you enough. Sending you all the love, girl!

To Kat, Jessica, and Kaylee for the early eyes on this story… multiple times over. I appreciate your insight and your patience, and the fact that you're always honest. Hugs to you all!

To Libby… if you haven't already read the dedication, go do that. You'll find your message there. xo

To Mason Castello and Stacy Powell for the amazing cover pic. You were both such a pleasure to work with, and I couldn't be happier with the outcome. Mason and Bri, I adore you both, and I am so grateful to have met you through this experience. Can't wait to see what the future brings you two!

To my readers for their patience with this book, as well. It took me a while to find my stride because life has been completely crazy, so if you're reading this, you've likely stuck with me through it all. I appreciate you so much!

Lastly, to my husband. Fuck, life is hard, isn't it? You keep supporting me, and I'll keep supporting you, and together, we will get through this. I love you, babe.

ABOUT THE AUTHOR

Molly McLain lives in a tiny Wisconsin town with her husband, three kiddos, and two adorable German Short-haired Pointers. She's addicted to 80's ballads, 90's rock, cheesecake, and office supplies, and she's been scribbling down love stories in spiral notebooks since she was old enough to daydream about hunky boys and happily-ever-afters. Now she turns those daydreams into steamy, small town novels.

Made in the USA
Las Vegas, NV
22 March 2023

69489298R00199